THE DEADLIEST GAMES

THE DEADLIEST GAMES

Tales of Psychological Suspense from
Ellery Queen's Mystery Magazine

Edited by Janet Hutchings

Carroll & Graf Publishers, Inc.
New York

Collection copyright © 1993 by Bantam Doubleday Dell Direct, Inc.

Introduction copyright © 1993 by Janet Hutchings

The acknowledgments listed on page five constitute an extension of this copyright page.

First Carroll & Graf edition 1993

Carroll & Graf Publishers, Inc.
260 Fifth Avenue
New York, NY 10001

Library of Congress Cataloging-in-Publication Data

The Deadliest games : tales of psychological suspense from Ellery
    Queen's mystery magazine / edited by Janet Hutchings.
      p.   cm.
    ISBN 0-7867-0001-7 : $19.95
    1. Detective and mystery stories, American. 2. Psychology—
Fiction. I. Hutchings, Janet. II. Ellery Queen's mystery
magazine.
PS648.D4D387   1993
813'.087208353—dc20   93-27040
                                                            CIP

Manufactured in the United States of America

Contents

INTRODUCTION by Janet Hutchings   9

THE MODEL by Joyce Carol Oates   11

BEAT YOUR NEIGHBOR OUT OF DOORS
by Jiro Akagawa   59

THE SERPENT AND THE MONGOOSE
by Edward D. Hoch   89

THE STRANGER by Florence V. Mayberry   105

BORN BAD by Andrew Vachss   123

SECRETS by June Thomson   131

THE BIG DANCE by Tom Verde   147

JEREMY by R. M. Kinder   159

THE JOURNEYER by Robert Campbell   165

THE 9:13 by Martin Naparsteck   185

A SALESMAN'S TALE by David Dean   203

HE WHO WAITS FOR YOU by David C. Hall   215

ACCOMMODATION VACANT
by Celia Fremlin   221

LIAR'S DICE by Bill Pronzini   239

THE MOMENT OF DECISION
by Stanley Ellin   247

INTRODUCTION

The critic and crime writer G.K. Chesterton once said, "The only thrill, even of a common thriller, is concerned somehow with the conscience and the will." His remark goes to the heart of the psychological thriller where the source of terror often involves something intangible such as the tell-tale heart invented by the murderer's own conscience in Edgar Allan Poe's classic tale of that name, a forerunner of the modern psychological suspense story. Chesterton is onto something too when he talks about the importance of the will in the creation of suspense. It is the will of the characters to act while caught up in a terrifying realm of uncertain perceptions and hidden agendas that keeps us on the edges of our seats.

At the same time, a strong sense of fatality runs through many stories of psychological suspense, as the forces of the subconscious mind move the characters closer and closer to the brink of disaster. In the hands of the skillful writers you will meet in these pages, our fear of what we do not see and may not be able to control in ourselves and others is used to chill and entertain. But some of the stories also conjure a profound question, one that philosophers have asked through the millenia, about the extent to which we are truly free when what surrounds our actions is a veil of sometimes deadly misperception.

The metaphor of the game used in the title to this volume was chosen because it seemed to fit with Chesterton's insight about the will as the focus of suspense and to emphasize the freedom of the will in the face of the powerful currents that oppose it. Yet our theme has as many variations as there are types of games, and some games, it should be remembered, are played only against oneself. There are games that involve a hunt, and those that involve deception, those played for a stake, and those that begin as sport only to end in entrapment or tragedy. Playfullness may enter into the story as well, sometimes as a gentle trifling that ends in a battle waged in deadly earnest. Some of players you will meet herein bring to the game a Machiavellian astuteness, while others prove too clever for their own good. Not every tale is meant to send a shiver up your spine, but pervading all is an undefined threat not designed to leave you sitting easy in your chair.

Unlike its cousin the detective story, the suspense story, in order to be successful, must create an intense concern for its characters. Absent is the cool detachment of rational investigation. The reader of the suspense story becomes a player in the game, a frightened participant who feels the urge to intervene for the other players' good, and who may in turn be taken in by the twists and turns of events. In the long history of the form, some of the twists have become classics, as with the pursuer who becomes the pursued. Other plot wrinkles originate with the authors of these fine stories.

All but one of the fifteen entries in this book are contemporary, the exception being "The Moment of Decision," a classic from the incomparable Stanley Ellin, first published in 1955. Joining him are current-day masters of the form, shown here at their best. So lock your doors and settle into your chair—it's now your move.

—Janet Hutchings

THE MODEL

By JOYCE CAROL OATES

1. The Approach of Mr. Starr

Had he stepped out of nowhere, or had he been watching her for some time, even more than he'd claimed, and for a different purpose?—she shivered to think that, yes, probably, she had many times glimpsed him in the village, or in the park, without really seeing him: him, and the long gleaming black limousine she would not have known to associate with him even had she noticed him: the man who called himself Mr. Starr.

As, each day, her eyes passed rapidly and lightly over any number of people both familiar to her and strangers, blurred as in the background of a film in which the foreground is the essential reality, the very point of the film.

She was seventeen. It was in fact the day after her birthday, a bright gusty January day, and she'd been running in the late afternoon, after school, in the park overlooking the ocean, and she'd just turned to head toward home, pausing to wipe her face, adjust her damp cotton headband, feeling the accelerated strength of her heartbeat and the pleasant ache of her leg muscles: and she glanced up, shy, surprised, and there he stood, a man she had never knowingly seen before. He was smiling at her, his smile broad and eager, hopeful, and he stood in such a way, leaning lightly on a cane, as to block her way on the path; yet tentatively too, with a gentlemanly, deferential air, so as to suggest that he meant no threat. When he spoke, his voice sounded hoarse as if from disuse. "Excuse me!—hello! Young lady! I realize that this is abrupt, and an intrusion on your privacy, but I am an artist, and I am looking for a model, and I wonder if you might be interested in posing for me? Only here, I mean, in the park—in full daylight! I am willing to pay, per hour—"

Sybil stared at the man. Like most young people she

11

was incapable of estimating ages beyond thirty-five—this strange person might have been in his forties, or well into his fifties. His thin, lank hair was the color of antique silver—perhaps he was even older. His skin was luridly pale, grainy, and rough; he wore glasses with lenses so darkly tinted as to suggest the kind of glasses worn by the blind; his clothes were plain, dark, conservative—a tweed jacket that fitted him loosely, a shirt buttoned tight to the neck, and no tie, highly polished black leather shoes in an outmoded style. There was something hesitant, even convalescent in his manner, as if, like numerous others in this coastal Southern California town with its population of the retired, the elderly, and the infirm, he had learned by experience to carry himself with care; he could not entirely trust the earth to support him. His features were refined, but worn; subtly distorted, as if seen through wavy glass, or water.

Sybil didn't like it that she couldn't see the man's eyes. Except to know that he was squinting at her, hard. The skin at the corners of his eyes was whitely puckered as if, in his time, he'd done a good deal of squinting and smiling.

Quickly, but politely, Sybil murmured, "No, thank you, I can't."

She was turning away, but still the man spoke, apologetically, "I realize this is a—surprise, but, you see, I don't know how else to make inquiries. I've only just begun sketching in the park, and—"

"Sorry!"

Sybil turned, began to run, not hurriedly, by no means in a panic, but at her usual measured pace, her head up and her arms swinging at her sides. She was, for all that she looked younger than her seventeen years, not an easily frightened girl, and she was not frightened now; but her face burned with embarrassment. She hoped that no one in the park who knew her had been watching—Glencoe was a small town, and the high school was about a mile away. Why had that preposterous man approached *her?*

He was calling after her, probably waving his cane after her—she didn't dare look back. "I'll be here tomorrow! My

name is Starr! Don't judge me too quickly—please! I'm
true to my word! My name is Starr! I'll pay you, per hour"
—and here he cited an exorbitant sum, nearly twice what
Sybil made babysitting or working as a librarian's assis-
tant at the branch library near her home, when she could
get hired.

She thought, astonished, He must be mad!

2. The Temptation

No sooner had Sybil Blake escaped from the man who
called himself Starr, running up Buena Vista Boulevard
to Santa Clara, up Santa Clara to Meridian, and so to
home, than she began to consider that Mr. Starr's offer
was, if preposterous, very tempting. She had never modeled of course, but, in art class at the high school, some of
her classmates had modeled, fully clothed, just sitting or
standing about in ordinary poses, and she and others had
sketched them, or tried to—it was really not so easy as it
might seem, sketching the lineaments of the human figure; it was still more difficult, sketching an individual's
face. But modeling, in itself, was effortless, once you over-
came the embarrassment of being stared at. It was, you
might argue, a morally neutral activity.

What had Mr. Starr said—*Only here, in the park. In full
daylight.*

I'm true to my word!

And Sybil needed money, for she was saving for college;
she was hoping too to attend a summer music institute at
U.C. Santa Barbara. (She was a voice student, and she'd
been encouraged by her choir director at the high school to
get good professional training.) Her Aunt Lora Dell Blake,
with whom she lived, and had lived since the age of two
years eight months, was willing to pay her way—was determined to pay her way—but Sybil felt uneasy about accepting money from Aunt Lora, who worked as a physical
therapist at a medical facility in Glencoe, and whose sal-
ary, at the top of the pay structure available to her as a

state employee, was still modest by California standards. Sybil reasoned that her Aunt Lora Dell could not be expected to support her forever.

A long time ago, Sybil had lost her parents, both of them together, in one single cataclysmic hour, when she'd been too young to comprehend what Death was, or was said to be. They had died in a boating accident on Lake Champlain, Sybil's mother at the age of twenty-six, Sybil's father at the age of thirty-one, very attractive young people, a "popular couple" as Aunt Lora spoke of them, choosing her words with care, and saying very little more. *For why ask,* Aunt Lora seemed to be warning Sybil,—*you will only make yourself cry.* As soon as she could manage the move, and as soon as Sybil was placed permanently in her care, Aunt Lora had come to California, to this sun-washed coastal town midway between Santa Monica and Santa Barbara. Glencoe was less conspicuously affluent than either of these towns, but, with its palm-lined streets, its sunny placidity, and its openness to the ocean, it was the very antithesis, as Aunt Lora said, of Wellington, Vermont, where the Blakes had lived for generations. (After their move to California, Lora Dell Blake had formally adopted Sybil as her child: thus Sybil's name was Blake, as her mother's had been. If asked what her father's name had been, Sybil would have had to think before recalling, dimly, "Conte.") Aunt Lora spoke so negatively of New England in general and Vermont in particular, Sybil felt no nostalgia for it; she had no sentimental desire to visit her birthplace, not even to see her parents' graves. From Aunt Lora's stories, Sybil had the idea that Vermont was damp and cold twelve months of the year, and frigidly, impossibly cold in winter; its wooded mountains were unlike the beautiful snow-capped mountains of the West, and cast shadows upon its small, cramped, depopulated, and impoverished old towns. Aunt Lora, a transplanted New Englander, was vehement in her praise of California —"With the Pacific Ocean to the west," she said, "it's like a room with one wall missing. Your instinct is to look out, not back; and it's a good instinct."

Lora Dell Blake was the sort of person who delivers

statements with an air of inviting contradiction. But, tall, rangy, restless, belligerent, she was not the sort of person most people wanted to contradict.

Indeed, Aunt Lora had never encouraged Sybil to ask questions about her dead parents, or about the tragic accident that had killed them; if she had photographs, snapshots, mementos of life back in Wellington, Vermont, they were safely hidden away, and Sybil had not seen them. "It would just be too painful," she told Sybil, "—for us both." The remark was both a plea and a warning.

Of course, Sybil avoided the subject.

She prepared carefully chosen words, should anyone happen to ask her why she was living with her aunt, and not her parents; or, at least, one of her parents. But—this was Southern California, and very few of Sybil's classmates were living with the set of parents with whom they'd begun. No one asked.

An orphan?—I'm not an orphan, Sybil would say. *I was never an orphan because my Aunt Lora was always there.*

I was two years old when it happened, the accident.

No, I don't remember.

But no one asked.

Sybil told her Aunt Lora nothing about the man in the park—the man who called himself Starr—she'd put him out of her mind entirely and yet, in bed that night, drifting into sleep, she found herself thinking suddenly of him, and seeing him again, vividly. That silver hair, those gleaming black shoes. His eyes hidden behind dark glasses. How tempting, his offer!—though there was no question of Sybil accepting it. Absolutely not.

Still, Mr. Starr seemed harmless. Well-intentioned. An eccentric, of course, but *interesting.* She supposed he had money, if he could offer her so much to model for him. There was something *not contemporary* about him. The set of his head and shoulders. That air about him of gentlemanly reserve, courtesy—even as he'd made his outlandish request. In Glencoe, in the past several years, there had been a visible increase in homeless persons and derelicts, especially in the oceanside park, but Mr. Starr was certainly not one of these.

Then Sybil realized, as if a door, hitherto locked, had swung open of its own accord, that she'd seen Mr. Starr before . . . somewhere. In the park, where she ran most afternoons for an hour? In downtown Glencoe? On the street?—in the public library? In the vicinity of Glencoe Senior High School?—in the school itself, in the auditorium? Sybil summoned up a memory as if by an act of physical exertion: the school choir, of which she was a member, had been rehearsing Handel's *Messiah* the previous month for their annual Christmas pageant, and Sybil had sung her solo part, a demanding part for contralto voice, and the choir director had praised her in front of the others . . . and she'd seemed to see, dimly, a man, a stranger, seated at the very rear of the auditorium, his features distinct but his grey hair striking, and wasn't this man miming applause, clapping silently? *There. At the rear, on the aisle.* It frequently happened that visitors dropped by rehearsals—parents or relatives of choir members, colleagues of the music director. So no one took special notice of the stranger sitting unobtrusively at the rear of the auditorium. He wore dark, conservative clothes of the kind to attract no attention, and dark glasses hid his eyes. But there he was. *For Sybil Blake. He'd come for Sybil.* But, at the time, Sybil had not seen.

Nor had she seen the man leave. Slipping quietly out of his seat, walking with a just perceptible limp, leaning on his cane.

3. The Proposition

Sybil had no intention of seeking out Mr. Starr, nor even of looking around for him, but, the following afternoon, as she was headed home after her run, there, suddenly, the man was—taller than she recalled, looming large, his dark glasses winking in the sunlight, and his pale lips stretched in a tentative smile. He wore his

clothes of the previous day except he'd set on his head a
sporty plaid golfing cap that gave him a rakish, yet wist-
ful, air, and he'd tied, as if in haste, a rumpled cream-
colored silk scarf around his neck. He was standing on the
path in approximately the same place as before, and leaning on his cane; on a bench close by were what appeared to
be his art supplies, in a canvas duffel bag of the sort students carried. "Why, hello!" he said, shyly but eagerly,
"—I didn't dare hope you would come back, but—" his
smile widened as if on the verge of desperation, the puckered skin at the corners of his eyes tightened, "—I *hoped.*"

After running, Sybil always felt good: strength flowed
into her legs, arms, lungs. She was a delicate-boned girl,
since infancy prone to respiratory infections, but such vigorous exercise had made her strong in recent years; and
with physical confidence had come a growing confidence in
herself. She laughed, lightly, at this strange man's words,
and merely shrugged, and said, "Well—this *is* my park,
after all." Mr. Starr nodded eagerly, as if any response
from her, any words at all, was of enormous interest. "Yes,
yes," he said, "—I can see that. Do you live close by?"

Sybil shrugged. It was none of his business, was it,
where she lived? "Maybe," she said.

"And your—name?" He stared at her, hopefully, adjust-
ing his glasses more firmly on his nose. "—My name is
Starr."

"My name is—Blake."

Mr. Starr blinked, and smiled, as if uncertain whether
this might be a joke. " 'Blake'—? An unusual name for a
girl," he said.

Sybil laughed again, feeling her face heat. She decided
not to correct the misunderstanding.

Today, prepared for the encounter, having anticipated it
for hours, Sybil was distinctly less uneasy than she'd been
the day before: the man had a business proposition to
make to her, that was all. And the park *was* an open,
public, safe place, as familiar to her as the small neat yard
of her Aunt Lora's house.

So, when Mr. Starr repeated his offer, Sybil said, yes,
she was interested after all; she did need money, she was

saving for college. "For college?—really? So young?" Mr.
Starr said, with an air of surprise. Sybil shrugged, as if
the remark didn't require any reply. "I suppose, here in
California, young people grow up quickly," Mr. Starr said.
He'd gone to get his sketch-pad, to show Sybil his work,
and Sybil turned the pages with polite interest, as Mr.
Starr chattered. He was, he said, an "amateur artist"—
the very epitome of the "amateur"—with no delusions regarding his talent, but a strong belief that the world is
redeemed by art—"And the world, you know, being profane, and steeped in wickedness, requires constant, ceaseless redemption." He believed that the artist "bears witness" to this fact; and that art can be a "conduit of
emotion" where the heart is empty. Sybil, leafing through
the sketches, paid little attention to Mr. Starr's tumble of
words; she was struck by the feathery, uncertain, somehow *worshipful* detail in the drawings, which, to her eye,
were not so bad as she'd expected, though by no means of
professional quality. As she looked at them, Mr. Starr
came to look over her shoulder, embarrassed, and excited,
his shadow falling over the pages. The ocean, the waves,
the wide rippled beach as seen from the bluff—palm trees,
hibiscus, flowers—a World War II memorial in the park—
mothers with young children—solitary figures huddled on
park benches—bicyclists—joggers—several pages of joggers: Mr. Starr's work was ordinary, even commonplace,
but certainly earnest. Sybil saw herself amid the joggers,
or a figure she guessed must be herself, a young girl with
shoulder-length dark hair held off her face by a headband,
in running pants and a sweatshirt, caught in mid-stride,
legs and swinging arms caught in motion—it *was* herself,
but so clumsily executed, the profile so smudged, no one
would have known. Still, Sybil felt her face grow warmer,
and she sensed Mr. Starr's anticipation like a withheld
breath.

Sybil did not think it quite right for her, aged seventeen, to pass judgment on the talent of a middle-aged
man, so she merely murmured something vague and polite and positive; and Mr. Starr, taking the sketch pad
from her, said, "Oh, I *know*—I'm not very good, yet. But I

propose to try." He smiled at her, and took out a freshly laundered white handkerchief, and dabbed at his forehead, and said, "Do you have any questions about posing for me, or shall we begin?—we'll have at least three hours of daylight, today."

"Three hours!" Sybil exclaimed. "That long?"

"If you get uncomfortable," Mr. Starr said quickly, "—we'll simply stop, wherever we are." Seeing that Sybil was frowning, he added, eagerly, "We'll take breaks every now and then, I promise. And, and—" seeing that Sybil was still indecisive, "—I'll pay you for a full hour's fee, for any part of an hour." Still Sybil stood, wondering if, after all, she should be agreeing to this, without her Aunt Lora, or anyone, knowing: wasn't there something just faintly odd about Mr. Starr, and about his willingness to pay her so much for doing so little? And wasn't there something troubling (however flattering) about his particular interest in her? Assuming Sybil was correct, and he'd been watching her . . . aware of her . . . for at least a month.

"I'll be happy to pay you in advance, Blake."

The name Blake sounded very odd in this stranger's mouth. Sybil had never before been called by her last name only.

Sybil laughed nervously, and said, "You don't have to pay me in advance—thanks!"

So Sybil Blake, against her better judgment, became a model, for Mr. Starr.

And, despite her self-consciousness, and her intermittent sense that there was something ludicrous in the enterprise, as about Mr. Starr's intense, fussy, self-important manner as he sketched her (he was a perfectionist, or wanted to give that impression: crumpling a half-dozen sheets of paper, breaking out new charcoal sticks, before he began a sketch that pleased him), the initial session was easy, effortless. "What I want to capture," Mr. Starr said, "—is, beyond your beautiful profile, Blake,—and you *are* a beautiful child!—the brooding quality of the ocean. That look to it, d'you see?—of it having consciousness of a kind, actually thinking. Yes, *brooding!*"

Sybil, squinting down at the white-capped waves, the rhythmic crashing surf, the occasional surfers riding their boards with their remarkable amphibian dexterity, thought that the ocean was anything but *brooding.*

"Why are you smiling, Blake?" Mr. Starr asked, pausing. "Is something funny?—am *I* funny?"

Quickly Sybil said, "Oh, no, Mr. Starr, of course not."

"But I *am,* I'm sure," he said happily. "And if you find me so, please *do* laugh!"

Sybil found herself laughing, as if rough fingers were tickling her. She thought of how it might have been . . . had she had a father, and a mother: her own family, as she'd been meant to have.

Mr. Starr was squatting now on the grass close by and peering up at Sybil with an expression of extreme concentration. The charcoal stick in his fingers moved rapidly. "The ability to *laugh,*" he said, "is the ability to *live*—the two are synonymous. You're too young to understand that right now, but one day you will." Sybil shrugged, wiping her eyes. Mr. Starr was talking grandly. "The world is fallen and profane—the opposite of 'sacred,' you know, *is* 'profane.' It requires ceaseless vigilance—ceaseless redemption. The artist is one who redeems by restoring the world's innocence, where he can. The artist gives, but does not take away, nor even supplant."

Sybil said, skeptically, "But you want to make money with your drawings, don't you?"

Mr. Starr seemed genuinely shocked. "Oh, my, no. Adamantly, *no.*"

Sybil persisted, "Well, most people would. I mean, most people need to. If they have any talent"—she was speaking with surprising bluntness, an almost childlike audacity—"they need to sell it, somehow."

As if he'd been caught out in a crime, Mr. Starr began to stammer apologetically, "It's true, Blake, I—I am not like most people, I suppose. I've inherited some money—not a fortune, but enough to live on comfortably for the rest of my life. I've been traveling abroad," he said, vaguely, "—and, in my absence, interest accumulated."

Sybil asked doubtfully, "You don't have any regular profession?"

Mr. Starr laughed, startled. Up close, his teeth were chunky and irregular, slightly stained, like aged ivory piano keys. "But, dear child," he said, *"this* is my profession —'redeeming the world!' "

And he fell to sketching Sybil with renewed enthusiasm.

Minutes passed. Long minutes. Sybil felt a mild ache between her shoulder blades. A mild uneasiness in her chest. *Mr. Starr is mad. Is Mr. Starr 'mad'?* Behind her, on the path, people were passing by, there were joggers, bicyclists—Mr. Starr, lost in a trance of concentration, paid them not the slightest heed. Sybil wondered if anyone knew her, and was taking note of this peculiar event. Or was she, herself, making too much of it? She decided she would tell her Aunt Lora about Mr. Starr that evening, tell Aunt Lora frankly how much he was paying her. She both respected and feared her aunt's judgment: in Sybil's imagination, in that unexamined sphere of being we call the imagination, Lora Dell Blake had acquired the authority of both Sybil's deceased parents.

Yes, she would tell Aunt Lora.

After only an hour and forty minutes, when Sybil appeared to be growing restless and sighed several times, unconsciously, Mr. Starr suddenly declared the session over. He had, he said, three promising sketches, and he didn't want to exhaust her, or himself. She *was* coming back tomorrow—?

"I don't know," Sybil said. "Maybe."

Sybil protested, though not very adamantly, when Mr. Starr paid her the full amount, for three hours' modeling. He paid her in cash, out of his wallet—an expensive kidskin wallet brimming with bills. Sybil thanked him, deeply embarrassed, and eager to escape. Oh, there *was* something shameful about the transaction!

Up close, she was able—almost—to see Mr. Starr's eyes through the dark-tinted lenses of his glasses. Some delicacy of tact made her glance away quickly but she had an impression of kindness—gentleness.

Sybil took the money, and put it in her pocket, and turned, to hurry away. With no mind for who might hear him, Mr. Starr called after her, "You see, Blake?—Starr is true to his word. Always!"

4. Is the Omission of Truth a Lie, or Only an Omission?

"Well!—tell me how things went with *you* today, Sybil!" Lora Dell Blake said, with such an air of bemused exasperation, Sybil understood that, as so often, Aunt Lora had something to say that really couldn't wait—her work at the Glencoe Medical Center provided her with a seemingly inexhaustible supply of comical and outrageous anecdotes. So, deferring to Aunt Lora, as they prepared supper together as usual, and sat down to eat it, Sybil was content to listen, and to laugh.

For it *was* funny, if outrageous too—the latest episode in the ongoing folly at the Medical Center.

Lora Dell Blake, in her late forties, was a tall, lanky, restless woman; with close-cropped greying hair; sand-colored eyes and skin; a generous spirit, but a habit of sarcasm. Though she claimed to love Southern California —"You don't know what paradise is, unless you're from somewhere else"—she seemed in fact an awkwardly transplanted New Englander, with expectations and a sense of personal integrity, or intransigence, quite out of place here. She was fond of saying she did not suffer fools gladly, and so it was. Overqualified for her position at the Glencoe Medical Center, she'd had no luck in finding work elsewhere, partly because she did not want to leave Glencoe and "uproot" Sybil while Sybil was still in high school; and partly because her interviews were invariably disasters—Lora Dell Blake was incapable of being, or even seeming, docile, tractable, "feminine," hypocritical.

Lora was not Sybil's sole living relative—there were Blakes, and Contes, back in Vermont—but Lora had discouraged visitors to the small stucco bungalow on Meridian Street, in Glencoe, California; she had not in fact troubled to reply to letters or cards since, having been granted custody of her younger sister's daughter, at the time of what she called "the tragedy," she'd picked up and moved across the continent, to a part of the country she knew nothing about—"My intention is to erase the past, for the child's sake," she said, "and to start a new life."

And: "For the child, for poor little Sybil—I would make any sacrifice."

Sybil, who loved her aunt very much, had the vague idea that there had been, many years ago, protests, queries, telephone calls—but that Aunt Lora had dealt with them all, and really had made a new and "uncomplicated" life for them. Aunt Lora was one of those personalities, already strong, that is strengthened, and empowered, by being challenged; she seemed to take an actual zest in confrontation, whether with her own relatives or her employers at the Medical Center—anyone who presumed to tell her what to do. She was especially protective of Sybil, since, as she often said, they had no one but each other.

Which was true. Aunt Lora had seen to that.

Though Sybil had been adopted by her aunt, there was never any pretense that she was anything but Lora's niece, not her daughter. Nor did most people, seeing the two together, noting their physical dissimilarities, make that mistake.

So it happened that Sybil Blake grew up knowing virtually nothing about her Vermont background except its general tragic outline: her knowledge of her mother and father, the precise circumstances of their deaths, was as vague and unexamined in her consciousness as a childhood fairy tale. For whenever, as a little girl, Sybil would ask her aunt about these things, Aunt Lora responded with hurt, or alarm, or reproach, or, most disturbingly, anxiety. Her eyes might flood with tears—Aunt Lora, who never cried. She might take Sybil's hands in both her own, and squeeze them tightly, and looking Sybil in the eyes, say, in a quiet, commanding voice, "But, darling, *you don't want to know.*"

* * *

So too, that evening, when, for some reason, Sybil brought up the subject, asking Aunt Lora how, again, exactly, *had* her parents died, Aunt Lora looked at her in surprise; and, for a long moment, rummaging in the pockets of her shirt for a pack of cigarettes that wasn't there (Aunt Lora had given up smoking the previous month, for perhaps the fifth time), it seemed almost that Lora herself did not re-member.

"Sybil, honey—why are you asking? I mean, why *now?*"

"I don't know," Sybil said evasively. "I guess—I'm just asking."

"Nothing happened to you at school, did it?"

Sybil could not see how this question related to her own, but she said, politely, "No, Aunt Lora. Of course not."

"It's just that out of nowhere—I can't help but wonder *why,*" Aunt Lora said, frowning, "—you should ask."

Aunt Lora regarded Sybil with worried eyes: a look of such suffocating familiarity that, for a moment, Sybil felt as if a band were tightening around her chest, making it impossible to breathe. *Why is my wanting to know a test of my love for you?—why do you do this, Aunt Lora, every time?* She said, an edge of anger to her voice, "I was seven-teen years old last week, Aunt Lora. I'm not a child any longer."

Aunt Lora laughed, startled. "Certainly you're not a child!"

Aunt Lora then sighed, and, in a characteristic gesture, meaning both impatience and a dutiful desire to please, ran both hands rapidly through her hair and began to speak. She assured Sybil that there was little to know, really. The accident—the tragedy—had happened so long ago. "Your mother, Melanie, was twenty-six years old at the time—a beautiful sweet-natured young woman, with eyes like yours, cheekbones like yours, pale wavy hair. Your father, George Conte, was thirty-one years old—a promising young lawyer, in his father's firm—an attrac-tive, ambitious man—" And here as in the past Aunt Lora paused, as if in the very act of summoning up this long-dead couple, she had forgotten them; and was simply re-peating a story, a family tale, like one of the more extreme of her tales of the Glencoe Medical Center, worn smooth by countless tellings.

"A boating accident—Fourth of July—" Sybil coaxed, "—and I was with you, and—"

"You were with me, and Grandma, at the cottage—you were just a little girl!" Aunt Lora said, blinking tears from her eyes, "—and it was almost dusk, and time for the fireworks to start. Mommy and Daddy were out in Daddy's speedboat—they'd been across the lake, at the Club—"

"And they started back across the lake—Lake Champlain—"

"—Lake Champlain, of course: it's beautiful, but treacherous, if a storm comes up suddenly—"

"And Daddy was at the controls of the boat—"

"—and, somehow, they capsized. And drowned. A rescue boat went out immediately, but it was too late." Aunt Lora's mouth turned hard. Her eyes glistening with tears, as if defiantly. "They drowned."

Sybil's heart was beating painfully. She was certain there must be more, yet she herself could remember nothing—not even herself, that two-year-old child, waiting for Mommy and Daddy who were never to arrive. Her memory of her mother and father was vague, dim, featureless, like a dream that, even as it seems about to drift into consciousness, retreats farther into darkness. She said, in a whisper, "It was an accident. No one was to blame."

Aunt Lora chose her words with care. "No one was to blame."

There was a pause. Sybil looked at her aunt, who was not now looking at her. How lined, even leathery, the older woman's face was getting!—all her life she'd been reckless, indifferent, about sun, wind, weather, and now, in her late forties, she might have been a decade older. Sybil said, tentatively, "No one *was* to blame—?"

"Well, if you must know," Aunt Lora said, "—there was evidence he'd been drinking. They'd been drinking. At the Club."

Sybil could not have been more shocked had Aunt Lora reached over and pinched the back of her hand.

"Drinking—?" She had never heard this part of the story before.

Aunt Lora continued, grimly, "But not enough, probably, to have made a difference." Again she paused. She was not looking at Sybil. "Probably."

Sybil, stunned, could not think of anything further to say, or to ask.

Aunt Lora was on her feet, pacing. Her close-cropped hair was disheveled and her manner fiercely contentious, as if she were arguing her case before an invisible audience as Sybil looked on. "What fools! I tried to tell her! 'Popular' couple—'attractive' couple—lots of friends—too many friends! That Goddamned Champlain Club, where everyone drank too much! All that money, and privilege! And what good did it do! She—Melanie—so proud of being asked to join—proud of marrying *him*—throwing her life away! That's what it came to, in the end. I'd warned her it was dangerous—playing with fire—but would she listen? Would either of them listen? To Lora?—to *me?* When you're that age, so ignorant, you think you will live forever —you can throw your life away—"

Sybil felt ill, suddenly. She walked swiftly out of the room, shut the door to her own room, stood in the dark, beginning to cry.

So that was it, the secret. The tawdry little secret— drinking, drunkenness—behind the "tragedy."

With characteristic tact, Aunt Lora did not knock on Sybil's door, but left her alone for the remainder of the night.

Only after Sybil was in bed, and the house darkened, did she realize she'd forgotten to tell her aunt about Mr. Starr—he'd slipped her mind entirely. And the money he'd pressed into her hand, now in her bureau drawer, rolled up neatly beneath her underwear, as if hidden. . . .

Sybil thought, guiltily, I can tell her tomorrow.

5. The Hearse

Crouched in front of Sybil Blake, eagerly sketching her likeness, Mr. Starr was saying, in a quick, rapturous voice, "Yes, yes, like that!—yes! Your face uplifted to the sun like a blossoming flower! Just so!" And: "There are only two or three eternal questions, Blake, which, like the surf, repeat themselves endlessly: 'Why are we here?'— 'Where have we come from, and where are we going?'—'Is there purpose to the Universe, or merely chance?' These questions the artist seems to express in the images he shows." And: "Dear child, I wish you would tell me about yourself. Just a little!"

As if, in the night, some change had come upon her, some new resolve, Sybil had fewer misgivings about modeling for Mr. Starr this afternoon. It was as if they knew each other well, somehow: Sybil was reasonably certain that Mr. Starr was not a sexual pervert, nor even a madman of a more conventional sort; she'd glimpsed his sketches of her, which were fussy, overworked, and smudged, but not bad as likenesses. The man's murmurous chatter was comforting in a way, hypnotic as the surf, no longer quite so embarrassing—for he talked, most of the time, not with her but at her, and there was no need to reply. In a way, Mr. Starr reminded Sybil of her Aunt Lora, when she launched into one of her comical anecdotes about the Glencoe Medical Center. Aunt Lora was more entertaining than Mr. Starr, but Mr. Starr was more idealistic.

His optimism was simpleminded, maybe. But it *was* optimistic.

For this second modeling session, Mr. Starr had taken Sybil to a corner of the park where they were unlikely to be disturbed. He'd asked her to remove her headband, and to sit on a bench with her head dropping back, her eyes partly shut, her face uplifted to the sun—an uncomfortable pose at first, until, lulled by the crashing surf below, and Mr. Starr's monologue, Sybil began to feel oddly peaceful, floating.

Yes, in the night some change had come upon her. She could not comprehend its dimensions, nor even its tone. She'd fallen asleep crying bitterly but had awakened feeling—what? Vulnerable, somehow. And wanting to be so. *Uplifted. Like a blossoming flower.*

That morning, Sybil had forgotten another time to tell her Aunt Lora about Mr. Starr, and the money she was making—such a generous amount, and for so little effort! She shrank from considering how her aunt might respond, for her aunt was mistrustful of strangers, and particularly of men. . . . Sybil reasoned that, when she did tell Aunt Lora, that evening, or tomorrow morning, she would make her understand that there was something kindly and trusting and almost childlike about Mr. Starr. You could laugh at him, but laughter was somehow inappropriate.

As if, though middle-aged, he had been away somewhere, sequestered, protected, out of the adult world. Innocent and, himself, vulnerable.

Today too he'd eagerly offered to pay Sybil in advance for modeling, and, another time, Sybil had declined. She would not have wanted to tell Mr. Starr that, were she paid in advance, she might be tempted to cut the session even shorter than otherwise.

Mr. Starr was saying, hesitantly, "Blake?—can you tell me about—" and here he paused, as if drawing a random, inspired notion out of nowhere "—your mother?"

Sybil hadn't been paying close attention to Mr. Starr. Now she opened her eyes and looked directly at him.

Mr. Starr was perhaps not so old as she'd originally thought, nor as old as he behaved. His face was a handsome face, but oddly roughened—the skin like sandpaper. Very sallow, sickly pale. A faint scar on his forehead above his left eye, the shape of a fish hook, or a question mark. Or was it a birthmark?—or, even less romantically, some sort of skin blemish? Maybe his roughened, pitted skin was the result of teenaged acne, nothing more.

His tentative smile bared chunky damp teeth.

Today Mr. Starr was bareheaded, and his thin, fine, uncannily silver hair was stirred by the wind. He wore plain, nondescript clothes, a shirt too large for him, a khaki-

colored jacket or smock with rolled-up sleeves. At close
range, Sybil could see his eyes through the tinted lenses of
his glasses: they were small, deep-set, intelligent, glistening. The skin beneath was pouched and shadowed, as if
bruised.

Sybil shivered, peering so directly into Mr. Starr's eyes.
As into another's soul, when she was unprepared.

Sybil swallowed, and said, slowly, "My mother is . . .
not living."

A curious way of speaking!—for why not say, candidly,
in normal usage, *My mother is dead.*

For a long painful moment Sybil's words hovered in the
air between them; as if Mr. Starr, discountenanced by his
own blunder, seemed not to want to hear.

He said, quickly, apologetically, "Oh—I see. I'm sorry."

Sybil had been posing in the sun, warmly mesmerized
by the sun, the surf, Mr. Starr's voice, and now, as if wakened from a sleep of which she had not been conscious, she
felt as if she'd been touched—prodded into wakefulness.
She saw, upside-down, the fussy smudged sketch Mr.
Starr had been doing of her, saw his charcoal stick poised
above the stiff white paper in an attitude of chagrin. She
laughed, and wiped at her eyes, and said, "It happened a
long time ago. I never think of it, really."

Mr. Starr's expression was wary, complex. He asked,
"And so—do you—live with your—father?" The words
seemed oddly forced.

"No, I don't. And I don't want to talk about this any
more, Mr. Starr, if it's all right with you."

Sybil spoke pleadingly, yet with an air of finality.

"Then—we won't! We won't! We certainly won't!" Mr.
Starr said quickly. And fell to sketching again, his face
creased in concentration.

And so the remainder of the session passed in silence.

Again, as soon as Sybil evinced signs of restlessness,
Mr. Starr declared she could stop for the day—he didn't
want to exhaust her, or himself.

Sybil rubbed her neck, which ached mildly; she
stretched her arms, her legs. Her skin felt slightly sun- or
wind-burnt and her eyes felt seared, as if she'd been star-

ing directly into the sun. Or had she been crying?—she couldn't remember.

Again, Mr. Starr paid Sybil in cash, out of his kidskin wallet brimming with bills. His hand shook just visibly as he pressed the money into Sybil's. (Embarrassed, Sybil folded the bills quickly and put them in her pocket. Later, at home, she would discover that Mr. Starr had given her ten dollars too much: a bonus, for almost making her cry?) Though it was clear that Sybil was eager to get away, Mr. Starr walked with her up the slope in the direction of the Boulevard, limping, leaning on his cane, but keeping a brisk pace. He asked if Sybil—of course, he called her Blake: "dear Blake"—would like to have some refreshment with him in a café nearby?—and when Sybil declined, murmured, "Yes, yes, I understand—I suppose." He then asked if Sybil would return the following day, and when Sybil did not say no, added that, if she did, he would like to increase her hourly fee in exchange for asking of her a slightly different sort of modeling—"A slightly modified sort of modeling, here in the park, or perhaps down on the beach, in full daylight of course, as before, and yet, in its way—" Mr. Starr paused nervously, seeking the right word, "—experimental."

Sybil asked doubtfully, " 'Experimental'—?"

"I'm prepared to increase your fee, Blake, by half."

"What kind of 'experimental'?"

"Emotion."

"What?"

"Emotion. Memory. Interiority."

Now that they were emerging from the park, and more likely to be seen, Sybil was glancing uneasily about: she dreaded seeing someone from school, or, worse yet, a friend of her aunt's. Mr. Starr gestured as he spoke, and seemed more than ordinarily excited. "—'Interiority.' That which is hidden to the outer eye. I'll tell you in more detail tomorrow, Blake," he said. "You *will* meet me here tomorrow?"

Sybil murmured, "I don't know, Mr. Starr."

"Oh, but you must!—please."

Sybil felt a tug of sympathy for Mr. Starr. He *was* kind,

and courteous, and gentlemanly; and, certainly, very generous. She could not imagine his life except to see him as a lonely, eccentric man without friends. Uncomfortable as she was in his presence, she yet wondered if perhaps she was exaggerating his eccentricity: what would a neutral observer make of the tall limping figure, the cane, the canvas duffel bag, the polished black leather shoes that reminded her of a funeral, the fine thin beautiful silver hair, the dark glasses that winked in the sunshine . . . ? Would such an observer, seeing Sybil Blake and Mr. Starr together, give them a second glance?

"Look," Sybil said, pointing, "—a hearse."

At a curb close by there was a long sleekly black car with dark-tinted, impenetrable windows. Mr. Starr laughed, and said, embarrassed, "I'm afraid, Blake, that isn't a hearse, you know—it's my car."

"Your car?"

"Yes. I'm afraid so."

Now Sybil could see that the vehicle was a limousine, idling at the curb. Behind the wheel was a youngish driver with a visored cap on his head; in profile, he appeared Oriental. Sybil stared, amazed. So Mr. Starr was wealthy, indeed.

He was saying, apologetically, yet with a kind of boyish pleasure, "I don't drive, myself, you see!—a further handicap. I did, once, long ago, but—circumstances intervened." Sybil was thinking that she often saw chauffeur-driven limousines in Glencoe, but she'd never known anyone who owned one before. Mr. Starr said, "Blake, may I give you a ride home?—I'd be delighted, of course."

Sybil laughed, as if she'd been tickled, hard, in the ribs.

"A ride? In that?" she asked.

"No trouble! Absolutely!" Mr. Starr limped to the rear door and opened it with a flourish, before the driver could get out to open it for him. He squinted back at Sybil, smiling hopefully. "It's the least I can do for you, after our exhausting session."

Sybil was smiling, staring into the shadowy interior of the car. The uniformed driver had climbed out, and stood, not quite knowing what to do, watching. He was a Filipino, perhaps, not young after all but with a small, wizened face; he wore white gloves. He stood very straight and silent, watching Sybil.

There was a moment when it seemed, yes, Sybil was going to accept Mr. Starr's offer, and climb into the rear of the long sleekly black limousine, so that Mr. Starr could climb in behind her, and shut the door upon them both; but, then, for some reason she could not have named—it might have been the smiling intensity with which Mr. Starr was looking at her, or the rigid posture of the white-gloved driver—she changed her mind and called out, "No thanks!"

Mr. Starr was disappointed, and Mr. Starr was hurt— you could see it in his downturned mouth. But he said, cheerfully, "Oh, I quite understand, Blake—I *am* a stranger, after all. It's better to be prudent, of course. But, my dear, I *will* see you tomorrow—?"

Sybil shouted, "Maybe!" and ran across the street.

6. The Face

She stayed away from the park. *Because I want to, because I can.*

Thursday, in any case, was her voice lesson after school. Friday, choir rehearsal; then an evening with friends. On Saturday morning she went jogging, not in the oceanside park but in another park, miles away, where Mr. Starr could not have known to look for her. And, on Sunday, Aunt Lora drove them to Los Angeles for a belated birthday celebration, for Sybil—an art exhibit, a dinner, a play.

So, you see, I can do it. I don't need your money, or you.

Since the evening when Aunt Lora had told Sybil about her parents' boating accident—that it might have been caused by drinking—neither Sybil nor her aunt had cared to bring up the subject again. Sybil shuddered to think of it. She felt properly chastised, for her curiosity.

Why do you want to know?—you will only make yourself cry.

* * *

Sybil had never gotten around to telling Aunt Lora about
Mr. Starr, nor about her modeling. Even during their long
Sunday together. Not a word about her cache of money,
hidden away in a bureau drawer.

Money for what?—for summer school, for college.

For the future.

Aunt Lora was not the sort of person to spy on a member
of her household but she observed Sybil closely, with her
trained clinician's eye. "Sybil, you've been very quiet
lately—there's nothing wrong, I hope?" she asked, and
Sybil said quickly, nervously, "Oh, no! What could be
wrong?"

She was feeling guilty about keeping a secret from Aunt
Lora, and she was feeling quite guilty about staying away
from Mr. Starr.

Two adults. Like twin poles. Of course, Mr. Starr was
really a stranger—he did not exist in Sybil Blake's life, at
all. Why did it feel to her, so strangely, that he did?

Days passed, and instead of forgetting Mr. Starr, and
strengthening her resolve not to model for him, Sybil
seemed to see the man, in her mind's eye, ever more
clearly. She could not understand why he seemed at-
tracted to her, she was convinced it was not a sexual at-
traction but something purer, more spiritual, and yet—
why? Why *her?*

Why had he visited her high school, and sat in upon a
choir rehearsal? Had he known she would be there?—or
was it simply accident?

She shuddered to think of what Aunt Lora would make
of this, if she knew. If news of Mr. Starr got back to her.

Mr. Starr's face floated before her. Its pallor, its sorrow.
That look of convalescence. Waiting. The dark glasses.
The hopeful smile. One night, waking from a particularly
vivid, disturbing dream, Sybil thought for a confused moment that she'd seen Mr. Starr in the room—it hadn't
been just a dream! How wounded he looked, puzzled, hurt.
Come with me, Sybil. Hurry. Now. It's been so long. He'd
been waiting for her in the park for days, limping, the

duffel bag slung over his shoulder, glancing up hopefully at every passing stranger.

Behind him, the elegantly gleaming black limousine, larger than Sybil remembered; and driverless.

Sybil?—Sybil? Mr. Starr called, impatiently.

As if, all along, he'd known her real name. And she had known he'd known.

7. The Experiment

So, Monday afternoon, Sybil Blake found herself back in the park, modeling for Mr. Starr.

Seeing him in the park, so obviously awaiting her, Sybil had felt almost apologetic. Not that he greeted her with any measure of reproach (though his face was drawn and sallow, as if he hadn't been sleeping well), nor even questioned her mutely with his eyes *Where have you been?* Certainly not! He smiled happily when he saw her, limping in her direction like a doting father, seemingly determined not to acknowledge her absence of the past four days. Sybil called out, "Hello, Mr. Starr!" and felt, yes, so strangely, as if things were once again right.

"How lovely!—and the day is so fine!—'in full daylight' —as I promised!" Mr. Starr cried.

Sybil had been jogging for forty minutes, and felt very good, strengthened. She removed her damp yellow headband and stuffed it in her pocket. When Mr. Starr repeated the terms of his proposition of the previous week, restating the higher fee, Sybil agreed at once, for of course that was why she'd come. How, in all reasonableness, could she resist?

Mr. Starr took some time before deciding upon a place for Sybil to pose—"It must be ideal, a synthesis of poetry and practicality." Finally, he chose a partly crumbling stone ledge overlooking the beach in a remote corner of the park. He asked Sybil to lean against the ledge, gazing out at the ocean. Her hands pressed flat against the top of the ledge, her head uplifted as much as possible, within comfort. "But today, dear Blake, I am going to record not just the surface likeness of a lovely young girl," he said, "—but *memory,* and *emotion,* coursing through her."

Sybil took the position readily enough. So invigorated did she feel from her exercise, and so happy to be back again in her role as model, she smiled out at the ocean as at an old friend. "What kind of memory and emotion, Mr. Starr?" she asked.

Mr. Starr eagerly took up his sketch pad and a fresh stick of charcoal. It was a mild day, the sky placid and featureless, though, up the coast, in the direction of Big Sur, massive thunderclouds were gathering. The surf was high, the waves powerful, hypnotic. One hundred yards below, young men in surfing gear, carrying their boards lightly as if they were made of papier-mâché, prepared to enter the water.

Mr. Starr cleared his throat, and said, almost shyly, "Your mother, dear Blake. Tell me all you know—all you can remember—about your mother."

"My mother?"

Sybil winced and would have broken her position, except Mr. Starr put out a quick hand, to steady her. It was the first time he had touched her in quite that way. He said gently, "I realize it's a painful subject, Blake, but—will you try?"

Sybil said, "No. I don't want to."

"You won't, then?"

"I *can't.*"

"But why can't you, dear?—any memory of your mother would do."

"*No.*"

Sybil saw that Mr. Starr was quickly sketching her, or trying to—his hand shook. She wanted to reach out to snatch the charcoal stick from him and snap it in two. How dare he! God damn him!

"Yes, yes," Mr. Starr said hurriedly, an odd, elated look on his face, as if, studying her so intently, he was not seeing her at all, "—yes, dear, like that. Any memory—any! So long as it's yours."

Sybil said, "Whose else would it be?" She laughed, and was surprised that her laughter sounded like sobbing.

"Why, many times innocent children are given memories by adults; contaminated by memories not their own," Mr. Starr said somberly. "In which case the memory is spurious. Inauthentic."

Sybil saw her likeness on the sheet of stiff white paper, upside-down. There was something repulsive about it. Though she was wearing her usual jogging clothes (a shirt, running pants) Mr. Starr made it look as if she were wearing a clinging, flowing gown; or, maybe, nothing at all. Where her small breasts would have been were swirls and smudges of charcoal, as if she were on the brink of dissolution. Her face and head were vividly drawn, but rather raw, crude, and exposed.

She saw too that Mr. Starr's silver hair had a flat metallic sheen this afternoon; and his beard was faintly visible, metallic too, glinting on his jaws. He was stronger than she'd thought. He had knowledge far beyond hers.

Sybil resumed her position. She stared out at the ocean —the tall, cresting, splendidly white-capped waves. Why was she here, what did this man want out of her? She worried suddenly that, whatever it was, she could not provide it.

But Mr. Starr was saying, in his gentle, murmurous voice, "There are people—primarily women!—who are what I call 'conduits of emotion.' In their company, the half-dead can come alive. They need not be beautiful women or girls. It's a matter of blood-warmth. The integrity of the spirit." He turned the page of his sketch pad, and began anew, whistling thinly through his teeth. "Thus an icy-cold soul, in the presence of one so blessed, can regain something of his lost self. Sometimes!"

Sybil tried to summon forth a memory, an image at least, of her mother. *Melanie. Twenty-six at the time. Eyes . . . cheekbones . . . pale wavy hair.* A ghostly face appeared but faded almost at once. Sybil sobbed involuntarily. Her eyes stung with tears.

"—sensed that you, dear Blake—*is* your name Blake, really?—are one of these. A 'conduit of emotion'—of finer, higher things. Yes, yes! My intuition rarely misguides me!" Mr. Starr spoke as, hurriedly, excitedly, he sketched Sybil's likeness. He was squatting close beside her, on his haunches; his dark glasses winked in the sun. Sybil knew, should she glance at him, she would not be able to see his eyes.

Mr. Starr said, coaxingly, "Don't you remember any-thing—at all—about your mother?"

Sybil shook her head, meaning she didn't want to speak.

"Her name. Surely you know her name?"

Sybil whispered, "Mommy."

"Ah, yes: 'Mommy.' To you, that would have been her name."

"Mommy—went away. They told me—"

"Yes? Please continue!"

"—Mommy was gone. And Daddy. On the lake—"

"Lake? Where?"

"Lake Champlain. In Vermont, and New York, Aunt Lora says—"

" 'Aunt Lora'—?"

"Mommy's sister. She was older. Is older. She took me away. She adopted me. She—"

"And is 'Aunt Lora' married?"

"No. There's just her and me."

"What happened on the lake?"

"—it happened in the boat, on the lake. Daddy was driv-ing the boat, they said. He came for me too but—I don't know if that was that time or some other time. I've been told, but I don't *know*."

Tears were streaming down Sybil's face now; she could not maintain her composure. But she managed to keep from hiding her face in her hands. She could hear Mr. Starr's quickened breath, and she could hear the rasping sound of the charcoal against the paper.

Mr. Starr said gently, "You must have been a little girl when—whatever it was—happened."

"I wasn't little to *myself*. I just *was*."

"A long time ago, was it?"

"Yes. No. It's always—there."

"Always where, dear child?"

"Where I, I—see it."

"See what?"

"I—don't *know.*"

"Do you see your mommy? Was she a beautiful woman? —did she resemble you?"

"Leave me alone—I don't *know.*"

Sybil began to cry. Mr. Starr, repentant, or wary, went immediately silent.

Someone—it must have been bicyclists—passed behind them, and Sybil was aware of being observed, no doubt quizzically: a girl leaning forward across a stone ledge, face wet with tears, and a middle-aged man on his haunches busily sketching her. An artist and his model. An amateur artist, an amateur model. But how strange, that the girl was crying! And the man so avidly recording her tears!

Sybil, eyes closed, felt herself indeed a conduit of emotion—she *was* emotion. She stood upon the ground but she floated free. Mr. Starr was close beside her, anchoring her, but she floated free. A veil was drawn aside, and she saw a face—Mommy's face—a pretty heart-shaped face—something both affectionate and petulant in that face—how young Mommy was!—and her hair up, brown-blond lovely hair, tied back in a green silk scarf. Mommy hurried to the phone as it rang, Mommy lifted the receiver. Yes? yes? oh hel*lo*—for the phone was always ringing, and Mommy was always hurrying to answer it, and there was always that expectant note to her voice, that sound of hope, surprise— Oh, hel*lo.*

Sybil could no longer maintain her pose. She said, "Mr. Starr, I am through for the day, I am *sorry.*" And, as the startled man looked after her, she walked away. He began to call after her, to remind her that he hadn't paid her, but, no, Sybil had had enough of modeling for the day. She broke into a run, she escaped.

8. A Long Time Ago . . .

A girl who'd married too young: was that it?

That heart-shaped face, the petulant pursed lips. The eyes widened in mock-surprise: Oh, Sybil, what have you *done* . . . ?

Stooping to kiss little Sybil, little Sybil giggling with pleasure and excitement, lifting her chubby baby arms to be raised in Mommy's and carried in to bed.

Oh honey, you're too big for that now. Too heavy!

Perfume wafting from her hair, loose to her shoulders, pale golden-brown, wavy. A rope of pearls around her neck. A low-cut summer dress, a bright floral print, like wallpaper. Mommy!

And Daddy, where *was* Daddy?

He was gone, then he was back. He'd come to her, little Sybil, to take her in the boat, the motor was loud, whining, angry as a bee buzzing and darting around her head, so Sybil was crying, and someone came, and Daddy went away again. She'd heard the motor rising, then fading. The churning of the water she couldn't see from where she stood, and it was night too, but she wasn't crying and no one scolded.

She could remember Mommy's face, though they never let her see it again. She couldn't remember Daddy's face.

Grandma said, You'll be all right, poor little darling, you'll be all right, and Aunt Lora too, hugging her tight, Forever now you'll be all right, Aunt Lora promised. It was scary to see Aunt Lora crying: Aunt Lora never cried, did she?

Lifting little Sybil in her strong arms to carry her in to bed but it wasn't the same. It would never be the same again.

9. The Gift

Sybil is standing at the edge of the ocean.

The surf crashes and pounds about her . . . water

streams up the sand, nearly wetting her feet. What a tu-
mult of cries, hidden within the waves! She feels like
laughing, for no reason. *You know the reason: he has returned to you.*

The beach is wide, clean, stark, as if swept with a giant
broom. A landscape of dreamlike simplicity. Sybil has
seen it numberless times but today its beauty strikes her
as new. *Your father: your father they told you was gone
forever: he has returned to you.* The sun is a winter sun,
but warm, dazzling. Poised in the sky as if about to rapidly descend. Dark comes early because, after all, it is
winter here, despite the warmth. The temperature will
drop twenty degrees in a half-hour. *He never died: he has
been waiting for you all these years. And now he has returned.*

Sybil begins to cry. Hiding her face, her burning face, in
her hands. She stands flatfooted as a little girl and the
surf breaks and splashes around her and now her shoes
are wet, her feet, she'll be shivering in the gathering chill.
Oh, Sybil!

When Sybil turned, it was to see Mr. Starr sitting on the
beach. He seemed to have lost his balance and fallen—his
cane lay at his feet, he'd dropped the sketch pad, his
sporty golfing cap sat crooked on his head. Sybil, concerned, asked what was wrong,—she prayed he hadn't
had a heart attack!—and Mr. Starr smiled weakly and
told her quickly that he didn't know, he'd become dizzy,
felt the strength go out of his legs, and had had to sit. "I
was overcome suddenly, I think, by your emotion!—whatever it was," he said. He made no effort to get to his feet
but sat there awkwardly, damp sand on his trousers and
shoes. Now Sybil stood over him and he squinted up at
her, and there passed between them a current of—was it
understanding? sympathy? recognition?

Sybil laughed to dispel the moment and put out her
hand for Mr. Starr to take, so that she could help him
stand. He laughed too, though he was deeply moved, and
embarrassed. "I'm afraid I make too much of things, don't
I?" he said. Sybil tugged at his hand (how big his hand

was! how strong the fingers, closing about hers!) and, as
he heaved himself to his feet, grunting, she felt the startling weight of him—an adult man, and heavy.

Mr. Starr was standing close to Sybil, not yet relin-
quishing her hand. He said, "The experiment was almost
too successful, from my perspective! I'm almost afraid to
try again."

Sybil smiled uncertainly up at him. He was about the
age her own father would have been—wasn't he? It
seemed to her that a younger face was pushing out
through Mr. Starr's coarse, sallow face. The hooklike quiz-
zical scar on his forehead glistened oddly in the sun.

Sybil politely withdrew her hand from Mr. Starr's and
dropped her eyes. She was shivering—today, she had not
been running at all, had come to meet Mr. Starr for purposes of modeling, in a blouse and skirt, as he'd requested.
She was bare-legged and her feet, in sandals, were wet
from the surf.

Sybil said, softly, as if she didn't want to be heard, "I
feel the same way, Mr. Starr."

They climbed a flight of wooden steps to the top of the
bluff, and there was Mr. Starr's limousine, blackly gleaming, parked a short distance away. At this hour of the
afternoon the park was well populated; there was a gay
giggling bevy of high school girls strolling by, but Sybil
took no notice. She was agitated, still; weak from crying,
yet oddly strengthened, elated too. *You know who he is.
You always knew.* She was keenly aware of Mr. Starr
limping beside her, and impatient with his chatter. Why
didn't he speak directly to her, for once?

The uniformed chauffeur sat behind the wheel of the
limousine, looking neither to the right nor the left, as if at
attention. His visored cap, his white gloves. His profile
like a profile on an ancient coin. Sybil wondered if the
chauffeur knew about her—if Mr. Starr talked to him
about her. Suddenly she was filled with excitement, that
someone else should *know.*

Mr. Starr was saying that, since Sybil had modeled so
patiently that day, since she'd more than fulfilled his ex-

pectations, he had a gift for her—"In addition to your fee, that is."

He opened the rear door of the limousine, and took out a square white box, and, smiling shyly, presented it to Sybil. "Oh, what *is* it?" Sybil cried. She and Aunt Lora rarely exchanged presents any longer, it seemed like a ritual out of the deep past, delightful to rediscover. She lifted the cover of the box, and saw, inside, a beautiful purse; an over-the-shoulder bag; kidskin, the hue of rich dark honey. "Oh, Mr. Starr—thank you," Sybil said, taking the bag in her hands. "It's the most beautiful thing I've ever seen." "Why don't you open it, dear?" Mr. Starr urged, so Sybil opened the bag, and discovered money inside—fresh-minted bills—the denomination on top was twenty dollars. "I hope you didn't overpay me again," Sybil said, uneasily, "—I never have modeled for three hours yet. It isn't fair." Mr. Starr laughed, flushed with pleasure. "Fair to whom?" he asked. "What is 'fair'?—*we* do what *we* like."

Sybil raised her eyes shyly to Mr. Starr's and saw that he was looking at her intently—at least, the skin at the corners of his eyes was tightly puckered. "Today, dear, I insist upon driving you home," he said, smiling. There was a new authority in his voice that seemed to have something to do with the gift Sybil had received from him. "It will soon be getting chilly, and your feet are wet." Sybil hesitated. She had lifted the bag to her face, to inhale the pungent kidskin smell: the bag was of a quality she'd never owned before. Mr. Starr glanced swiftly about, as if to see if anyone was watching; he was still smiling. "Please do climb inside, Blake!—you can't consider me a stranger, now."

Still, Sybil hesitated. Half teasing, she said, *"You* know my name isn't Blake, don't you, Mr. Starr?—how do you know?"

Mr. Starr laughed, teasing too. *"Isn't* it? What is your name, then?"

"Don't you know?"

"Should I know?"

"Shouldn't you?"

There was a pause. Mr. Starr had taken hold of Sybil's wrist; lightly, yet firmly. His fingers circled her thin wrists with the subtle pressure of a watchband.

Mr. Starr leaned close, as if sharing a secret. "Well, I did hear you sing your solo, in your wonderful Christmas pageant at the high school! I must confess, I'd sneaked into a rehearsal too—no one questioned my presence. And I believe I heard the choir director call you—is it 'Sybil'?"

Hearing her name in Mr. Starr's mouth, Sybil felt a sensation of vertigo. She could only nod, mutely, yes.

"*Is* it?—I wasn't sure if I'd heard correctly. A lovely name, for a lovely girl. And 'Blake'—is 'Blake' your surname?"

Sybil murmured, "Yes."

"Your father's name?"

"No. Not my father's name."

"Oh, and why not? Usually, you know, that's the case."

"Because—" And here Sybil paused, confused, uncertain what to say. "It's my mother's name. Was."

"Ah, really! I see," Mr. Starr laughed. "Well, truly, I suppose I *don't,* but we can discuss it another time. Shall we—?"

He meant, shall we get into the car; he was exerting pressure on Sybil's wrist, and, though kindly as always, seemed on the edge of impatience. Sybil stood flatfooted on the sidewalk, wanting to acquiesce; yet, at the same time, uneasily thinking that, no, she should not. Not yet.

So Sybil pulled away, laughing nervously, and Mr. Starr had to release her, with a disappointed downturning of his mouth. Sybil thanked him, saying she preferred to walk. "I hope I will see you tomorrow, then?—'Sybil'?" Mr. Starr called after her. "Yes?"

But Sybil, hugging her new bag against her chest, as a small child might hug a stuffed animal, was walking quickly away.

Was the black limousine following her, at a discreet distance?

Sybil felt a powerful compulsion to look back, but did not.

She was trying to recall if, ever in her life, she'd ridden in such a vehicle. She supposed there had been hired, chauffeur-drawn limousines at her parents' funerals, but she had not attended those funerals; had no memory of anything connected with them, except the strange behavior of her grandmother, her Aunt Lora, and other adults—their grief, but, underlying that grief, their air of profound and speechless shock.

Where is Mommy, she'd asked, where is Daddy, and the replies were always the same: Gone away.

And crying did no good. And fury did no good. Nothing little Sybil could do, or say, or think did any good. That was the first lesson, maybe.

But Daddy isn't dead, you know he isn't. You know, and he knows, why he has returned.

10. "Possessed"

Aunt Lora was smoking again!—back to two packs a day. And Sybil understood guiltily that she was to blame.

For there was the matter of the kidskin bag. The secret gift. Which Sybil had hidden in the farthest corner of her closet, wrapped in plastic, so the smell of it would not permeate the room. (Still, you could smell it—couldn't you? A subtle pervasive smell, rich as any perfume?) Sybil lived in dread that her aunt would discover the purse, and the money; though Lora Dell Blake never entered her niece's room without an invitation, somehow, Sybil worried, it *might* happen. She had never kept any important secret from her aunt in her life, and this secret both filled her with a sense of excitement and power, and weakened her, in childish dread.

What most concerned Lora, however, was Sybil's renewed interest in *that*—as in, "Oh, honey, are you thinking about *that* again? *Why?*"

That was the abbreviated euphemism for what Lora might more fully call "the accident"—"the tragedy"—"your parents' deaths."

Sybil, who had never shown more than passing curiosity about *that* in the past, as far as Lora could remember, was now in the grip of what Lora called "morbid curiosity." That mute, perplexed look in her eyes! That tremulous, though sometimes a bit sullen, look to her mouth! One evening, lighting up a cigarette with shaking fingers, Lora said, bluntly, "Sybil, honey, this tears my heart out. What *is* it you want to know?"

Sybil said, as if she'd been waiting for just this question, "Is my father alive?"

"What?"

"My father. George Conte. *Is* he—maybe—alive?"

The question hovered between them, and, for a long pained moment, it seemed almost that Aunt Lora might snort in exasperation, jump up from the table, walk out of the room. But then she said, shaking her head adamantly, dropping her gaze from Sybil's, "Honey, no. The man is not alive." She paused. She smoked her cigarette, exhaled smoke vigorously through her nostrils; seemed about to say something further; changed her mind; then said, quietly, "You don't ask about your mother, Sybil. Why is that?"

"I—believe that my mother is dead. But—"

"But—?"

"My—my father—"

"—isn't?"

Sybil said, stammering, her cheeks growing hot, "I just want to *know*. I want to see a, a—grave! A death certificate!"

"I'll send to Wellington for a copy of the death certificate," Aunt Lora said slowly. "Will that do?"

"You don't have a copy here?"

"Honey, why would I have a copy here?"

Sybil saw that the older woman was regarding her with a look of pity, and something like dread. She said, stammering, her cheeks warm, "In your—legal things. Your papers. Locked away—"

"Honey, no."

There was a pause. Then Sybil said, half-sobbing, "I was too young to go to their funeral. So I never saw. Whatever it was—I never *saw*. Is that it? They say that's the reason for the ritual—for displaying the dead."

Aunt Lora reached over to take Sybil's hand. "It's one of the reasons, honey," she said. "We meet up with it all the time, at the medical center. People don't believe that loved ones are dead—they know, but can't accept it; the shock is just too much to absorb at once. And, yes, it's a theory, that if you don't see a person actually dead—if there isn't a public ceremony to define it—you may have difficulty accepting it. You may—" and here Aunt Lora paused, frowning, "—be susceptible to fantasy."

Fantasy! Sybil stared at her aunt, shocked. *But I've seen him, I know. I believe him and not you!*

The subject seemed to be concluded for the time being. Aunt Lora briskly stubbed out her cigarette and said, "I'm to blame—probably. I'd been in therapy for a couple of years after it happened and I just didn't want to talk about it any longer, so when you'd asked me questions, over the years, I cut you off; I realize that. But, you see, there's so little to say—Melanie is dead, and *he* is dead. And it all happened a long time ago."

That evening, Sybil was reading in a book on memory she'd taken out of the Glencoe Public Library: *It is known that human beings are "possessed" by an unfathomable number of dormant memory-traces, of which some can be activated under special conditions, including excitation by stimulating points in the cortex. Such traces are indelibly imprinted in the nervous system and are commonly activated by mnemonic stimuli—words, sights, sounds, and especially smells. The phenomenon of déjà vu is closely related to these experiences, in which a "doubling of consciousness" occurs, with the conviction that one has lived an experience before. Much of human memory, however, includes subsequent revision, selection, and fantasizing. . . .*

Sybil let the book shut. She contemplated, for the dozenth time, the faint red marks on her wrist, where Mr. Starr—the man who called himself Mr. Starr—had gripped her, without knowing his own strength.

Nor had Sybil been aware, at the time, that his fingers were so strong; and had clasped so tightly around her wrist.

11. "Mr. Starr"—or "Mr. Conte"

She saw him, and saw that he was waiting for her. And her impulse was to run immediately to him, and observe, with childish delight, how the sight of her would illuminate his face. *Here! Here I am!* It was a profound power that seemed to reside in her, Sybil Blake, seventeen years old—the power to have such an effect upon a man whom she scarcely knew, and who did not know her.

Because he loves me. Because he's my father. That's why. And if he isn't my father—

It was late afternoon of a dull, overcast day. Still, the park was populated at this end; joggers were running, some in colorful costumes. Sybil was not among them, she'd slept poorly the previous night, thinking of—what? Her dead mother who'd been so beautiful?—her father whose face she could not recall (though, yes surely, it was imprinted deep, deep in the cells of her memory)?—her Aunt Lora who was, or was not, telling her the truth, and who loved her more than anyone on earth? And Mr. Starr of course.

Or Mr. Conte.

Sybil was hidden from Mr. Starr's gaze as, with an air of smiling expectancy, he looked about. He was carrying his duffel bag and leaning on his cane. He wore his plain, dark clothes; he was bare-headed, and his silvery hair shone; if Sybil were closer, she would see light winking in his dark glasses. She had noticed the limousine, parked up on the Boulevard a block away.

A young woman jogger ran past Mr. Starr, long-legged, hair flying, and he looked at her, intently—watched her as she ran out of sight along the path. Then he turned back, glancing up toward the street, shifting his shoulders impatiently. Sybil saw him check his wristwatch.

Waiting for you. You know why.

And then, suddenly—Sybil decided not to go to Mr. Starr after all. The man who called himself Starr. She changed her mind at the last moment, unprepared for her decision except to understand that, as, quickly, she walked away, it must be the right decision: her heart was beating erratically, all her senses alert, as if she had narrowly escaped great danger.

12. The Fate of "George Conte"

On Mondays, Wednesdays, and Fridays Lora Dell Blake attended an aerobics class after work, and on these evenings she rarely returned home before seven o'clock. Today was a Friday, at four: Sybil calculated she had more than enough time to search out her aunt's private papers, and to put everything back in order, well before her aunt came home.

Aunt Lora's household keys were kept in a top drawer of her desk, and one of these keys, Sybil knew, was to a small aluminum filing cabinet beside the desk, where confidential records and papers were kept. There were perhaps a dozen keys, in a jumble, but Sybil had no difficulty finding the right one. "Aunt Lora, please forgive me," she whispered. It was a measure of her aunt's trust of her that the filing cabinet was so readily unlocked.

For never in her life had Sybil Blake done such a thing, in violation of the trust between herself and her aunt. She sensed that, unlocking the cabinet, opening the sliding drawers, she might be committing an irrevocable act.

The drawer was jammed tight with manila folders, most of them well-worn and dog-eared. Sybil's first response was disappointment—there were hundreds of household receipts, financial statements, Internal Revenue records dating back for years. Then she discovered a packet of letters dating back to the 1950s, when Aunt Lora would have been a young girl. There were a few snapshots, a few formally posed photographs—one of a strikingly beautiful,

if immature-looking, girl in a high-school graduation cap
and gown, smiling at the camera with glossy lips. On the
rear was written "Melanie, 1969." Sybil stared at this likeness of her mother—her mother long before she'd become
her mother—and felt both triumph and dismay: for, yes,
here was the mysterious Melanie, and, yet, *was* this the
Melanie the child knew?—or, simply, a high school girl,
Sybil's own approximate age, the kind who, judging from
her looks and self-absorbed expression, would never have
been a friend of Sybil's?

Sybil put the photograph back, with trembling fingers.
She was half grateful that Aunt Lora had kept so few
mementos of the past—there could be fewer shocks, reve-
lations.

No photographs of the wedding of Melanie Blake and
George Conte. Not a one.

No photographs, so far as Sybil could see, of her father
"George Conte" at all.

There was a single snapshot of Melanie with her baby
daughter Sybil, and this Sybil studied for a long time. It
had been taken in summer, at a lakeside cottage; Melanie
was posing prettily, in a white dress, with her baby snug
in the crook of her arm, and both were looking toward the
camera, as if someone had just called out to them, to make
them laugh—Melanie with a wide, glamorous, yet sweet
smile, little Sybil gaping open-mouthed. Here Melanie
looked only slightly more mature than in the graduation
photograph: her pale brown hair, many shades of brown
and blond, was shoulder-length, and upturned; her eyes
were meticulously outlined in mascara, prominent in her
heart-shaped face.

In the foreground, on the grass, was the shadow of a
man's head and shoulders—George Conte, perhaps? The
missing person.

Sybil stared at this snapshot, which was wrinkled and
dog-eared. She did not know what to think, and, oddly,
she felt very little: for was the infant in the picture really
herself, Sybil Blake, if she could not remember?

Or did she in fact remember, somewhere deep in her
brain, in memory-traces that were indelible?

From now on, she would "remember" her mother as the pretty, self-assured young woman in this snapshot. This image, in full color, would replace any other.

Reluctantly, Sybil slid the snapshot back in its packet. How she would have liked to keep it!—but Aunt Lora would discover the theft, eventually. And Aunt Lora must be protected against knowing that her own niece had broken into her things, violated the trust between them.

The folders containing personal material were few, and quickly searched. Nothing pertaining to the accident, the "tragedy"?—not even an obituary? Sybil looked in adjacent files, with increasing desperation. There was not only the question of who her father was, or had been, but the question, nearly as compelling, of why Aunt Lora had eradicated all trace of him, even in her own private files. For a moment Sybil wondered if there had ever been any "George Conte" at all: maybe her mother had not married, and that was part of the secret? Melanie had died in some terrible way, terrible at least in Lora Dell Blake's eyes, thus the very fact must be hidden from Sybil, after so many years? Sybil recalled Aunt Lora saying, earnestly, a few years ago, "The only thing you should know, Sybil, is that your mother—and your father—would not want you to grow up in the shadow of their deaths. They would have wanted you—your mother especially—to be *happy.*"

Part of this legacy of happiness, Sybil gathered, had been for her to grow up as a perfectly normal American girl, in a sunny, shadowless place with no history, or, at any rate, no history that concerned her. "But I don't want to be *happy,* I want to *know,"* Sybil said aloud.

But the rest of the manila files, jammed so tightly together they were almost inextricable, yielded nothing.

So, disappointed, Sybil shut the file drawer, and locked it.

But what of Aunt Lora's desk drawers? She had a memory of their being unlocked, thus surely containing nothing of significance; but now it occurred to her that, being unlocked, one of these drawers might in fact contain something Aunt Lora might want to keep safely hidden. So, quickly, with not much hope, Sybil looked through these drawers, messy, jammed with papers, clippings, further packets of household receipts, old programs from plays they'd seen in Los Angeles—and, in the largest drawer, at the very bottom, in a wrinkled manila envelope with "MEDICAL INSURANCE" carefully printed on its front, Sybil found what she was looking for.

Newspaper clippings, badly yellowed, some of them spliced together with aged cellophane tape—

WELLINGTON, VT. MAN SHOOTS WIFE, SELF
SUICIDE ATTEMPT FAILS

AREA MAN KILLS WIFE IN JULY 4 QUARREL
ATTEMPTS SUICIDE ON LAKE CHAMPLAIN

GEORGE CONTE, 31, ARRESTED FOR MURDER
WELLINGTON LAWYER HELD IN SHOOTING
DEATH OF WIFE, 26

CONTE TRIAL BEGINS
PROSECUTION CHARGES PREMEDITATION
Family Members Testify

So Sybil Blake learned, in the space of less than sixty seconds, the nature of the tragedy from which her Aunt Lora had shielded her for nearly fifteen years.

Her father was indeed a man named George Conte, and this man had shot her mother Melanie to death, in their speedboat on Lake Champlain, and pushed her body overboard. He had tried to kill himself too but had only critically wounded himself with a shot to the head. He'd undergone emergency neurosurgery, and recovered; he was arrested, tried, and convicted of second-degree murder; and sentenced to between twelve and nineteen years in prison, at the Hartshill State Prison in northern Vermont.

Sybil sifted through the clippings, her fingers numb. So this was it! This! Murder, attempted suicide!—not mere drunkenness and an "accident" on the lake.

Aunt Lora seemed to have stuffed the clippings in an envelope in haste, or in revulsion; with some, photographs had been torn off, leaving only their captions—"Melanie and George Conte, 1975," "Prosecution witness Lora Dell Blake leaving courthouse." Those photographs of George Conte showed a man who surely did resemble "Mr. Starr": younger, dark-haired, with a face heavier in the jaws and an air of youthful self-assurance and expectation. *There. Your father. "Mr. Starr." The missing person.*

There were several photographs too of Melanie Conte, including one taken for her high-school yearbook, and one of her in a long, formal gown with her hair glamorously upswept—"Wellington woman killed by jealous husband." There was a wedding photograph of the couple looking very young, attractive, and happy; a photograph of the "Conte family at their summer home"; a photograph of "George Conte, lawyer, after 2nd-degree murder verdict" —the convicted man, stunned, down-looking, being taken away handcuffed between two grim sheriff's men. Sybil understood that the terrible thing that had happened in her family had been of enormous public interest in Wellington, Vermont, and that this was part of its terribleness, its shame.

What had Aunt Lora said?—she'd been in therapy for some time afterward, thus did not want to relive those memories.

And she'd said, *It all happened a long time ago.*

But she'd lied, too. She had looked Sybil full in the face and lied, lied. Insisting that Sybil's father was dead when she knew he was alive.

When Sybil herself had reason to believe he was alive.

My name is Starr! Don't judge me too quickly!

Sybil read, and reread, the aged clippings. There were perhaps twenty of them. She gathered two general things: that her father George Conte was from a locally prominent family, and that he'd had a very capable attorney to defend him at his trial; and that the community had greatly enjoyed the scandal, though, no doubt, offering condolences to the grieving Blake family. The spectacle of a beautiful young wife murdered by her "jealous" young husband, her body pushed from an expensive speedboat to

sink in Lake Champlain—who could resist? The media
had surely exploited this tragedy to its fullest.

Now you see, don't you, why your name had to be
changed. Not "Conte," the murderer, but "Blake," the vic-
tim, is your parent.

Sybil was filled with a child's rage, a child's inarticulate
grief—Why, why! This man named George Conte had, by
a violent act, ruined everything!

According to the testimony of witnesses, George Conte
had been "irrationally" jealous of his wife's friendship
with other men in their social circle; he'd quarreled pub-
licly with her upon several occasions, and was known to
have a drinking problem. On the afternoon of July Fourth,
the day of the murder, the couple had been drinking with
friends at the Lake Champlain Club for much of the afternoon, and had then set out in their boat for their summer
home, three miles to the south. Midway, a quarrel
erupted, and George Conte shot his wife several times
with a .32 caliber revolver, which, he later confessed, he'd
acquired for the purpose of "showing her I was serious."
He then pushed her body overboard, and continued on to
the cottage where, in a "distraught state," he tried to take
his two-year-old daughter Sybil with him, back to the boat
—saying that her mother was waiting for her. But the
child's grandmother and aunt, both relatives of the murdered woman, prevented him from taking her, so he returned to the boat alone, took it out a considerable distance onto the lake, and shot himself in the head. He
collapsed in the idling boat, and was rescued by an emergency medical team and taken to a hospital in Burlington
where his life was saved.

Why, why did they save *his* life?—Sybil thought bitterly. She'd never felt such emotion, such outrage, as she
felt for this person George Conte: "Mr. Starr." He'd
wanted to kill her too, of course—that was the purpose of
his coming home, wanting to get her, saying her mother
wanted her. Had Sybil's grandmother and Aunt Lora not
stopped him, he would have shot her too, and dumped her
body into the lake, and ended it all by shooting himself—

but not killing himself. A bungled suicide. And then, after recovering, a plea of "not guilty" to the charge of murder.

A charge of second-degree murder, and a sentence of only twelve to nineteen years. So, he was out. George Conte was out. As "Mr. Starr," the amateur artist, the lover of the beautiful and the pure, he'd found her out, and he'd come for her.

And you know why.

13. "Your Mother Is Waiting For You"

Sybil Blake returned the clippings to the envelope so conspicuously marked "MEDICAL INSURANCE," and returned the envelope to the very bottom of the unlocked drawer in her aunt's desk. She closed the drawer carefully, and, though she was in an agitated state, looked about the room to see if she'd left anything inadvertently out of place; any evidence that she'd been in here at all.

Yes, she'd violated the trust Aunt Lora had had in her. Yet Aunt Lora had lied to her too, these many years. And so convincingly.

Sybil understood that she could never again believe anyone fully. She understood that those who love us can, and will, lie to us; they may act out of a moral conviction that such lying is necessary, and this may in fact be true —but, still, they *lie.*

Even as they look into your eyes and insist they are telling the truth.

Of the reasonable steps Sybil Blake might have taken, this was the most reasonable: she might have confronted Lora Dell Blake with the evidence she'd found and with her knowledge of what the tragedy had been, and she might have told her about "Mr. Starr."

But she hated him so. And Aunt Lora hated him. And, hating him as they did, how could they protect themselves against him, if he chose to act? For Sybil had no doubt, now, her father had returned to her to do her harm.

If George Conte had served his prison term, and been released from prison, if he was free to move about the country like any other citizen, certainly he had every right to come to Glencoe, California. In approaching Sybil Blake, his daughter, he had committed no crime. He had not threatened her, he had not harassed her, he had behaved in a kindly, courteous, generous way; except for the fact (in Aunt Lora's eyes this would be an outrageous, unspeakable fact) that he had misrepresented himself.

"Mr. Starr" was a lie, an obscenity. But no one had forced Sybil to model for him, nor to accept an expensive gift from him. She had done so willingly. She had done so gratefully. After her initial timidity, she'd been rather eager to be so employed.

For "Mr. Starr" had seduced her—almost.

Sybil reasoned that if she told her aunt about "Mr. Starr," their lives would be irrevocably changed. Aunt Lora would be upset to the point of hysteria. She would insist upon going to the police. The police would rebuff her, or, worse yet, humor her. And what if Aunt Lora went to confront "Mr. Starr" herself?

No, Sybil was not going to involve her aunt. Nor implicate her in any way.

"I love you too much," Sybil whispered. "You are all I have."

To avoid seeing Aunt Lora that evening, or, rather, to avoid being seen by her, Sybil went to bed early, leaving a note on the kitchen table explaining that she had a mild case of the flu. Next morning, when Aunt Lora looked in Sybil's room, to ask her worriedly how she was, Sybil smiled wanly and said she'd improved; but, still, she thought she would stay home from school that day.

Aunt Lora, ever vigilant against illness, pressed her hand against Sybil's forehead, which did seem feverish. She looked into Sybil's eyes, which were dilated. She asked if Sybil had a sore throat, if she had a headache, if she'd had an upset stomach or diarrhea, and Sybil said no, no, she simply felt a little weak, she wanted to sleep. So Aunt Lora believed her, brought her Bufferin and fruit juice and toast with honey, and went off quietly to leave her alone.

Sybil wondered if she would ever see her aunt again.

But of course she would: she had no doubt, she could force herself to do what must be done.

Wasn't her mother waiting for her?

A windy, chilly afternoon. Sybil wore warm slacks and a wool pullover sweater and her jogging shoes. But she wasn't running today. She carried her kidskin bag, its strap looped over her shoulder.

Her handsome kidskin bag, with its distinctive smell.

Her bag, into which she'd slipped, before leaving home, the sharpest of her aunt's several finely honed steak knives.

Sybil Blake hadn't gone to school that day but she entered the park at approximately three forty-five, her usual time. She'd sighted Mr. Starr's long elegantly gleaming black limousine parked on the street close by, and there was Mr. Starr himself, waiting for her.

How animated he became, seeing her!—exactly as he'd been in the past. It seemed strange to Sybil that, somehow, to him, things were unchanged.

He imagined her still ignorant, innocent. Easy prey.

Smiling at her. Waving. "Hello, Sybil!"

Daring to call her that—"Sybil."

He was hurrying in her direction, limping, using his cane. Sybil smiled. There was no reason not to smile, thus she smiled. She was thinking with what skill Mr. Starr used that cane of his, how practiced he'd become. Since the injury to his brain?—or had there been another injury, suffered in prison?

Those years in prison, when he'd had time to think. Not to repent—Sybil seemed to know he had not repented— but, simply, to think.

To consider the mistakes he'd made, and how to unmake them.

"Why, my dear, hello!—I've missed you, you know," Mr. Starr said. There was an edge of reproach to his voice but he smiled to show his delight. "I won't ask where *were* you, now you're *here*. And carrying your beautiful bag—"

Sybil peered up at Mr. Starr's pale, tense, smiling face. Her reactions were slow at first, as if numbed; as if she were, for all that she'd rehearsed this, not fully wakened —a kind of sleepwalker.

"And—you *will* model for me this afternoon? Under our new, improved terms?"

"Yes, Mr. Starr."

Mr. Starr had his duffel bag, his sketch pad, his charcoal sticks. He was bareheaded, and his fine silver hair blew in the wind. He wore a slightly soiled white shirt with a navy-blue silk necktie and his old tweed jacket; and his gleaming black shoes that put Sybil in mind of a funeral. She could not see his eyes behind the dark lenses of his glasses but she knew by the puckered skin at the corners of his eyes that he was staring at her intently, hungrily. She was his model, he was the artist, when could they begin? Already, his fingers were flexing in anticipation.

"I think, though, we've about exhausted the possibilities of this park, don't you, dear? It's charming, but rather common. And so *finite,*" Mr. Starr was saying, expansively. "Even the beach, here in Glencoe. Somehow it lacks —amplitude. So I was thinking—I was hoping—we might today vary our routine just a bit, and drive up the coast. Not far—just a few miles. Away from so many people, and so many distractions." Seeing that Sybil was slow to respond, he added, warmly, "I'll pay you double, Sybil—of course. You know you can trust me by now, don't you? Yes?"

That curious, ugly little hook of a scar in Mr. Starr's forehead—its soft pale tissue gleamed in the whitish light. Sybil wondered was that where the bullet had gone in.

Mr. Starr had been leading Sybil in the direction of the curb, where the limousine was waiting, its engine idling almost soundlessly. He opened the door. Sybil, clutching her kidskin bag, peered inside, at the cushioned, shadowy interior. For a moment, her mind was blank. She might have been on a high board, about to dive into the water, not knowing how she'd gotten to where she was, or why. Only that she could not turn back.

Mr. Starr was smiling eagerly, hopefully. "Shall we? Sybil?"

"Yes, Mr. Starr," Sybil said, and climbed inside.

BEAT YOUR NEIGHBOR OUT OF DOORS

By JIRO AKAGAWA

—MONDAY—

"That's my seat!"

Kyosuke looked up in surprise.

"I beg your pardon . . ."

"I said that's my seat!"

The man was well over sixty, grey and wrinkled. His skin was dry and his sunken eyes threatened to burst out of their sockets with rage.

"What do you mean, 'your seat'?" Kyosuke replied, looking around the carriage. "There are any number of other empty seats."

Although the train was only comprised of two carriages, there were very few other passengers, but despite the fact that Kyosuke was only stating the obvious, the old man became even madder.

"This is my seat!" he shouted. "I always sit here!"

The old man was shaking with rage, and realizing that it would be pointless to antagonize him any further, Kyosuke shrugged and stood up. He sat down again in a nearby seat, but the old man, far from thanking him, commented in a loud voice for everyone to hear:

"I don't know what's become of young people these days, they've got no respect for their elders. They're just a bunch of ill-mannered, selfish loafers . . ."

Kyosuke decided to ignore the old man's tirade and looked around the carriage. There were eight other passengers altogether. Five had got on at the last station with him; they were his new neighbors.

Kyosuke Ikegami had spent the weekend moving into his new house and today was the first day he would be commuting from there to his office. He had been deter-

59

mined to buy a house of his own by the time he was thirty, but his wages weren't very high and his company, being comparatively small, could not offer its employees cheap mortgages. He had managed it at last, however. Even though he had had to borrow a lot of money, he had bought his first home.

It took him one hour and fifty minutes to get to the office, three times as long as it did from his previous apartment, and this meant getting up at six o'clock in the morning. The expresses did not stop at the local station; there were not even any staff there, so the train would just pull in unannounced and leave again without any warning. It was a fifteen minute walk to the station from his house along a road surrounded by woods and fields all the way, with not a single building to break the monotony.

A large real-estate company had planned to develop the area but it had gone bankrupt soon after it started and all that remained to show of its plans were six houses, huddled together in a vast expanse of nothing. The shopping centers and restaurants which had been in the original plans had all come to nothing and the isolated houses had to rely on propane gas. It was a twenty minute walk to the nearest shops.

Despite all this, Kyosuke had chosen to move here. He only had three months before the lease on his apartment expired and the house was the best he could afford.

Even though he had been forced by circumstances to move to this house, he was more than satisfied with it and felt like shouting to the world, "This is my house! I have bought my very own home!"

The train had to wait fifteen minutes for an express to pass. While he was sitting there, Kyosuke could not help but think it a coincidence that the occupants of all six houses should just happen to catch the same train every morning. However, when he thought about it, he realized that it was only natural. There was not another train for more than thirty minutes, so even if they all arrived at work a little early, they were sure to be late if they waited for the next train.

Kyosuke thought that he should introduce himself to

his neighbors. He had been so busy with the move that he had not had a chance over the weekend, and although he had seen them all set off for the station that morning, they seemed to be avoiding him and he could not bring himself to approach them. Now, however, they were all going to be sitting together in the same carriage for the next hour or more and surely they would not object to a little conversation. The only problem was that they were not sitting together and he could not make up his mind whom he should approach first. He looked them over, one by one.

The old man who had picked the argument with him was without a doubt the eldest of the group and judging by his age, it was likely that he had started his present job after retirement. Thinking about this, it occurred to Kyosuke that it was probably as a result of having to work at some boring job at his age that the man was so bad-tempered . . .

After seeing Kyosuke off that morning, Kimiko had kept herself as busy as a bee. She was a small, slim person, but she was quite energetic and a good worker.

The night before, Kyosuke had taken her to bed before she even had time to hang the curtains and they had found it so exhilarating to have sex in their new house that they had both forgotten how tired they were. Another reason why they had found it so exciting was that now that they had a home of their own, they wanted to start a family, so they did not need to bother with any precautions. They had made love countless times until they had both fallen into an exhausted sleep, but Kimiko did not feel tired at all. This was a major event in their marriage and she felt like a newlywed all over again.

Although late November in the suburbs is rather chilly, she was so busy arranging things and moving the furniture around that her forehead was beaded with perspiration and she decided to take a short break after taking the empty packing cases out into the garden. The garden was very small and while she was breaking up the cardboard boxes, she felt someone's eyes on her. She looked up and saw a skinny old woman looking at her over the hedge.

That must be our new neighbor, she thought as she pushed her hair back unconsciously with one hand. What was her name now . . . ? Oh yes, Muramatsu, that's it.

She made her way over to the hedge which divided their garden from the next and smiling warmly, she said:

"Good morning, I am Kimiko Ikegami, we have just moved in. You must be Mrs. Muramatsu."

The old lady looked Kimiko slowly up and down. Kimiko was wearing jeans and a T-shirt.

"Please excuse the state I'm in . . ." Kimiko said, smiling embarrassedly.

The old lady did not return her smile.

"I thought it was only good manners to introduce yourself to your neighbors when you first move into a new home. You should save the informalities until later."

Kimiko was astounded by the antagonism in the other's voice.

"I'm very sorry. I meant to come over as soon as I had finished tidying up . . ."

"You young people don't seem to know the meaning of manners," the woman said stingingly. "Anyway, the name is Murakoshi, not Muramatsu."

Watching her as she made her way back into her house, Kimiko gave a deep sigh.

"I can see that we are going to have problems with our neighbors," she said to herself.

Kyosuke looked at the other four men.

One was a swarthy, plump fellow who sat clutching a black leather case as if he was afraid it would fall off his lap any moment. He looked about fortyish and gave the impression of being very nervous. His eyes behind his thick glasses were closed, but he didn't seem to be asleep. He was probably scared that someone might meet his eye.

Kimiko pressed the doorbell and after a second she heard a reply in a high-pitched voice. She straightened her hair again. She was wearing a smart dress and had made herself up. She thought that she should get the introductions over with before she made any more enemies.

"Oh, you must be the person who has just moved in. How do you do? Please come in."

The woman started to rattle on as soon as she came to the door and Kimiko hardly had the chance to introduce herself.

She was hustled into the house before she could refuse. Kozue Takasugi was the type of woman Kimiko disliked the most. She did nothing but complain about her husband, who was an accountant, and the cost of living, watching television the whole time she was speaking.

"I am afraid that I have to visit the other neighbors . . ." Kimiko said, and heaved a sigh of relief when she finally managed to get out.

Kyosuke looked at the man who was sitting directly opposite him. He was about forty-five or forty-six, wearing a very expensive coat and looking every inch a gentleman. Kyosuke guessed that he was probably involved in some kind of intellectual profession.

Kimiko was relieved to find someone whom she could relax and talk with.

"Yes, our son is in senior high now," Keiko Yagisawa was saying as she poured out some tea. "He says that he doesn't want to commute from here so he's got himself an apartment in town."

"That must be very lonely for you."

"Yes, my husband doesn't get back from work until late. He's a university professor, you know . . ."

"Oh really? A professor?"

"It is not all that good a job, but . . ." Keiko smiled. "He teaches in the evenings as well and doesn't get back until ten o'clock, eleven if he misses the train."

The small living room was lined with shelves which were crammed full of books. It was obviously the house of an intellectual. Keiko was rather a weak-looking person, but had a beautiful character and Kimiko felt that living here was not going to be so bad after all.

* * *

The fourth man was a typical office worker. He was about thirty-two and of average weight and height. He would appear to have rushed out as his hair was not combed and his necktie was crooked. He was reading a golf magazine and practicing his swings as he sat there. As soon as the train started to move after the express had passed, Mr. Office-worker fell asleep with his mouth open.

Everything about him is typical, Kyosuke thought, smiling to himself.

The last person was the one sitting farthest from Kyosuke and in his student days, he had obviously been an athlete. He had broad shoulders and a strong-looking body. His crew cut made him look quite young, but judging from his paunch, he was probably about thirty-five.

These five men were his new neighbors and this time he was not living in rented accommodation so he would be with them for a long time. There was no need to hurry. If he took his time and chatted with them, little by little they would grow to understand each other.

Kyosuke was not a believer in first impressions. He worked in a very busy office where the staff changed with bewildering speed and often he would meet someone who looked very interesting, but after he got to know them better, they would turn out to be just the opposite. The only person who truly lived up to his first impression was Kimiko, he thought fondly.

Anyway, it's still only the first day, he thought as he tried to get comfortable on the hard seat.

The only thing that worried him a bit was that apart from the bad-tempered old man, none of them had so much as looked his way and he got the feeling that they were trying to avoid him.

"The one who was reading the golf magazine was probably Mr. Aso."

"Ah so?"

"Idiot!" Kimiko said, laughing as she served him a second bowl of rice. "There were lots of golf magazines in his house."

"What's his wife like?"

"She looks very tough. They've got two children, one is three and the other is only one, but she is five months pregnant already."

"Ah! That's probably why her husband fell asleep on the train."

"The sportsman type was probably Mr. Eguchi. His wife is a pretty woman and she's got a really good taste in clothes. Although they are quite different types, she seems to be very friendly with Mrs. Aso; it's probably because they both have three-year-old children."

"Anyway," Kyosuke said, sipping his hot tea, "they're all our neighbors so we'll just have to do our best to get on well with them."

"Yes, particularly in a deserted place like this, we can't pick and choose."

"It took all we had to get this place, so we'll have to stay," Kyosuke said. "It will be twenty years at least until we can pay off the loan."

"Say, I know we have already eaten, but how about a drink? I'd like to propose a toast." Although she did not drink as a rule, Kimiko brought out a bottle of beer and pouring it into two glasses, she gave one to Kyosuke. Raising her own, she said: "To a happy future in this house."

"Cheers," Kyosuke said, and the two glasses touched with a gentle clink.

At that moment the lights all went out.

—TUESDAY—

"I say . . . over here."

Kyosuke looked over at the man who had called him and after a moment remembered who it was.

"Oh, good afternoon. Thanks for all your help."

They were in a coffee bar on the first floor of the building where he worked and the man who had telephoned and asked him to come, mysteriously not giving his name, worked for the real-estate agency which had sold him the house. His name was Ishihara.

"I'm glad that I could have been of assistance."
Kyosuke sat down opposite him and ordered a coffee.
"I'm sorry to call you out during office hours."
"That's okay, I'm always having to visit people on business so I'm often out of the office. What can I do for you?"
"I was wondering if everything was okay at your new house. Nothing has happened, has it?"
"That's very kind of you, but I'm pleased to be able to tell you that everything is just fine. Of course, it's a bit inconvenient with regard to the shops, but we knew that before we moved in."
"That's good."
Ishihara seemed to be relieved for some reason.
"Oh yes, the only thing is that the power went off last night."
"A power cut? Did you find the cause?"
"Yes, it was just a fuse, although we weren't using any heavy appliances. But anyway, it's nothing for you to worry about."
"That's a relief. Should anything come up, however, please don't hesitate to get in touch with me."
"Thank you very much, it's very kind of you."
"Not at all."
So saying, Ishihara went out, leaving Kyosuke drinking his coffee.
He is a very conscientious agent, he thought. Fancy coming to ask for complaints without my having called him. All the same . . .
For some reason he was a bit disturbed by the way in which Ishihara had asked if nothing had happened, almost as if he had half-expected something would . . .

"Mrs. Ikegami . . ."
Kimiko was hanging out the bedclothes to air when Mrs. Takasugi called out to her from the other side of the hedge.
"Good morning."
"You wouldn't like to come to the supermarket with me, would you? Tomorrow is a holiday so there will be lots of bargains."

Kimiko hesitated for a moment. She did not enjoy Kozue's company all that much and she still had a lot of work to do in the house. She had plenty of food in the larder and did not need anything urgently. She was about to refuse when she realized that Kozue might take offense and after all, they were going to be living together for a long time to come . . .

"Yes, I'd love to."

"Go and get ready then, I'll wait here."

Kimiko started for the house when she glanced up at the sky. It was sunny at the moment, but there were also quite a few clouds. Maybe it would be safer to take the sleeping quilts indoors.

Kozue seemed to guess what was on her mind for she said: "Don't worry about the quilts, just leave them there. You can get Mrs. Murakoshi to keep her eye on them."

"But I don't like to ask—"

"Nonsense, I'll ask her for you, but you'll have to leave the back door open or she won't be able to get in."

Kimiko did not like to leave the door unlocked and felt that it would probably be easier if she just took the quilts indoors herself, but looking over, she saw that Kozue was already talking to Mrs. Murakoshi and realized that it was too late to refuse. She unlocked the door.

"Hello." It was a deep, husky voice. "Is that Mr. Ikegami?"

"Yes, that's right," Kyosuke replied without stopping his work. "Who is speaking, please?"

The person on the other end of the line did not answer. "I believe you've just bought a house, haven't you?"

"Yes, what about it?"

"You're not wanted there."

"What?"

"Get out while you still have the chance."

"Who are you? Who is this speaking?"

The line went dead.

"Damn it!"

Kyosuke slammed the phone down so violently that the man on the next desk looked up.

"What's wrong?"

"It's just someone playing some kind of practical joke."

He tried to get back to his work but found that he could not concentrate properly. Why should that call make him so uneasy? And what was the meaning of that threat, "while you still have the chance?"

Whoever it was knew that he had bought the house and also knew his work number. What was going on?

He suddenly thought of Kimiko and stretched out his hand to the phone, but then he remembered that their new house had not been connected yet and he did not know which of the neighbors would take a message for him.

As he said, it was probably just a joke, someone trying to irritate him.

The rain was so heavy that it bounced back from the road's thin surface, making it look like a grey river.

"Just look at the rain," Kozue said.

They had gone to a restaurant for lunch after they had finished their shopping and it was not until they came to leave that they realized it was raining. Kimiko went and bought a cheap plastic umbrella which they both sheltered under as they walked home, but it was a twenty-minute walk and Kimiko was soaked by the time they got there. Even though it was she who had bought the umbrella, Kozue had insisted on holding it, leaving Kimiko exposed on one side.

"Goodbye," Kozue said at her porch as she handed back the umbrella. "Wasn't it a good thing I asked Mrs. Murakoshi to take in your quilts for you?"

Kimiko had to struggle to keep her temper. Instead of thanking her for the use of the umbrella, she actually seemed to expect Kimiko's gratitude. She realized that it was not worth making an enemy over a small thing like that so mumbling something that could be taken for a thank you, she hurried back to her own house.

She was so wet that she thought she would go in through the kitchen to avoid messing up their new house. She went through the side gate and stopped dead in her tracks. She could not believe her eyes.

"She couldn't . . . The old . . ." she murmured unconsciously. There in the garden were the two quilts. They were so sodden that the poles she had hung them on were bending under the weight.

"Stop crying," Kyosuke said, a bit fed up.

"I can't help it—I'm so mad—" No matter how hard she tried, she could not stop the tears. "How could she do a thing like that?"

"She's very old, she's probably getting a bit absent-minded and forgot."

"No, I bet she left them out on purpose. I'm to blame, too. I should never have gone out and left them in the garden—I'm sorry."

"It's nothing. It's not as if we can't use them anymore."

"But they are wringing wet. It was all I could do to carry them into the bathroom they were so heavy. Even when they dry out, I don't know if we'll be able to use them."

"We can buy some new ones then. They were only old ones we brought with us so it's no real loss."

"Mmm . . ."

Kimiko had stopped crying so Kyosuke changed the subject.

"I heard from the phone company today. We'll be connected next week."

"Really? That's good." Kimiko smiled.

"Until then, is there anyone here that I could ask to give you a message?"

"Mmm—well, we can forget about next door, and I'm not too keen on Mrs. Takasugi— Why?"

"Oh nothing in particular, just in case. You know."

"Yes, well, I'll ask Mrs. Yagisawa then."

"What, the professor's wife?"

"That's right, she's a nice woman."

Kyosuke decided it would probably be better not to tell her about the phone call he had had that afternoon, it would only make her worry.

"What are we going to do about our bed tonight?" Kimiko asked.

"What's wrong with the visitor's quilts?"

"But there's only one set."

"That will be ample . . . ample," Kyosuke said with a lecherous grin.

"You've got a one-track mind!" Kimiko exclaimed, blushing.

—WEDNESDAY—

When the doorbell rang, Kimiko was in the bathroom doing the laundry.

"Just a minute!"

She washed the detergent off her hands and wiped them on the towel before going to the door, so she took a few minutes getting there.

"Yes," she said, opening the door on the chain. There was nobody there. She guessed that it was a mistake or some children playing a joke—but there were not any children around there who would do something like that.

She undid the chain and opening the door, she noticed a small paper bag on the porch . . .

"Leave that house."

It was the same voice as yesterday and Kyosuke realized that whoever it was, he was trying to disguise his voice.

"Who are you?" Kyosuke asked, trying to keep calm. "One of the neighbors?"

"No!" The man shouted with unexpected violence, and in doing so, he forgot to disguise his voice.

I know that voice from somewhere, Kyosuke thought. "Why are you giving me this warning?"

"It's for your own sake."

So saying, the man hung up. Kyosuke bit his lip thoughtfully as he replaced the receiver and noticed that his hand was shaking slightly.

Kimiko took a portable tape recorder out of the bag and put it on the kitchen table.

What is it, I wonder . . .

She looked at the used recorder for a few minutes in perplexity. Finally she decided that at least she should listen to the tape that was left in it.

To begin with she thought that the tape must be blank, but then she noticed that there was some faint background noise. She turned the volume up full and heard a muffled whispering.

I wonder what it is . . .

She strained her ears and after a short while she had a horrible premonition. Her cheeks became scarlet with embarrassment and as the tape continued, she realized that she was right.

The voices on the tape were her own and Kyosuke's. It was a recording of them making love the night before.

She could hear herself almost crying as she climaxed. She could also hear Kyosuke whispering that he loved her . . .

She slammed her hand down on the stop button, her cheeks burning with shame. Tearing out the cassette, she pulled all the tape out, tore it into shreds, and threw it on the floor.

She ran to the front door, flung it open, and looked around for the perpetrator of this foul joke to vent her rage on. Of course, there was nobody there.

Who could have done it? Her anger turned to fear. Whoever it was had not only spied on them, but had taped everything and then delivered the tape to her. There was a definite threat indicated by this behavior.

Before going back indoors, she went around to the bedroom window and there, in the mud from the previous day's rain, was a set of woman's footprints, different from her own. However, unlike in a detective story, they were not very clear and had no special characteristics.

Kimiko went back into the house and just sat in a daze for several hours. The fact that someone would hate her enough to have done this came as a terrible shock to her.

* * *

"What's wrong?" Kyosuke asked.

"Nothing, I just thought it would be nice to eat out for a change."

She had come into town and rung him from a phone near his office. She waited for him to finish and then they both went to a restaurant together. It was a long time since they had had a date like this.

"I don't mind at all, but are you sure nothing happened?"

Kimiko could not bring herself to tell him about the tape as she did not want to worry him unnecessarily. She told herself that this was probably the last she would ever hear of it so it would be best to just forget about it.

Kyosuke could tell from her behavior that something was wrong, but he forced himself not to worry too deeply about it. He was more worried about the mystery phone calls. He was convinced now that they weren't a joke and even considered going to the police about them. However, he had no idea who could be responsible and so the police probably could not do anything to help him.

Anyway, he would keep quiet for the time being.

They each had their own problems but they were both pretending that nothing had happened.

They were both surprised when Yagisawa suddenly spoke to them.

"You are Mr. Ikegami, aren't you? We're neighbors but I don't even know your face very well. My name is Yagisawa."

This was the first time Kyosuke had met one of the five on his homeward journey.

"What do you think of the house now that you are settled in?"

True to his profession, he had a good carrying voice.

"Well, it's difficult to say, we have only been there a few days so far." Kyosuke replied in a noncommittal way.

"I suppose you find it quite inconvenient." Mr. Yagisawa smiled at Kimiko in a most friendly fashion. "I expect you find it quite lonely, too."

"Not at all, I'm so busy and all the other ladies are such

nice people." Kimiko was surprised that she could lie so easily, even though she had said it half in sarcasm.

They chatted about neutral subjects such as work for some time and then fell into silence until they reached their station. Standing up, Yagisawa said in a casual way:

"Well, what do you think? Do you intend to live here for long?"

Kyosuke was speechless for a moment.

"Of course—after all, it is my house."

"I see . . . well, good night."

Yagisawa nodded slightly, then, moving with remarkable agility, he got off the train and walked home ahead of them.

"I wonder what he meant by that," Kimiko said as they walked along the road back from the station in silence.

Kyosuke took some time with the key, trying to open the front door.

"What's wrong?" Kimiko asked.

Kyosuke turned the knob and finally got the door open.

"The door, it wasn't locked," he said, looking Kimiko in the eye.

—THURSDAY—

"Hey, what's wrong? You don't seem yourself today," one of Kyosuke's colleagues asked and tapped him on the shoulder. Kyosuke laughed and tried to cover up, but he felt irritated because it was true, he could not concentrate on his work.

Last night Kimiko had insisted that she had locked the door and they had ended up having an argument. The door had been open, but nothing in the house had been touched and nothing stolen, so if someone had picked the lock, what was their object? When Kimiko had told him about the tape, he had been shocked. It was an obvious case of harassment, but they did not know who was responsible so they had no choice but to let it stand. It was not, however, something that could be ignored.

Kimiko was very angry and demanded that he do something about it. He did his best to make a joke of the whole affair, though, as he thought that if he showed her he was worried, it would only add to her unrest.

He wondered if there was someone he could discuss it with, and at that moment, the phone rang.

"Hello, Ikegami here."

"You know what I want." It was the same voice. "Get out of that house, now!"

"Not unless you give me a good reason."

"It's for your own good."

"So you say . . ."

Kyosuke broke off. A police car was driving by his building and for some reason its siren sounded strange. As the siren passed the window, he could also hear it in the phone.

He put the phone down on his desk and flew down the stairs from his third-floor office. The man had to be phoning from one of the phone booths on the first floor.

The phones just came into view when he saw a familiar figure disappearing out of the building.

"Wait!"

He leapt forward, and grabbing the man's arm, he pulled him back. The man turned around nervously—it was the real-estate agent, Ishihara.

Kimiko had hardly slept a wink the night before. Who had opened the front door, and for what reason? She could distinctly remember locking the door when she went out, but as Kyosuke had said, why would a thief force open the door and then leave without stealing anything?

However, if the object had been intimidation, she could understand it. They were demonstrating how easily they could enter the house any time they wanted to. That was it! She would change the locks on the front door and the French windows for stronger ones . . .

She was still thinking about all this when morning came and it was time to get up.

She did the housework and laundry as usual and was sitting down to read the paper before she realized how tired she was. She decided to lie down for a minute and folding a cushion in half to make a pillow, she closed her eyes. She was not going to sleep, just relax for a few minutes.

Before she knew what had happened, she was sound asleep.

"What?! Do you mean we are not the first people to live in that house?"

Kyosuke was so surprised that he could hardly believe his ears.

"That's right. There were two other people, two families that is, who were there before you."

Ishihara had lost his threatening stance and as they sat in the coffee bar, he seemed anything but an intimidator.

"But—" Kyosuke was having trouble understanding what he was hearing. "Do you mean there is something wrong with the deeds on the place?"

"Oh, no, not at all. You are the first people to actually buy the house. The others had only rented it and of course, when they died, the lease automatically—"

"Hang on a minute," Kyosuke interrupted. "Did you just say 'when they died'?"

Ishihara wiped the perspiration off his forehead.

"Yes, that's right."

Kyosuke swallowed heavily and settled himself in his chair.

"Why don't you tell me the whole story?"

"Well, you see, both of the other families that lived in that house died in accidents—within two weeks of their having moved in."

Kyosuke could feel the blood draining from his face.

"You mean that you hid something as important as that when you sold us the place?!"

"But you must look at our side of it. If we told people about the deaths, we would never be able to sell it."

Of course Kyosuke understood this, but he could not help but feel deceived.

"But why did you make those threatening phone calls then?"

"I thought that you should know about the history of the house, but my superiors strictly forbid it. All the same, I couldn't get it off my conscience. I was very anxious in case something should happen to you or your wife so I—"

"So you made those threatening calls to try and make me leave before it was too late."

"I am very sorry."

Kyosuke calmed down. This man had only been thinking of his well-being and had even gone against a strict order from his superiors in telling him all this.

"I understand," he said. "I won't tell anyone in your firm that you told me about this."

"Thank you very much."

"But what does it all mean?"

"I am sure that it is just a coincidence. The first was a family of three and they died in an accident when they were out for a drive nearby. The second family were newlyweds and one day—it was in winter and it had been snowing—the husband was coming back from a party drunk when he fell over in the woods by the road. He froze to death and his wife committed suicide a few days later."

"In that house?"

"No, she drowned in a river near her parents' home."

Kyosuke gave a sigh of relief.

"Anyway, after that our company did the house up to make it look like new and sold it to you."

"But none of the neighbors told us about any of this."

"Well, it's not really the kind of thing people want to talk about."

All the same, could there be any connection between the cassette tape and these two accidents?

Leaving the repentant real-estate agent, Kyosuke went up to the third floor and was immediately called by one of his colleagues.

"Hey, Ikegami. Where have you been?"

"Why? Do you want something?"

"You had a phone call from a Mrs. Yagisawa. She said that you were to go straight home, your wife has gassed herself . . ."

* * *

"Kimiko!" Kimiko was lying in bed and smiled weakly at him. "Are you all right?"

"Yes, Mrs. Yagisawa found me in time . . ."

"I wanted to borrow some soy sauce and came over to see if you had any." Mrs. Yagisawa was sitting by Kimiko's bed.

"I don't know how to thank you," Kyosuke said, bowing his head to the floor.

"There is no need, I only did what anyone would in that situation."

"No, I'll come over later and thank you properly."

"Oh, please don't bother." She smiled at Kimiko. "Anyway, your husband is home now so I will leave you both together. Look after yourself."

"Thank you—for everything."

Kyosuke saw her to the front door and then came back to Kimiko.

"Kyosuke!" Kimiko rushed into his arms and collapsed in tears. "I'm scared—I'm so scared."

Kyosuke held her close and spoke to her soothingly.

"There is no need to worry, it's all right."

Kimiko shook her head violently.

"No, you are wrong, you don't understand. They say that I fell asleep and that the kettle boiled over and put the flame out—but I did not have anything on the gas! I know for sure that I didn't!"

After they had finished dinner and had a bath, Kimiko seemed to have recovered.

"What shall we do?"

"Do about what?"

"Somebody hates us and tried to kill me."

"Don't be silly."

"But it's true. That tape could be considered a bad joke, but trying to gas me shows a genuine murderous intent. If Mrs. Yagisawa hadn't happened to find me, I would have been—I would be dead now."

Kyosuke became thoughtful. The accidents which killed the previous tenants of the house, the car crash and the man falling over in the woods and freezing to death—it was feasible that they could both have been murder.

"But why should anyone want to kill us?"

"I don't know."

After a while Kyosuke said: "I'll go and discuss it with Mr. Yagisawa."

"Yagisawa?"

"I think we can trust him, don't you?"

"But he did say something a bit strange last night, didn't he?"

"Yes, but it was his wife who saved your life today."

Kimiko nodded unwillingly.

"That's true."

"I might as well go straightaway," Kyosuke said, rising to his feet.

Yagisawa nodded. "Yes, it is true. The other people who lived in that house all met with accidents. Didn't you know?"

"The real-estate company forgot to mention it."

"Yes, I can understand that—would you care for a whiskey?"

"No, thank you, I'm fine."

"Oh, well you wouldn't mind if I helped myself, would you?"

Yagisawa poured himself a whiskey and water and took a sip.

"I'm sure you must realize that we don't really like to talk about the deaths either."

"Yes, of course. Personally, I'm prepared to believe that they were both unrelated accidents, but I am more concerned with that tape recording and the attempted gas poisoning today. It seems to be taking a practical joke too far when it threatens somebody's life. I want to know who it was and what they expect to gain by it."

"And what do you expect of me?"

"You are a professor and have good standing in society. You must be used to judging people, and I feel sure that you must be able to guess who would be likely to do a thing like that."

"Mmm . . . That's a very difficult thing to ask. It's true that I have known my neighbors ever since I moved here and have a good idea as to what kind of people they are, but you are asking that I should condemn one of them without a shred of evidence."

"I realize it's an unreasonable request to make . . ."

Yagisawa gazed at Kyosuke for a while with a strange expression on his face.

"Mr. Ikegami."

"Yes?"

"If your wife is so scared, maybe the best thing would be for you to move somewhere else."

"I'm afraid I can't do that," Kyosuke replied. "I've finally managed to buy my own house and I'm not about to give it up now."

"I see," Yagisawa said, nodding. "So you intend to live here indefinitely then?"

"Yes," Kyosuke said definitely.

Yagisawa sat for a while gazing at the floor, apparently deep in thought. He looked at Kyosuke for a while then said:

"I understand."

—THURSDAY MIDNIGHT—

The men were all gathered in the Murakoshis' living room.

"He has no intention of leaving," Yagisawa said. "He said so quite clearly."

They all gave a sigh of disappointment. Only Murakoshi seemed pleased by the news.

"Well, we needn't wait any longer. We all know what we must do."

"Hold on a minute, Mr. Murakoshi," Yagisawa said. "This is a serious problem and we mustn't let ourselves get carried away."

"What do you mean? We've got no intention of letting

that couple live here and if they won't move of their own volition, there is only one option left to us."

"I know all that, but this isn't something that can be settled so simply. After all, there is the danger to be considered."

"We did not have problems the previous two times."

"We were lucky."

"Yes, we had God on our side." Murakoshi's voice became quite high-pitched and he shook with excitement.

"But if we keep doing it, someone's going to get suspicious," Yagisawa said quietly. "We should hear everyone's opinion first."

The other three men all looked rather uncomfortable and glanced at each other as if they were waiting for someone else to speak first.

"Takasugi," Yagisawa prompted. The accountant adjusted his glasses and looked up. "What do you think?"

Takasugi cleared his throat and mumbled, "Well, to be quite honest—that is—personally—"

"You can't decide," Yagisawa finished for him and he nodded silently.

"Since when were you such a weakling?" Murakoshi asked, raising his voice. "You can't expect to protect your land without being a bit more positive."

"Aso, how about you?"

Yagisawa raised his voice slightly.

"I've given the matter a lot of thought. Well—there's no rush and we don't want to make a decision we might regret later on—I think we should wait a little longer and see what happens."

Murakoshi snorted in disgust at the office worker's answer.

"The way I look at it," the sportsman, Eguchi, said, "the last two times we had good reason for what we did. The first man almost killed Aso's child with his reckless driving and the second one . . ." He hesitated.

"It's okay," Takasugi said. "He and my wife . . ."

"There's no need to go into that again," Yagisawa said, interrupting.

Eguchi continued:

"This new couple, however, haven't done anything directly, and although I'm not suggesting that we should leave them alone, I don't think that it is necessary to do anything so drastic." He looked around the other faces. "What do you say? Shall we continue to act indirectly?"

"You're all chicken!" Murakoshi exploded with anger. "Since when were you such a weak-minded lot?!" His eyes flashed as he looked them over, one by one. "Have you forgotten what it was like when we first moved here? Not a street light from here to the station, and when it rained the road became so muddy we could hardly walk! Swarms of mosquitoes in the summer and in the winter the road would be closed by the slightest snowfall.

"How many times did we have to go to the council offices before things improved? Tens, no hundreds of times!"

He looked around the circle of faces, but nobody could meet his gaze.

"Why is it we can come home safely at night? Because we've got streetlights all the way to the station! Come on, tell me I'm wrong!

"We paid for the road to be surfaced out of our own pockets. In summer we went out and sprayed all the puddles where the mosquitoes were likely to breed and as a result, our children can play outside at last."

His voice rose in pitch.

"Our sweat is in this land! These outsiders think they can come here when everything is finished and enjoy the fruits of our labors for free! Did we do all this for them? I should say not! This area is ours and ours alone!"

He stood panting, his emotion temporarily spent. No one said a word.

"Well," Yagisawa said after a minute. "What shall we do?"

The other three all looked at each other.

"Let's do it," Eguchi said. "Mr. Murakoshi has made me change my mind."

Takasugi joined in.

"I agree. They don't show any indication of leaving, so let's do it."

Aso shrugged: "If that's what everyone wants . . ."

Yagisawa nodded and said, "So we are all agreed then. Any objections?"

There were none.

"Very well. It's unfortunate, but it looks as if our new neighbors will meet with an accident."

Murakoshi smiled with satisfaction.

"How are we going to do it?"

"When are we going to do it?"

"I think we should do it straightaway before we change our minds," Yagisawa said. "How about tomorrow morning?"

—FRIDAY—

Eh? Kyosuke thought as he walked out of the front door in the morning to find his five neighbors standing in a group on the misty road. I wonder what they're doing there.

"Good morning, Mr. Ikegami," Yagisawa said, leaving the group and walking towards him.

"Good morning," Kyosuke replied a little stiffly as Yagisawa approached, smiling broadly. "What can I do for you?"

A look of surprise came over the other's face.

"Nothing. We just thought it was about time we all became friends."

"Friends?"

"Yes, we are all stuck out here together whether we like it or not, so why should you have to walk to the station on your own?"

"Oh, I'm sorry."

He didn't really understand what was going on, but he couldn't very well refuse, so he allowed Yagisawa to lead him over to the others.

Why should they suddenly change their attitude toward me like this? he thought uneasily.

"I'm sorry we didn't wait for you before," Yagisawa said as they walked down the road. "It's just that this is such an inconvenient place that we didn't think that you would actually want to stay here long. Anyway, we thought we would wait until you made up your mind before we became too friendly, otherwise it would only have made the parting all that much more difficult."

"As I told you last night, I don't intend to go anywhere."

"Exactly, that's why we waited for you today; we're all very pleased."

Upon this, the other four men all greeted him warmly. Surprisingly enough, even the antagonistic old Murakoshi smiled warmly and slapped him on the shoulder.

"I'm sorry if I was a bit rude to you on Monday," he said. "I'm afraid that you tend to get a bit grumpy when you reach my age. I hope you won't hold it against me."

"Oh . . ." Kyosuke was taken aback and wondered what had brought this on.

"Oh yes," the old man continued. "I hear from my wife that she forgot to take your quilts in when it rained the other day. I am very sorry, but she is getting a bit forgetful in her old age. Of course, we'll pay for new quilts."

"No, that's okay."

"But I insist."

"It really doesn't matter. They were old quilts anyway."

"Well, if you are quite sure . . . but in that case you must come around for dinner one night. My wife wants to apologize in person, but she is so ashamed that she has been avoiding you."

"That's very kind of you."

Takasugi spoke next.

"I'm afraid that I owe you an apology, too."

"Really?"

"Yes, it's about that tape . . ."

"What?"

"My wife was responsible."

Kyosuke was too amazed to feel angry. He looked at Takasugi blankly.

"It's very embarrassing for me to talk about, but I'm afraid I'm not altogether fit and can't satisfy her—well, she—she was jealous of you two and made that tape. When I found out what she had done, I was very angry and told her to get rid of the tape, but I never imagined that she would leave it on your doorstep like that."

"Forget it."

Kyosuke nodded towards him, but he still could not understand what was going on. He only needed someone to admit to opening his door and trying to gas Kimiko and all the events of the last week would be explained. At that moment he looked around at his surroundings.

"Just a minute, this isn't the road to the station."

"Who can that be?" Kimiko said in surprise as the front doorbell rang. She went to the door and found Mrs. Murakoshi, Mrs. Takasugi, and Mrs. Yagisawa lined up on the porch.

"We are very sorry to butt in on you like this," Mrs. Yagisawa said. "But we had something we wanted to discuss with you."

"It's no bother, please come in."

Kimiko led them into the living room and hurriedly laid out cushions for them to sit on.

"I'll pour you some tea."

"That's okay, please don't bother. You just carry on with your washing; we'll wait here."

Kimiko went out to the kitchen and finished boiling water for the washing, then poured out some tea.

"Well, if you are sure you don't mind, I'll just finish the laundry."

"Don't worry about us, go ahead."

Kimiko went into the bathroom and poured the remainder of the boiling water into the washing machine. She glanced back and saw Mrs. Murakoshi standing in the entrance, looking at her.

"It's hard work, isn't it?"

"Yes."

Kimiko bent over the bathtub and suddenly Mrs. Murakoshi rushed over and pushed her in.

"You're going to kill me?" Kyosuke asked in shock. Eguchi, Takasugi, and Aso were holding his arms and he was unable to resist.

They were standing in the woods some way from the station. There were no other houses for miles so even if he were to cry out for help, nobody was likely to hear him.

"The express will pass here in a few minutes," Yagisawa said, looking at his watch. "And you will commit suicide by jumping in front of it."

"Wait a minute! What have I done? Why do you want to kill me?"

"It's difficult to explain," Yagisawa said quietly. "I suppose you could call it a kind of defense mechanism. Our five houses comprise a harmonious society and your intrusion has disturbed our daily routines. In order to protect our way of life, we must act like the white corpuscles in the body and destroy the invader—you."

"So the last two occupants of that house—"

"That's right."

"You're all insane!" Kyosuke cried, horrified. "You'll get caught one day and then it will be prison for the lot of you!" He gave a sudden start. "What about Kimiko?"

"Your pretty little wife should have been taken care of by now," Murakoshi said with a cold smile.

"You're insane! You're all mad!"

Kyosuke tried to struggle, but he could not do anything against three of them. Yagisawa pricked up his ears.

"It's coming . . ."

In the silence, the noise of the distant train could be heard. The rails began to sing.

"This is goodbye then, Ikegami," Yagisawa said.

It was hopeless to struggle as he was dragged up to the small cliff over the tracks.

The train rushed towards them . . .

Kimiko struggled violently when her head plunged into the bath. The water got into her nose and mouth and she choked. She did not know which way was up, she just fought blindly until she found her head out of the water.

Through misty eyes, she saw Murakoshi brandishing the lid of the bath over her head, a horrifying expression on her face. Kimiko instinctively grabbed the woman and the lid came down on her shoulder. Using all her weight,

Kimiko dragged Murakoshi to the bath and pushing her in head first, held her under the water, oblivious to her flailing arms and legs.

When she finally came to her senses, Kimiko was horrified to find that the other woman had stopped moving.

I never even knew her first name, she thought absently.

She climbed out of the bath and saw Mrs. Takasugi and Mrs. Yagisawa standing in the doorway, looking at her.

"—Er—she—" Kimiko tried to explain, but Mrs. Yagisawa stopped her, saying:

"It's all right, it's best this way."

They ran out of the woods. As soon as the train stopped there would be a commotion and they could not afford to be seen by any of the passengers.

Once they got back to the road, Yagisawa stopped and looked back.

"Are you okay?" he asked.

Kyosuke was still in a state of shock and could not understand what had happened.

A moment before the express had rushed through the cutting below his feet, Yagisawa had pushed Murakoshi from behind. The old man had fallen without a sound and they could see him lying facedown on the tracks until the train hid him from view.

"Why . . . ? Why . . . ?" Kyosuke murmured.

"Murakoshi knew nothing but hatred," Yagisawa said. "He would have ruined us all if we had continued listening to him, so the four of us got together and decided that this was the only solution—Don't worry, your wife is safe, but what are you going to do now?"

"Do?"

"We thought you might like to take Murakoshi's place and become the fifth member of our little community."

"But— You—you just committed murder!"

"That was just a small sacrifice to protect our society. What are you going to do? Are you going to rush to the police, or—"

Eguchi slapped Kyosuke on the shoulder.

"Let's be friends."

"That's right," Yagisawa said, smiling. "That's your house, isn't it—the house that you've struggled so hard to buy? You don't think you'd be able to live there on your own, do you, if we all got arrested? You said yourself that you intended to stay . . ."

—EPILOGUE—

"See you later," Kyosuke said as he gave Kimiko a kiss on the cheek.

"Look after yourself."

"And you. Don't overdo things."

"Don't worry."

Kimiko's pregnancy was already noticeable.

"Well, goodbye then."

"Goodbye."

The other four men were waiting for him outside and after they had exchanged greetings, all five of them set off for the station.

"Spring is here at last," Yagisawa said, looking up at the buds on the trees.

Murakoshi's death had been put down as suicide resulting from the shock of finding his wife dead in the bathroom. His son soon sold the house to a real-estate agent and it had been standing empty ever since.

Ishihara, the man who had warned Kyosuke to move, had changed companies and the five households were able to enjoy life together without any worries.

That day was warm and there was a light fog hanging over the surrounding woodland. They had almost reached the station when a truck came towards them through the mist. It stopped in front of them.

"Excuse me," the young man behind the wheel said, opening the window. "I'm looking for five or six houses that are supposed to be around here somewhere. Do you know where they are?"

"Just keep straight on down this road," Yagisawa said. "You can't miss them."

"Thank you."

The removal truck, loaded with furniture, swayed heavily down the road. The five men looked at each other, then turned to watch the truck disappear into the distance.

—translated by Gavin Frew

THE SERPENT AND THE MONGOOSE

By EDWARD D. HOCH

Durning awoke shortly after dawn and pushed aside the curtains of the stateroom window. The cruise ship was passing a large island which he took to be Martinique. There were white buildings along the shore and up the sides of the mountains that betrayed the island's volcanic origins. A peaceful place, he thought, only just awakening for the day beneath a blanket of clouds.

Carol stretched and opened her eyes. "What time is it?"

"Five-thirty. You'd better get back down to your quarters before you're missed."

"Just a little longer," she begged. "Come on! Get back in with me."

"Hurry up and get dressed! We have too much riding on this for you to get in trouble now."

Grumbling softly, she slid from the bed and grabbed her clothes on the way into the tiny bathroom. He went back to gazing out the stateroom window. When she emerged a few minutes later she was fully dressed, even to the flying-fish pendant that always dangled from the gold chain around her neck. She paused for a quick kiss and slipped out the door, heading for the elevator which would take her down to the crew's deck.

Durning spent the next hour going over plans for the following days. The *Starshine* stopped at a different island each day, and that meant people to contact, arrangements to be made. Yesterday in Barbados it had been easy. He'd gone into Bridgetown with the other tourists in the morning and stopped at the little map store on Broad Street. The smiling man behind the counter had taken his boarding card and gone off to the cruise ship while Durning lingered in town for a couple of hours. Then the man had returned the card to him and the transaction had been

89

completed. Durning watched a cricket match at Kensington Oval for a time before returning to the ship.

He'd been on board only a few minutes when he heard Carol's voice come over the ship's public-address system. "Welcome aboard to all our returning passengers. We hope you had a pleasant day in Barbados. Bridge games with the cruise staff are now getting under way in the card room."

Durning knew from the wording she used that all had gone well on her end. That night when she visited his stateroom she'd filled him in on the details. Today, with luck, things would go equally well on Martinique.

He dressed and left his cabin shortly after seven, when the ship's dining room opened for breakfast. He greeted the others at his table and scanned the familiar menu, finally deciding on the elaborate buffet. While standing in line for it his eyes scanned the other tables and came to rest on a man seated alone in the smoking section. He was short and bearded, looking a bit like the traditional representations of the devil. Durning knew the man and had reason to avoid him. His name was Felix Pond and he was a hired killer of an unusual sort.

That was when Durning decided it would be best to spend the entire day ashore, as far away from the ship as he could get. His appointment with the contact in Fort-de-France was not until noon, but after breakfast he signed up for a morning tour of a botanic garden situated some distance north of the city. About thirty of his fellow passengers were along and they made the trip in several hired taxis.

The guided tour lasted the better part of an hour, leading them along trails past exotic shrubs and formal gardens. The native guide spoke of more than a thousand different varieties of tropical and local plants. At one point they came to a high fence protecting them from a steep drop-off. Down below Durning could see nothing but a jumble of tropical vegetation.

"They call this the bottomless pit," the guide said with a smile. "It is a long way down."

"What's at the bottom?" a woman asked.

"Ah! The fer-de-lance lives there!" The guide seemed to take a special pride in it. "One of the deadliest snakes in the world. Luckily we have mongooses down there too, to keep them under control."

"Do they fight?" Durning asked.

"Oh, yes! Sometimes fights are staged here on the island."

"I understand a mongoose can kill a cobra."

"Yes, and a fer-de-lance, too. People sometimes make bets on the fights between them."

"But if the mongoose always wins—"

"Ah, the mongoose *usually* wins! But sometimes the fer-de-lance wins."

Durning nodded. "I'd like to see one of those."

"What time does your ship sail?"

"Not till seven o'clock."

The guide wrote an address on one of his business cards. "My name is Rodolphe Marin. Come here at four this afternoon and there will be a mongoose and snake fight."

"Is this illegal?" Durning asked a bit uneasily. He did not need a run-in with the law.

"No, no! But sometimes the events are private when large stakes are involved."

By the time they'd finished their tour of the botanic garden dark clouds were beginning to gather overhead. Durning wondered if a brief shower was on the way.

The clouds had yielded only the briefest of drizzles by the time he returned to Fort-de-France shortly before noon. Walking through La Savane Park in the heart of the city he paused to study the white marble statue of Napoleon's wife, the Empress Josephine, the island's most famous resident. A plaque explained that she'd been born in the village of La Pagerie in 1763, but there was nothing to indicate when or how the head had been broken from the large statue. Perhaps it had been an act of protest from citizens who were not always as peaceful as they now appeared.

Exactly at noon, Durning crossed the park to the ferry

dock. In the men's room there he met his contact, a tall Englishman dressed like a tourist. "This is my boarding card for the *Starshine*," Durning told the man. "It will get you on without question. Go to cabin six twenty-five and someone will be waiting there for you. Then return the boarding card to me here in one hour. You understand?"

"Certainly," the tall man said. He took the card and departed.

After a moment Durning left the men's room himself. He walked outside and watched the Englishman strolling in the direction of the cruise ship, like a passenger returning early from town. No one would question the camera case he carried. Durning's insistence upon retrieving the boarding card was mainly to keep it from falling into police hands if the contact was arrested later. Carol had supplied him with a duplicate to get him back on board if needed. This time there was no necessity for it. The man returned promptly and handed the card back to Durning.

"I hope you had a rewarding visit," Durning told him.

"Very rewarding, thank you. We will do business again."

They shook hands and parted.

Shortly before four o'clock Durning went to the address Rodolphe Marin had given him. It was on the rue Victor Hugo, near the city's main shopping area, and proved to be a small pet shop filled with exotic fish and tropical birds. The woman clerk spoke to him in French as he entered, but when he asked about the mongoose fight she motioned him toward the back room.

It proved to be larger than the shop in front, and already a dozen or so men were gathered there, talking in French and English as they placed their bets. A round wooden ring occupied the center of the room, with a few inches of sawdust in the bottom. Perhaps, Durning thought, this was to absorb any blood. The ring was about ten feet in diameter, and though it was empty, the milling crowd avoided it. Presently, at just after four o'clock, Rodolphe Marin himself appeared and stepped into the ring. He spoke quickly in French and then translated his remarks into English.

"Good afternoon, gentlemen. In a few moments you will witness a rare sight—a fight to the death between a fer-de-lance and a mongoose. Wagering is allowed on the outcome and after I speak you will have ten minutes more to place your bets. First let me tell you a little about these two animals. The mongoose has a long history of fighting and killing cobras in India, recorded by no less than Rudyard Kipling in his story 'Rikki-Tikki-Tavi.' They have up to forty teeth, well developed for shearing flesh. The mongoose was not originally native to Martinique, but was imported during the 1870s to kill rats on the sugarcane plantations. Some countries, like the United States, ban their importation because they kill many useful animals in addition to rats and snakes. Birds and chickens are among their favorite prey. The mongoose is not immune to snake venom. It is simply agile enough to avoid the strikes by jumping to one side or even into the air."

A wooden box about a foot long was brought in and placed at the edge of the ring. Marin watched it in silence and then continued. "The fer-de-lance is found only on the island of Martinique, although many related pit vipers are called by that name, and are found on the other islands and the mainland of Central and South America. The venom of the fer-de-lance is especially deadly. It is fast-acting and causes internal bleeding. For those of you wondering about the odds in the battle between these two enemies, let me say only that the mongoose usually wins, but sometimes the serpent wins. Now you have ten minutes to place your bets."

As the spectators milled about and odds were discussed, a heavy burlap sack was carried in by two men and deposited by the ring, opposite the mongoose's box. The spectators realized at once that the snake had arrived, and gave the sack a wide berth. Some were betting with each other, while others placed their bets with Rodolphe Marin. Durning was still deciding what, if anything, to do, when a voice behind him said, "Mr. Durning, isn't it?"

He turned and saw Felix Pond standing there, his black beard trimmed to a satanic point. "I don't believe we've met."

"Oh, surely we have! Someone introduced us at the nightclub called Eden last year, in New York."

Durning remembered all too well. A man he knew slightly had been gunned down the following day and it was general knowledge that Felix Pond or his people had carried out the execution. Pond was a new sort of hired killer, often employed by large multinational corporations when all else failed. If this bearded devil was interested in him, it was bad news indeed.

"Yes," Durning assented. "I remember now."

"Who do you like in the fight?"

"We haven't seen either animal, but I'd have to go with the mongoose. His box is quite well made. The owner must take pride in him, which suggests he's been around for a while."

Felix Pond merely smiled, then suggested, "The box may have served many animals in turn. It proves nothing. Would you like to wager on the mongoose?"

"You'd take the fer-de-lance?"

"I would, sight unseen."

"What sort of odds do you want?"

"Oh, even money, Mr. Durning. My bets are always even money."

Durning felt suddenly confident. "A thousand dollars."

"We'll shake on it," Pond said, holding out his hand.

Marin reappeared a moment later, summoning everyone back to the ring. The crowd had increased now to about twenty, and there was an air of anticipation as the serpent was released from its sack. The fer-de-lance was about five feet long, as near as Durning could determine, with a thick reddish-brown body and tapering tail. The lance-shaped head that provided its name moved back and forth as if searching for the enemy it knew must be present. There was a low murmur from the spectators, and Durning noted the slight smile of triumph on Felix Pond's face. Perhaps he recognized the snake from some past encounter, or knew from its markings it was a good fighter.

The owner of the mongoose unlatched the end of the wooden box and opened it. "Rikki," someone said. The creature, named after Kipling's animal, was known to many of the local people, and this encouraged Durning. It had fought and won before. Rikki was about two feet long, with a grizzled brownish-black body, long tail, and short feet. It immediately rose up on its hind legs, the weasel-like head turning to search for enemies. Spotting the serpent at once, it dropped back down and hugged the sawdust.

As the fer-de-lance slithered slowly forward, the mongoose moved closer too, sniffing along the ground. While still some distance away, the fer-de-lance struck without warning straight at Rikki. The mongoose leaped into the air as the lance-shaped head passed beneath him, then came down almost on the serpent's back, biting quickly but releasing his jaws at once as the serpent's tail lashed around like a whip. A few drops of blood appeared on the lacerated skin as the fer-de-lance coiled, waiting for a chance to strike again.

"The snake is wounded," Durning told Pond.

"That is nothing. The fer-de-lance needs only one bite."

It was true. The snake's fangs were uncovered as its head shot forward, this time barely missing the mongoose. Frustrated, it whipped around once more and gave a savage hiss. But Rikki was still too fast for it, darting this way and that, leaping out of danger at the last possible second. The sharp teeth of the mongoose flashed, and it sprang, landing on the serpent's back, biting deep and high on the body, just below the lance-shaped head. His teeth struck again, before the snake could move, ripping at the flesh. The tail of the fer-de-lance flicked once and then it was still.

"It is paralyzed now," Rodolphe Marin said quietly. "The end will be quick."

The mongoose ripped at another piece of flesh, and it was clear that the fight was over. A cheer went up among the winners. Money was exchanged.

Felix Pond shrugged. "Sometimes the serpent wins," he said simply, and peeled off ten hundred-dollar bills from the roll in his pocket.

Durning accepted the money and stuffed it into his pocket. "What do you want with me?"

"We are both in business, Mr. Durning. Let us go outside and talk like businessmen."

As they were leaving he saw the remains of the fer-de-lance being returned to the sack. Perhaps it would be burned, or dumped in the harbor. Outside it was still cloudy but at least it was not raining. They walked to the corner and Pond led him down a side street. After another turn and more walking, the short man started to speak. "You and your confederate have been engaged in a conspiracy against SeaKing Lines. Naturally they are very upset about it. Their entire cruise ship business could be ruined."

"Conspiracy? What conspiracy?"

"Do I need to spell it out, Mr. Durning?" He reached into his pocket and took out a color snapshot. It had been taken with available light and Durning recognized a street in San Juan, toward evening on the day they'd sailed. He was easily recognizable, speaking with a young woman wearing the blue and white uniform of the *Starshine*'s crew. Luckily, Carol's face was completely obscured by shadows.

"That looks like me," he said innocently. "Where'd you get this?"

Pond ignored the question. "You have a woman confederate aboard the ship," he said. "I believe she brings stolen diamonds and other gems aboard on the cruise. You make arrangements with jewelry merchants in each port to trade the gems for cocaine. While you are on shore, they board the *Starshine* with your boarding card and close the deal with this woman in one of the cabins. They leave with the jewels, which quickly find their way into legitimate markets, and she sells the cocaine to the passengers and crew. With a potential market of nearly two thousand people, it's gone before the ship returns to San Juan."

"A nice story. You should write for television."

"The SeaKing people have been aware of this for some time, but they weren't able to determine exactly how the drugs got on board or who was involved. The police on these various islands hardly want to disrupt the lucrative tourist industry by barring ships or searching passengers."

"What are you supposed to do about it?" Durning asked.

"Stop this business, if necessary by taking out the company employee involved."

"Taking out?" Durning repeated, feeling a chill down his spine.

"There's another way, of course. Simply cease all operations. Tell your confederate to resign her position, whatever it is."

"I don't feel like making an admission of guilt, thanks."

Felix Pond exhaled softly, making a sound something like the hissing of the fer-de-lance. "Your guilt is already known. It's only a matter of identifying your partner."

"You won't do it from that snapshot. You'll end up killing an innocent person."

"I never kill an innocent person. I make very certain of that."

"I've heard enough," Durning told him, picking up his pace. "Stay out of my way."

Behind him, the voice of Felix Pond had the last word. "You have been warned."

Durning had been back on the ship only a short while when the public-address system came to life and he heard Carol's voice summoning him. "Passenger Adam Durning, please report to the tour desk for your tickets."

He waited five minutes in case Pond was watching and then casually made his way to the tour desk. "You paged me?" he asked her with a bland expression.

"Mr. Durning?"

"That's correct."

"Here are the tickets you requested for tomorrow's tours on St. Maarten. Will you be visiting the nude beach?"

"I think I'll pass that by."

Still keeping the same casual smile on her face, she dropped her voice and said, "He didn't have much today. I sold it all in the first hour. You have to do better than that."

"He told me he had more."

"Never mind. I'll see you after midnight in your room."

"Be careful. A man named Felix Pond is aboard."

"What about him?"

"I'll tell you later. Don't come to the room if there's any-one else in the corridor."

They chatted casually for another minute or two, but no one seemed to be watching.

There was a knock on his stateroom door at 12:15. He opened it a crack and saw Carol's dark hair glistening in the light from overhead. She slipped into the cabin and sat down on the bed. "There was someone who seemed to be watching me tonight, during the amateur show," she told him. "When I was introducing the acts a man at a front table kept staring at me."

"Short man with a pointed black beard?"

"That's him."

Durning let out a sigh. He hadn't been careful enough. "It's Felix Pond. He's been hired by the ship's owners to get rid of us, however he can. They're afraid for their tour-ist business."

She grinned as she removed the flying-fish pendant from around her neck. "I'll bet they'd increase business if they started listing our services in their advertising."

"They're not likely to do that." He was in no mood for joking.

"How was your day ashore?"

"I saw a fight between a mongoose and a fer-de-lance."

"What happened?"

"The mongoose won. It usually does. That was the best thing that happened to me all day. I won a thousand dol-lars."

"Who from?"

"Felix Pond. He probably put it on his expense account."

After she'd undressed they slipped into the narrow bed together. "He bothers you, doesn't he?"

"Pond is a hit man of sorts. Corporations, especially for-eign corporations, hire him to deal with embarrassments like us."

She thought about that. "Does he know who I am?"

"No, but anyone who bought from you could probably tell him."

"I'm very careful with my customers. I've dealt with some of them for years."

"Pond has a snapshot of us together in San Juan, but it's dark and he can't identify you."

"Let's keep it that way."

"Maybe we should skip St. Maarten, lay low for the rest of the trip."

"I've got disappointed customers from today, Adam."

He thought about it, weighing the risks. "All right," he said finally. "One more time."

They both slept later than planned in the morning, and by the time they'd awakened it was well after six. Carol dressed quickly and hurried from the room, throwing him a goodbye kiss. He checked the corridor, but no one was waiting to catch them together.

During breakfast, Carol's voice came over the ship's public-address system. "I'm afraid I have some disappointing news for those of you looking forward to the nude beach at St. Maarten. The water near the shore is a bit rough and we won't be able to dock. Instead, we're going on to Antigua today. We should be there in another hour. For those of you who haven't gotten enough gambling on board the *Starshine,* there's a large gambling casino just across from the dock at Antigua. We'll have information on available tours shortly, and your account will be credited for any St. Maarten tours you were planning to take."

There were a great many jewelry stores on St. Maarten, and Durning was sorry to miss it. But the islands were quite close and perhaps they'd go back there the following day. After breakfast he returned to his stateroom, already made up by the cabin steward, and unlocked his suitcase. He found the coded list of contacts on Antigua and chose one he'd dealt with successfully in the past.

He left the ship before noon, as soon as it had docked at St. John's. Despite the casino Carol had mentioned, the port lacked the glamour of some of their other stops. Virtually all the jewelry stores were confined to the Heritage Quay area and surrounding streets near the docks.

Durning was heading for his destination, strolling across the little park at the center of the quay, when Felix Pond seemed to appear from nowhere and intercepted him. "Hello, there! It's quite a chore beating off the cab-drivers in these places. They all want to take you on a tour of the island."

"They are persistent," Durning admitted, trying not to betray his sense of frustration at Pond's sudden appearance.

"Can I walk a bit with you?" the bearded man asked.

"Of course, so long as you offer no more threats." His mind was racing, trying to work out a plan.

After fifteen minutes of visiting shops together, it seemed obvious that Felix Pond would not be leaving his side. He suggested they stop for a beer in a bar adjoining the casino and Pond readily agreed. Halfway through the drink, Durning excused himself to go to the men's room. He'd noticed a pay telephone on the back wall, and the *Starshine* was newly equipped with ship-to-shore telephones in every room.

Pond's back was to him as he reached the ship and was connected to Carol's desk. "Pond is with me," he said, speaking softly but rapidly. "Can you get off the ship and make the contact yourself?"

"I suppose I could get off for an hour. What's the name?"

"Redcliffe Street, runs up the right side of Heritage Quay. Look for number thirty-eight and ask for Mr. Simmons."

"He'll have the goods?"

"Or he can get them in five minutes. The usual deal. Be careful."

"I'm always careful."

"I'll keep Pond occupied. Good luck."

He hung up and returned to the table. Pond looked up at him and smiled. "I would like to get my thousand dollars back. Are there any mongoose fights on Antigua?"

"Not that I know of. But the casino is just through that door."

"There's a casino on the ship. I'm looking for something a bit more exciting."

"Sorry I can't help." He finished his beer. "I think I'll wander back to the ship, maybe go for a dip in the pool."

He fully expected Pond to follow along, but when they reached the gangway the bearded man changed his mind. "You go ahead," he told Durning. "I'm going to look around town, maybe walk up to that church on the hill."

A male voice over the loudspeaker, reading a routine schedule of bingo games and dance instruction, seemed to confirm that Carol had gone ashore. Durning changed into his trunks and swam around the pool for a while, thinking of her. Maybe it was time they both got out of the business. It had been profitable over two seasons, but with the shipowners hiring someone like Felix Pond, the risks were beginning to outweigh the gains.

He was lounging in a deck chair about an hour later when Pond returned, taking the chair next to him. "Did you get to that church?" Durning asked.

"No, I had some other business to attend to."

Durning caught something in his voice. "What was that?"

"The matter is cleared up now. I'll be reporting to my employers in San Juan."

"You talk in circles."

"I'll be more direct. Your operation is ended. Your mysterious partner was Carol Evans, the ship's social director. She died—" he glanced at the expensive watch on his wrist "—exactly twenty-five minutes ago."

Durning tried to hold himself steady, to keep his hands from shaking, to keep from leaping at Felix Pond and tearing his throat out. "I don't know what you're talking about."

"It was a clever plot, using her position on the ship as a way of communicating with would-be customers. Everyone heard her voice over the loudspeaker several times a day, only her words carried a special meaning for those in need of a fix or a snort."

"I don't believe you," Durning said quietly. "You wouldn't kill an innocent person. You said so yourself."

"It was a matter of business, Durning. You must understand that. The Caribbean cruise business is very profitable, but very competitive. SeaKing could not afford the bad publicity an arrest would bring." He stood up and moved to the railing. "This way it's best for everyone."

Durning rose and followed. "I don't believe she's dead."

Felix Pond merely smiled and reached into his pocket. "Here," he said, tossing something gold and glittery through the air between them. "I took it off her body myself."

Durning caught it and stood staring down at Carol's flying-fish pendant on its gold chain. "My God, Pond!"

"Satisfied?"

"You bastard! She was only trying to make a little money. She never harmed a fly!"

"She harmed a great many people, including my employers."

"You could have given her a chance!"

"I warned you. The warning extended to both of you. Fly back home and never set foot on a SeaKing ship again, and I'll do nothing more."

"She—she was only a kid!" He realized his voice was breaking.

"She was an example."

Durning rubbed his eyes and turned toward shore. At the end of the pier a pushcart vendor was selling tropical fruit. Some others were heading back to the ship. One of them—

"You lied to me! That's Carol down there. She's not dead!"

He saw her walking quickly with that firm determined stride, carrying a package in one hand. Felix Pond had bluffed him. "So it is," the bearded man said, leaning over the railing as if to wave.

Then it was all in slow motion. Durning saw the pushcart vendor lift something black and tubular from beneath his fruit, just as Carol was passing. There was no sound but Durning saw a puff of smoke and Carol seemed to stumble into the cart, toppling the fruit to the ground. The vendor fired one more time with his silenced weapon, then tossed it into the harbor water and walked away fast.

Durning screamed, *"Carol!"*

But it was too late.

"I had to be sure," Felix Pond whispered into his ear. "The cabin steward found her flying-fish pendant in your room this morning, but I still had to be sure. I couldn't kill an innocent person."

Durning hugged the rail and felt the world collapsing around him. Down below, on the pier, passengers were gathering around Carol's lifeless body. "How could you do it like this?" he asked with an anguished cry.

"It was as they told you," Felix Pond replied. "Sometimes the serpent wins."

THE STRANGER

By FLORENCE V. MAYBERRY

The small outboard motorboat, its blue paint streaked and faded by harsh exposure to weather and water, moved in and out of the deep, narrow cove for the greater part of the day. As though the tall, hunch-shouldered man at its wheel who occasionally stood up when the motor was cut, hands shading eyes to gaze around him, was uncertain where to drop a fish line. Or searching for something, or someone, on the lake's shore.

Earlier in the day this had not troubled Karen, but as afternoon wore on she began to worry about his purpose. He lifted no rod to drop into the fish-rich lake. But if not here for fishing, why hover in this one cove? And if searching, for what or whom? To check out possibility of game? Surely not people, there were no neighboring cabins. Could be deer, these animals often skimmed through the forest that surrounded her property. She saw no gun or fishing rod but one or the other would be lying low in the boat. But if a hunter, why remain in the boat all day?

Karen's studio-cabin was the lone dwelling in this north end of the long cove-indented lake which speared close to the Canadian border. The shores surrounding the cold blue-green water were thick with pine and tamarack, their trunks sheltered by spreading bushes, an area little traveled by even hardy vacationers. She had discovered it herself only because of her driving passion to immerse herself in untouched nature, to be alone with it and her need to lock its beauty forever in raw brilliance upon her canvases, no disturbance from the rush and push of people at cross purposes. Here, alone, a kind of exalted moodiness seemed to drop upon the land from the branches of the tall needled trees. She had caught this mood in some of her paintings, brooding, shadowy, here and there a searching, shocking light piercing a haunted forest.

Why would that stranger be searching for whatever in

this lonely place? Nothing about him made him seem to be an artist seeking a subject, or fisherman or hunter, or house builder cogitating about a likely building spot. He didn't act like anything. Should she call to him, ask if he was lost, point the way to the town at the far southern end of the lake? The scattered few houses or cabins between her property and the small town some twenty miles to the south were normally inhabited only during the brief summer. Now it was late October. Only she with Lad, her Scottish terrier, remained on this shore. Toward the mountains there could be a few trappers and hunters wintering in until spring. She never saw them.

Even Karen intended to shutter and lock her cabin within the coming two weeks, head back to Seattle and her job as illustrator for an advertising firm, from which she had taken three months' leave. Soon she would pack her car with the paintings produced during those special months, a wrenching departure to leave her retreat. Hopefully its essence had been captured on canvases with which she intended to storm Seattle and Portland galleries. If they had the impact she hoped for, next year she would return to her cabin to live and paint as long as she wished.

She peered once more through the small casement window. The stranger was giving no sign of leaving the cove and the worry that nibbled at her intensified. Fleetingly she wondered if her rapturous enthusiasm over buying this secluded cabin had been foolish, even dangerous. Dangerous for a single female, thirty-three years old, no neighbors to call upon, and not yet, during her introductory summer, able to put in a telephone. What with buying the cabin, the cost of setting up poles to this outlying spot, without neighbors to share the expense, had been beyond her ability to finance. Too, she would soon be leaving, not to return for perhaps a year.

Anyway, too late to fret now. Surely the man would leave soon, go home. The day's cold had sharpened, it would be miserable out in the open.

She saw the stranger arise in the boat, stand rubbing his hands together, then stare intently at the cabin. He was too distant for his features or expression to be clearly discerned but somehow he had a familiar look. Those slumped shoulders, the sidewise slant of head as he gazed up the slope, pinged a distant ring of memory in her. She struggled to bring it close, tag the figure to a place, an incident. There was nothing unusual about the man, clothes common to this Northwest, outdoors country, sagging jeans, heavy short jacket, plaid shirt, long-billed cap. No beard, no moustache. Long-legged, rangy. Nothing distinctive.

But that furtive slant of the head, the almost boneless slouch, where had she seen that before? Perhaps down in the town, at the general store? Or lounging in the garage where she filled up with gasoline, or at the town dock where she had inquired about renting a boat.

The faint familiarity of the man became a nagging nuisance. She shook her head in irritation against it, her grey eyes dark with growing unease. The terrier, a fey Scotsman, responded to her discomfort by rubbing against her ankle, muttering in his throat. "Lad, that man's been here too long, it's not right him hanging about. I want him to go!" The Scottie tipped his whiskered head, muttered again.

Yes, now she believed she remembered where she had seen the stranger. At the general store, standing by the stove while she talked with the store owner's wife about the problem of bringing in a telephone, an exorbitant cost for a few months' use, the woman agreeing with her. If it was the same man, he could have easily heard her, stored up the information. In this unstructured, almost pioneering setting, the thought of danger never entered her mind.

But it did now and she swiftly began to plan a defense. If the man would sit down again, turn his boat into the open lake, well and good. But if instead he turned the boat toward her dock, made it fast, she and Lad would run for her car, drive to town. And what would she tell them in the town? That a man had been running his boat all day on a public lake that belonged to the state, open to everyone's use, then insist he was a trespasser with evil intentions? *Did he attack you? No, I fled.* What would be the town's reaction? Decide she was a hysterical city green-horn? Plus being a fool for not having a telephone.

"Leave, leave!" she whispered at the window. "Go away!" The vehemence of the "Go" made the Scottie's tail swing with happy anticipation. She added, "Not yet, Lad, the man's still on the lake, he may turn around, leave."

She left the window, added a stick of wood to the old-fashioned cooking range, checked the steaming teakettle kept on it continuously to counteract the dryness of the wood-heated air. Came back to the window, looked for the stranger. Her heart plunged. The boat was rubbing against the dock.

The man's left hand grasped the sawed end of one of the dock's log flooring planks. His right hand clutched a long, slim, dark object close to his right side. Too dark, too broad for a fishing rod. The man laid it on the dock, pulled himself up after it. It was a rifle.

Even in the approaching twilight she could make out the stranger's features: sharp nose, chin slanted into his neck, eyes sunk beneath deep brows. He squinted at the cabin, as though to pierce sight through the barrier of its log walls.

Karen rushed back to the range, banked its fire, closed the stove's drafts. Grabbed a down-filled jacket off a nail by the door, slipped it on, found her purse and car keys, slid the bolt on the front entrance door, called Lad. With the dog at her heels she hurried to the cabin's narrow back door, which opened into a low-ceilinged attached woodshed, its sides stacked with split wood. She locked the door, headed for the small car parked at the foot of the steep, rutted drive which led to the rough county road, grateful she had left the car faced down the drive, no need to back and turn it.

Lad frisked ahead, jumped against the car door.

A rifle shot cracked.

"Lad, heel! Heel!" she screamed.

The dog wheeled, raced back, unhurt.

Two more shots in quick succession. The back tires of the car softened, began to sink.

She jabbed the key at the backdoor lock, missed, jabbed,

made contact, opened the door. Ordered the dog inside, started to follow, then turned, picked up the axe beside the chopping block. At least no axe for the stranger to chop his way in after her.

Inside she relocked the door, shoved a chair under its knob, set two empty buckets on it to warn her by their clatter if the door was forced. She looked down at the axe she had dropped to the floor. A weapon for her? She shuddered at the thought.

She picked up the axe, carried it into the main room, dropped it beside the stove. Jammed a chair-back beneath the knob of the bolted front door. Walked to the casement window, cautiously pulled its gingham curtains together, peeped through their joining slit.

The stranger, shadowed by nightfall, stood on the dock, rifle half raised, took a few slow steps toward shore. She slid open the window a crack, shouted, "Go away! I have a weapon too! And I'll use it!"

He stepped back, slid over the dock's edge into the boat, hunkered down. He was a coward. A bully and a coward too. But he had a gun. She had only an axe that terrified her.

She kept watching for his next move, now and then a nervous sigh escaping her. Her hand patted her lips against a soundless scream. In the low-ceilinged room, lighted only by the glow shed through the isinglass of the stove's firebox, Karen's oval face became mystic, strangely beautiful, a troubled Modigliani character. The dog rumbled uncertainly, paced from his mistress to the door, back to her. The furniture took on shadowy, unnatural shapes as the dark deepened. But now the moon was rising. Soon it would spill light upon lake, cabin, upon a skulking, approaching figure.

She shivered from the room's increasing chill, went to the stove, opened the damper, fed the firebox more wood. Closed the iron door quickly against the glimmer it cast on the wall.

She contemplated the chance of success if she and Lad again slipped from the back door. After that to dart into the surrounding forest, hike the almost twenty miles in the frosty night to the town, problematically discover a cabin along the way. But under moonlight movement quickly revealed its source. Lad might bark, even rush the intruder, be shot.

To gain better perspective upon movement the man might make, Karen hastened up the short stairway to her slant-roofed attic studio, her low bed on one side under the eaves. Her canvas on its easel to one side of the window gave off ghostly reflected moonlight as she stood beside it to peer toward the dock.

The boat gently rocked at the mooring. It was empty, the man vanished, lost in the night. He could be behind a tree, back of the cabin in the woodshed, anywhere.

She returned downstairs, locked all windows, their panes heavy storm glass difficult to break. But not difficult to shoot out. She checked the chairs bracing the doorknobs. Firm. Then eased into the rocker near the stove, the axe at her feet. Her chair creaked, she stilled it, sat tense and listening.

A brush of movement sounded from the deck, beside the door. A footstep, then a second. The dog barked, plunged against the door and snorted fiercely at the sill.

The doorknob rattled.

She forced Lad away from the door. A bullet could pierce the wood.

"Hey, sister! You in there, better listen up!" The voice held a raw joviality, as though sharing a common eagerness. "No use tryin' to fool me, you ain't got no gun, or you woulda popped it when I came off the dock. So why get me all riled up when all I'm lookin' for is some good comp'ny 'cause I'm lonesome. Ain't you kinda lonesome too? Way out here all alone, no man."

She clutched the dog closer, remained silent.

Now the voice was eager, confident. "Maybe you think I ain't comin' in after you, then you gotta 'nother think comin'. Now listen, I don't wanna ruin this door, but I will. Open up like a smart girl, nobody gonna get hurt. Not even that dog if you shut him up somewheres. Just use old common sense, we can have a nice friendly visit, make up to you for all the time you been out here all alone."

Silence.

The voice turned gritty. "You don't open up, I got the gun ready, you better step aside if you don't wanna—"

"Wait! I'm getting the key!" She was remotely shocked to hear her voice clean and strong. She tiptoed to the chair, eased the dog to the floor, whispered, "Stay!" Picked up the axe, returned beside the door, raised the axe.

"Hurry it up!" Arrogance in the voice now, assured. "I said hurry! I'm not kiddin' around, it's freezin' cold out here."

Could she hit fast and hard enough to knock the gun from his grasp, have the stomach to strike into living flesh, wound or kill the marauder? She stood motionless, waiting, scarcely breathing. Into the silence a new sound intruded, soft but insistent, almost like a whispered message. Steam arising from the large old-fashioned iron teakettle on the range performing its duty of humidifying the atmosphere. A sibilant, bubbling response to her silent inner cry for help.

Back at the stove she grasped the kettle's handle, sped upstairs with it, Lad behind her. She crossed the studio to the small window that overlooked the deck, where at one side the waiting man pounded on the door. Above his head was a narrow makeshift roof shielding the cabin's entrance. Other than that the deck was open to sky and weather.

Through the windowpane she could glimpse the stranger's long legs only, his head and upper torso concealed by the flimsy roof. She slid open the window, called, "Here! Up here at the window. Please come closer, there's something I need to ask you before I open the door. I don't want to shout, I just want to talk, ask you something, something kind of—well, personal, it might solve all this trouble."

"Yeah?" He sounded doubtful. "So why not just yell it out, we're all alone, who's to care?"

She made her voice coy, hesitant. "I care, I just need to sort of talk, it's, well, very private, I wish I could whisper it. Please, this is difficult for a woman—"

"You got somethin' wrong with you?"—He stepped out of

the roof's shadow. "Whyn't you just come on downstairs, open the door, tell me real close?"

"I—I just couldn't, I need to know first how—oh, please—"

He left the shelter, stood beneath the window, looked up. The moon, now risen, put the man and his rifle in clear view. He was close, she could hear his breathing. The rifle raised, both of his hands on it. "Okay, spill it, it better be worth my—"

His last word escalated into a tormented shriek as boiling water spilled over his head, face, hands. Scalded hands let the rifle slip onto the deck as more liquid fire spilled. He jerked backwards, stumbled over the weapon, fell, and began a crablike scramble on elbows and knees to reach shelter under the entry's roof.

"Damn you to hell! Murderin' bitch!" he yelled. "Oh Christ, my eyes! You've blinded me!"

"Kick that gun onto the ground! Else you'll get something worse than boiling water. And I have another weapon that doesn't need bullets, and that a blinded man can't dodge. Plus I'll set the dog on you! So do as I say!"

"I gotta have help, my face is on fire, eyes swelled shut! Oh God!"

He began a cautious backward crawl, feet scooting back and forth across the flooring, met the rifle, kicked it. It spun to the ground.

Karen and the dog hurried downstairs, she opened the entry door, Lad plunged toward the intruder. "Heel!" she ordered. The twenty-pound terrier, outsize white fangs ready and gleaming for business, reluctantly backed away but kept watchful gaze upon the moaning figure.

Karen shut and locked the door behind her. "Stay where you are, don't move! Lad, keep guard, guard him! You better do as I say, this dog doesn't like you." The dog edged closer to the man, growling, trembling with eagerness to be about his job.

Karen jumped off the deck, picked up the rifle, ran to the dock, along its length, flung the gun far into the dark water. Hurried back to the deck, unlocked the door, stepped inside briefly. Called, "Now get to your feet, turn toward me, can you open your eyes enough to glimpse me and the door? Okay, come inside and I'll try to help you."

The man awkwardly arose, approached the entry, his puffed hands held limply before him. Karen edged back of the door, her hands gripped behind her on the axe handle. As he stumbled past her she slipped the weapon out of sight beneath the cook range. She lighted an oil lamp, said, "There's a rocking chair just ahead of you to your left. Sit down and I'll see what I can do. Lad, on guard!"

The man sat down, the dog anxiously half-circling the chair.

Swiftly Karen dipped cold water from the bucket on her rough drainboard, filled a deep pan. More gently than she felt she eased off his jacket, lifted the red puffed hands into the water, placed a cold wet cloth across his forehead and eyes. He groaned, more softly, relieved as the water cooled his flesh. She dipped water into a second basin, dropped a clean towel into it, unbuttoned the top button of his shirt, placed the cold wet cloth on the scalded skin of his neck and cheeks. For a long time she did this, dipping the cloth, changing the water, dipping again, the man whimpering under his breath. She was silent.

"Ain't helpin' much, I'm still on fire," he whined. "Hell, you mighta burnt out my eyes, got me blinded for life, you d—" He choked off the remainder of that word but anger snaked in and out of what followed. "You'd oughta knowed I was just talkin', just makin' a little try, woulda done nothin'." His whine rose, "All I was lookin' for was a little comp'ny, don't know nobody around here, folks around here not friendly, just wanted a little—"

"Shut up! Stop lying. Real bullets tore my tires. You threatened me with a gun. So shut up!"

The dog was alerted by the anger in her voice. His lips skinned back from his teeth, a growl rumbled in his throat, and the man shrank against the chair. "Keep that dog away from me, my right leg's scalded too up on the thigh. I could stand cold water there too if I could get my pants down." The petulant whine became sly, "Maybe you could give me a little help, I can't stand no pressure on my hands."

"No!"

"Hey, I didn't mean nothin'. Just anxious, I could get infected way out in this God-forsaken place. No doctor even in that one-horse town, need to get to a bigger place. Listen, you done the scalding, you oughta get me to town. I know a guy at the garage, he might could drive me on to a doctor. I hurt bad, you oughta at least get me to town, not have me die out here."

"That's a burn, not a gunshot. And how should I drive you to town? In my car with shot-out tires. Or maybe you can walk it. By yourself."

"Oh God!" He began to tremble, rock back and forth. Sweat gleamed on his face and his shaking increased. "I mean it, I hurt awful. It's stingin' like a thousand matches on me."

She went to a chest beneath the stairway, took out a thick blanket, wrapped it around his shoulders. "There's your boat, I can handle a boat. Maybe in the morning I could run you into town." (*And hand you over to whoever is the town authority, get someone to bring me home with new tires, or fix these.*) "I'm afraid to try the boat at night, especially without lights. Your boat doesn't have lights, does it?"

"No. But maybe you got a big lantern you could fasten in front."

"Too dangerous. The lake has too many deep coves, twists and turns, even floating logs. Easy to get turned around in the dark, spend the night on the lake. Tip over, maybe, get drowned. We need to wait for dawn. And hope it's not raining or snowing by then."

They sat through the night, she on the stairs, awake and watchful, the dog between her and the man who dozed fitfully in the blanketed chair. As the first grey light of morning filtered through the heavy mist hovering over the lake, the blanketed man, the woman, and the dog walked onto the dock, got in the boat. The motor sputtered, coughed, died, caught after several tries. Karen clenched her teeth against a ragged sigh of relief.

The boat chugged out of the cove, turned south, held to

the lake's center to avoid submerged logs and the ragged beds of water weeds that grew along the shore.

Perhaps twenty minutes of travel passed, the only sounds that of the motor and the rushing water as the boat skimmed through it, when suddenly a muttered curse and heavy, lurching movement startled her, swung her head about, threw her off balance. She staggered against the wheel, saw that the stranger was braced on elbows against the boat's side, towel-wrapped hands dangling and one leg lowering from what could have been a kick. Lad had vanished.

She cut the throttle, stared into the boat's wake. A small dark object bounced in the wave path. Lad.

She sharply wheeled the boat, fought its rocking, gunned it into the opposite direction. The man's elbows awkwardly jabbed at the boat's sides as he attempted to stand; instead he slid to the boat's bottom, yelping with pain. "Damn fool woman! Wreck us for a sonabitchin' dog! Gonna bite me! Can't half see with swelled-up eyes, musta sent him off wrong way, was gonna bite— Hey, for God's sake, turn around—"

For answer, the boat sped toward the swimming animal. The man, now half bent, half standing, lunged at her, staggered from the boat's bouncing, and pitched sideways into the lake.

The boat held course toward the dog. Reaching him, Karen cut the throttle, stretched over the boat's side, grabbed Lad's ruff, lost hold. Grabbed again, hung on until she grasped his collar, yanked him aboard. He shook himself, coughed, gagged out water.

She turned the boat toward the floundering man, his waterlogged arms splashing at the water. She tossed out the painter. "Grab the rope! Hang onto it! Catch it between your hands, squeeze hard, even if it hurts, you have to! Don't let loose! I'll pull you to the boat, try to lift you in."

With the motor idling, she reached for the man bobbing at the rear of the boat, he grimaced as swathed hands squeezed at the rope. She pulled him close, caught hold of his shoulder. He let go the rope, grappled at her down jacket, his desperation pulling her toward the water. "Let loose! If you pull me in with you I'll never get you out!" She dropped his shoulder, yanked her jacket, but his grasp was tenacious. She braced her feet against it, swiftly unzipped the jacket, shucked it off.

As the man submerged the jacket floated free. He resurfaced, hands flailing to re-contact the rope. She pushed it toward him, he caught it. "This time, hang on, don't drop that rope! I'll pull you to shore. It's impossible to lift you in out here on the lake."

"I'm freezing! The water's like ice!" Chattering teeth, blanched face bore out his statement.

Her jacket gone, she grabbed the blanket the man had dropped before he pitched overboard, threw it about her shoulders, headed the boat toward shore. Now a raw east wind cut from shore to shore and the boat bumped heavily over the lake's cross current. She looked back anxiously at the towed man. Momentarily his white, terrified face lifted to stare at her through the boat's spray.

She moved ahead cautiously, edged into the reed-bound shore, reached a small stretch of muddy beach. "Going in! Hold on!" she yelled. The boat bumped against solid ground, she cut the motor, turned to pull the man to shore.

The rope was drifting free, curling aimlessly on the water's surface, no weight pulling it downward. She scanned the water, its wave-roughened breadth shadowed by an even more menacing sky. Far out a head bobbed above the lake's surface, an arm reaching up beside it. She restarted the motor, reversed the craft, aimed for the bobbing head.

The head sank, briefly rose. As the boat fought the current, the tiny dark object seemed to flee from the pursuing boat. It sank again.

She forced the boat against the choppy waves, gained the vicinity where the head last surfaced. She made a slow, wide circle, fearful that the injured, chill-paralyzed man might be under the boat, to be sliced by its propeller. Holding onto the wheel, she leaned far over the boat's side, stared helplessly into the storm-darkened water.

A first light sting of snow struck her cheeks. Within

minutes the storm could become blinding, driven by wind into tunnels of white-out in which no direction existed.

She lifted the emergency oar, stirred it into the water in an attempt to discover the submerged body. The oar helplessly fought the storm-stressed water. The current had swept the man away. To where on this turbulent lake?

In the distance she glimpsed a dark floating object and her heart leapt. She raced toward it. But it was her own dark blue jacket she had shed. She jabbed for it with the oar but the wind skimmed it beyond capture. She cupped her hands about her mouth, shouted, "Here! Here! Show where you are!"

Only wind and the hiss of snow as it struck against the boat responded. With unreasonable, frantic irritation she thought, *He didn't even tell me his name, I don't even know who he is.*

She searched for him in ever widening circles, then backtracked by narrowing them. No sign, no mark to go by. In a shock of recollection she recalled an overheard conversation at the town's general store between the owner's wife and a woman customer. About an Indian legend of this lake handed down from old times, that this lonely northern lake was jealous of the bodies it claimed for its own. For reasons known only to the Lake Spirit it would release some drowned bodies, but others simply vanished, never to resurface. Some geologists offered the explanation that the lake bed had deep, bottomless holes here and there, cones of ancient submerged volcanoes that sucked those chosen bodies into them. But, said the store owner's wife to the customer, the old-timers clung to the belief that the Lake Spirit was moody and unpredictable, had an affinity and yearning for certain lonely souls to match its cold loneliness.

"I'm lonesome," the stranger had told her. Wasn't lonesome the same as lonely? "Ain't you kinda lonesome too, out here all alone?" Did the Lake Spirit go on a rampage today, try for two bodies plus a dog?

"Nonsense!" she shouted into the wind.

She turned the boat again toward the shoreline, straining for a glimpse of the lost white face, silently praying it would suddenly appear caught in the water weeds. The snow had thickened. As the boat moved against its slanting force, the flakes compacted into a blinding white siphon sucking her into an unknown vortex.

Despite her art, her dreams, was she lonely too—did the lake yearn for her?

She left the shore, waves buffeting her progress. Lad huddled at her feet, whined uneasily. She estimated to be roughly fifteen miles north of the town dock, her own property five miles or so north. If she turned back, followed the shore, she might reach home, escape the lake's hunger. The longer southward journey, coupled with the accelerating storm, could divert her into one of the numerous convoluted coves, cause loss of direction, even capsize the boat. If the boat should be beached it would be too far to walk to town for help through the approaching blizzard.

Besides, who would challenge this storm to search for the lost man when even she would be confused as to the location of his disappearance. Too late for the stranger. Hypothermia. Drowned. Lost to the lake.

With the decision to return home came fatalistic relaxation. She became aware of her own body's needs, of the cold, her wet flannel shirt clammy on her flesh, driving chill into her bones. Drawing the blanket close, she headed north.

At her dock she lifted Lad to its top. She brushed aside the dark, snow-weighted bangs that dripped water down her cheeks like tears, followed the dog up the steep bank. Her head throbbed with misery as she struggled to ferret out the mystery of why tragedy had so abruptly entangled two utter strangers. For what purpose? Only to punish the invader? To reveal herself to herself? Her weakness, self-centeredness, foolishness? Even though it had seemed idiocy at the time, should she have jumped into the water after the man, attempted to hold him afloat? No, not that, both would have drowned, pulled beneath the surface by his panic. Could it be that the Indians were right, the lake was a mystic entity, greedy for lonely people? Was she lonely, not merely alone?

"Not lonely!" she argued aloud. "I have painting, I have Lad."

In the driveway she knelt beside her car, examined the rear tires. Neat bullet holes punctured them, but the wheels seemed undamaged. Her one spare tire could go on one wheel, but twenty miles on the opposite punctured tire would make a ghastly trip over the storm-gouged county road, now snow-covered.

But the stranger ought to be found soon, pulled from the lake. Shouldn't he? If this storm was the start of an early, hard winter, the lake would freeze the body in the ice.

She looked downhill at the boat tied to the dock. She had two spare cans of gasoline. When, or if, the storm let up she could put gas in the boat's tank, run down to the village, report the whole terrible situation. Start a search.

If the lake froze, and the crippled car proved too difficult, she would have to walk. And after she reached town, then what? The sheriff would come, investigate. Perhaps drag this cove below her cabin to find the rifle she said she had tossed away. Or maybe it too would be claimed by the lake, no evidence left to back up her story. Reporters too, on the scene, keen for intrigue, spicy drama, sending out stories wild with conjecture, *Maybe you led the guy on,* pretty girl out in the woods all alone, maybe lonesome, and the guy came on too strong, scalded him you say, you do play rough, tipping him in the lake—

"Oh God!" she whispered. "What am I into? What shall I do?"

Lad was shaking with cold. He pawed her legs, whined. She led him to the cabin, unlocked the door, put him inside, started to follow. She stopped on the threshold, her head still whirling with conjecture. After a few minutes, she nodded, responding to an inner decision.

She returned to the dock, stepped down into the boat. Ignoring her own chill, methodically she gathered up blanket, purse, all her belongings and placed them on the dock. Then steeled herself to jump into the water, shuddered as it circled her waist, lapped at her breast. She untied the boat, pushed it from the dock, down the cove until the water reached her shoulders. She edged to the rear of the craft, kicked herself and her burden forward.

At the cove's entrance the wind-stressed water wrenched the boat from her grasp and the boat rocked northward on a haphazard path. Karen, dog-paddling, watched it bounce into the distance until, shrouded in snow, it vanished. She clenched her jaw to control the chatter of her teeth and swam back to the dock.

She gathered up her belongings, stumbled up the bank to the cabin. Inside, the load dropped from her suddenly nerveless hands, startling Lad, who was curled up beneath the stove. She stared at the scattered articles as though unable to comprehend what they were or where they came from.

"My jacket?" she asked herself weakly. "Where's my jacket?"

Out in the icy water. With the drowned man.

Suppose the jacket is found, tangled with him, in macabre intimacy.

When the storm abates the boat might ricochet from a jutting bank, turn south, float to the town. Or, hopefully, it could break up in the storm, no longer recognizable. Did the stranger own the boat? Or was it rented, its owner eager to find his property and its renter? Was any of what happened real, the stranger, herself, the boat, the gun, any of it, all enveloped in phantasmagoric illusion? Mightn't the body remain disappeared within the lake as illusions should?

Or, dear God, would it turn out completely, even exaggeratedly, real, into a frozen face glaring through the ice as skaters sped over it when the storm abated? Or, most terrible of all, suppose the wind changed direction in the night and drove the body back to its launching place, her dock, to stare at her in the morning with frozen dead eyes. "No, no!" she whispered vehemently.

Inside her mind, silent but equally vehement, came a secret whisper, "Yes, yes, perhaps." She shrugged, helpless before the mystery of fate.

In an effort to regain normality, she built up the fire. As

she stood beside the warming stove peeling off wet clothes, she faced the fact of two strangers. The man. And the woman beside the stove uselessly trying to drive out the deep chill she had discovered within herself.

BORN BAD

By ANDREW VACHSS

The man was husky, with a big chest and thick wrists, wearing a tweed jacket over an oxford-cloth white shirt and plain dark tie. His hair was cropped short, eyes alert behind aluminum-framed glasses. He handed his battered leather medical satchel to the guard standing by the metal detector.

"Morning, Jackson," he said.

"Good morning to you, Doc. Carrying any weapons today?"

Doc tapped his head, smiled. The guard looked carefully through the satchel, ran his electronic wand over Doc's body.

"Everybody there?"

"Waiting on you, Doc."

He threw a half-salute at the guard and strolled down the sterile concrete corridor, the bag swinging at his side, taking his time.

He came to an institutional green door with a hand-lettered sign taped on its front. Task Force. He knocked. The door was opened by a heavyset, thick-necked man wearing a shoulder holster. He stepped aside and the man the guard had called Doc entered.

The room was long and narrow. He was facing a row of windows. Barred windows. The wall behind him was covered with corkboard, littered with randomly fastened charts, graphs, maps. A battered wood podium stood at the head of a double-length conference table; behind it, a small movie screen pulled down like a window shade. In the upper corner of the room, a TV set stood on an elevated platform, a VCR on a shelf underneath. Cigarette smoke hung in the air, blue-tinted in the slanting sunlight.

Doc took his seat, looked around. They were all there, waiting.

"How come you're always the last to show up, Doc?" Oscar asked. The slim black investigator pretended an irritation he didn't feel. "We moved the Task Force into this looney bin just 'cause you work here, the least you could do is make the damn meetings on time."

"Sorry, hoss. There was a little problem on one of the wards."

"Never mind that now," a red-haired woman said, the chief prosecutor in the Homicide Bureau. "Tell him what happened."

A tall blond man stepped to the podium, moving with the authority he carried from his long-ago days as a street cop, a sheaf of papers in his hand. He carefully extracted a single sheet, smoothed it flat, flicked on an opaque projector. One page of a neatly typed letter sprang into life on the screen.

"It's from him?" a Hispanic with a duelist's mustache asked. He was the group's forensics expert.

"Yeah," the blond man answered. "We Xeroxed the whole thing. Seven pages. The lab boys went over it with an electron microscope. Typed on a computer, probably that laptop he carries around. It was printed out on a laser printer. Generic paper, standard number ten business envelope. Untraceable. But we know it's him—he left us a perfect thumbprint below the signature."

"Damn!" the black man said.

"Postmark?" the redhead asked.

"Tucson, Arizona. Four days ago," the blond answered. "Central Post Office. He won't be there now."

On the screen, the letter stood out in bold contrast to the darkened room. Justified margins, single spaced with the paragraphs indented.

"He's always so neat, so precise," the woman said.

"Yeah," the blond agreed. He looked across the table. "Looks like your idea worked, Doc. When you wrote that article about the Surgeon—the one where you said he had to have been an abused child—it made him mad. Smoked him out. Look at this letter—he's boiling over. Slashed at your theory like he's been doing at women all around the country."

Doc nodded, waiting patiently for the recap he knew was coming as soon as he'd spotted new faces in the room.

The blond man swept his eyes around the table, willing everyone to silence. "Mark Anthony Monroe," he began, nodding his head toward a blown-up black-and-white photograph on the wall to his left. "White male, age forty-one last birthday. Five foot eleven, one hundred and sixty pounds. Blond and blue. Undergraduate degree in physics, graduate work in computer technology. No scars, marks, or tattoos. No known associates. Mother and father divorced when he was two. Mother remarried when he was five. Divorced again when he was eight. No contact with either father or stepfather since, whereabouts of both unknown. Mother died when he was in his late twenties. You with me so far?"

Nods and grunts of assent from around the room. Doc drew a series of tiny boxes on his notepad, not looking up.

"First arrest, age thirteen," the blond man continued. "Fire-setting. He convinced the juvie officers it was an accident—dismissed. Next time down, he was fourteen. He put a cat in a shoebox, poured gasoline over it, dropped a match. He got probation, referred for counseling. The counselor said he didn't mean to hurt the cat—some kind of scientific experiment. At sixteen, he was dropped for attempted rape. Attacked a schoolteacher on a stairwell right outside the gym. Cut her too. Sent to a juvenile institution. Did almost five years. After his discharge, he was quiet for a while. We have an admission, voluntary admission to a psychiatric hospital when he was in his mid-twenties. He was treated for depression, signed himself out after a few months. Nothing since.

"He went to college, like I said. Far as we can tell, he's never worked a real job.

"For the last two and a half years, he's been roaming the country. Killing. He kills them different ways. All women. But no matter how he kills them, he always cuts out the heart. Neat, clean cuts. He knows what he's doing. That's why the newspaper guys call him the Surgeon.

"We got thirteen confirmed kills, and a whole bunch of Unsolved that may be his.

"He's smooth and slick. Talks nice, got a lot of employment skills. And a good deal of cash . . . money his
mother left him when she died. He don't look like a killer
. . . hell, he don't look like much of anything. He could be
anywhere."

He looked around the room. "Any questions?"

"You do a profile on him, Marty?" the redhead asked.

"Profile? Yeah, we did a damn profile, Suzanne. No-
madic, prolific driver, rootless, pathological hate for females. Serial killer . . . that's what we got. Big deal."

The Hispanic looked up from his place at the end of the
table. "He . . . do anything to the women? Besides kill
them?"

"No. At least nothing we can tell. No semen found on or
in any of the bodies."

"Why's he do it, then?"

"Because he likes to," Doc said, so softly some of the
assembled hunters had to lean forward to hear his voice.

"Yeah, well let's all see what he says about it," the blond
man said, stepping to the corner and switching off the
overhead lights. He adjusted a dial until the letters on the
screen were big enough to read from anywhere in the
room.

My dear, ignorant Dr. Ruskin:

I read your fascinatingly stupid "analysis" of my moti-
vations in the June 15 issue of *Parade*. It was so pathet-
ically uninformed, so lacking in insight, so bereft of logic
that I felt compelled to provide the education you so
obviously neglected in medical school.

It is my understanding that you have been "studying"
my case for some months now. How unfortunate that
your politics interfere with your judgment—that is
highly unprofessional. You are clearly one of those irre-
deemably ignorant individuals who takes it on faith
that nobody is "born bad." You believe there must be
some etiology of a monster—some specific cause and effect. I quote from your purple prose: "There is no bioge-
netic code for serial killer. There may be some hard-

wired personality propensities, but the only way to produce such a monster is early, chronic, systematic child abuse." How I pity your lack of intelligence—and what contempt I have for your cowardice. Like all liberals, you hide your head in the sand of religion, convincing yourself that evil does not exist.

Pay attention, you little worm: I *was* born bad. I came out of the womb evil. My only pleasure is power, and I learned early on that the ultimate power is to possess life. To extinguish it at my will. You know how some men break hearts? Well, I *take* hearts. And I keep them.

Was I an "abused child"? Certainly not. My mother was, if anything, over-indulgent. I was always treated with kindness, love, and respect. And I repaid that investment in blood. I am not insane, and never have been. When I admitted myself to the psychiatric hospital, it was to avoid the consequences of my own act—the rape of a little girl. I was never caught. Never even charged. And I probably never will be.

I am not insane, despite your fervent wish that I be so. The behavior you so carefully chart is not the prodromal phase of psychosis, it is entirely volitional. Should you be interested in propounding a more accurate, precise diagnosis, you might check your holy DSM-III, your biblical attempt to quantify human behavior. I'll guide your dim brain to the right spot, Doctor: Anti-Social Personality Disorder, 301.70. Such high-flown verbiage to describe what I am. Dangerous. Remorseless. Evil.

By now I am certain you stand in abject awe of my protean grasp of psychiatric jargon. Do not be surprised, I have been studying your ancient tablets for many years—preparing my defense. You see, Doctor, I have none of the grandiosity that characterizes others who have walked my same road. Such subhumans are not of my ilk. Ted Bundy was a contemptible, whining worm— an obsessive-compulsive the media made into a criminal genius simply because he possessed the slightly above-average IQ sufficient to enter law school. Arrogance without intellect personified. And John Wayne Gacy, a repulsive gargoyle. Were the media not so utterly enthralled by high body counts, he would not have merited a line of type. Lust-driven cowards, with not the remotest concept of higher orders. Your pedestrian theories fit such creatures quite well, Doctor—both abused children, screaming in rage against their past.

As I said, I am not grandiose, or narcissistic. I acknowledge that capture is possible. Should such luck (and it will take considerable luck) befall you, I expect to be acquitted at any trial. You will all judge me "insane." Because you fear the truth.

So please spare me your insipid wish fulfillment. I am not a "sexual sadist," I have no "fetish." My rituals are of my own making, designed for my pleasure, not the subject of any compulsion. They are, in fact, private ceremonies—homage to my sociopathic genius. I am capable of modifying my behavior. Indeed, I have done so on many occasions. The unexpected presence of potential witnesses has caused me to forsake my trophies several times. But, if you look closely, you will note unmistakable forensic evidence of my passage even when I have not had the opportunity to take the hearts from my victims. Read the last sentence carefully, you stupid slug: *my* victims. They belong to me, forever.

My many homicides are not a "cry for help." I have no desire to be caught. I have taken great pains to avoid capture. But, should that unlikely event come to pass, I know I can rely on religious cowards such as yourself to leap to my defense, to stridently proclaim my "insanity" to a court. And should a different result emerge, my situation will not change materially. I have no need of sex, and less of human companionship. Serial Killer Chic has infected American consciousness. (Perhaps you should be studying *that* phenomenon instead of wasting your time trying to analyze me.) I will be an object of fascination. Women will offer to marry me. Publishers will clamor for my life story. Wealthy morons will buy my paintings, telling their friends they have seen into my soul.

You are not my nemesis, Doctor, you are my safety net.

Oh, don't you wish I were insane? Don't you pray to your ineffectual gods that I am the product of an abusive home? Doesn't the truth terrify you?

Let me appeal to your scientific mind—if only to that portion not clouded by your so-called "education." You claim to be an environmentalist, a determinist, if you will. I cannot, in your narrow-minded view, be "born" bad. It must be attributable to something in the way I was nurtured, yes? Unfortunately for your indefensible theories, there is irrefutable evidence to the contrary. My mother, despite her impeccable conduct toward me, was no saint. She had her own demons. I was, as I said, raised in an environment of total love. Yet my brother, my half-genetic counterpart (we had different biological fathers), was not. Unlike myself, he was the target of my mother's insanity. Yes, Doctor, my mother was conventionally insane. Bipolar, schizoid, with more than a touch of pedophilia. Ah, wouldn't your liberal heart bleed for my poor brother—locked and chained in a dark basement closet for literally days at a time, beaten with a wide variety of objects, burned with cigarettes. The poor tyke was violated by one of my mother's gentleman friends while my mother held him. A Polaroid camera provided many hours of entertainment for my mother, and, later, a considerable source of income as well. And yet, my brother is a fine, upstanding citizen. He has never committed a transgression against society in his entire life. A credit to the community, welcome anywhere. If your lamentably weak little theories had any basis in fact, my brother would have been a prime candidate for what your stupid article called the "negative fallout" from child abuse: drugs, alcohol, promiscuity, suicide, crime. None of the above ever occurred. Perhaps you should do some research, Doctor. Have you ever read the seminal work of Denis M. Donovan in the field of traumatology? His concept of "inescapable shock syndrome" is most illuminating, although I fear it would be wasted on a man of your distinctly limited scope.

Your theories are lies. I am the living, life-taking proof.

Absent fortuitous circumstance, you will never catch me. I am invisible. People like you make it certain that we don't see evil. I am a shark in a suburban swimming pool. Safe and deadly forever, feeding as I will.

Take my warning, Doctor. So long as you promulgate your explanations for evil, it will flourish. Face the truth. And fear it forever.

The blond man waited patiently until the entire Task Force had finished reading. Then he flicked on the lights and looked across the room at Doc.

"You know, Doc, you and me, we've been having this go-round for years. I always said your theories were nonsense, didn't I? I been a cop too long. I got to hand it to this freak—he told it like it is. I mean, there's your evidence, right? Two brothers, raised in the same household. Look how different they turned out. One's treated like a prince, he turns out to be a monster. The other's tortured all kinds of ways, he turns out to be a decent guy. I think we all learned something today. The freak's right: all the stuff about child abuse causing crime is just so much liberal claptrap. You got anything to say?"

Doc took off his glasses, cleaned them patiently with a handkerchief. The red-haired woman lit a cigarette. Others leaned forward, watching from the sidelines.

"Come on, Doc. You've been studying the Surgeon for years, going over the ground inch by inch," the black man said. "You got any comeback for what Marty said?"

The husky man said, "Yes," very quietly, and got to his feet. He looked into the face of each person in the room, one by one, eyes shining with sadness and with truth.

"He doesn't have a brother," he said.

SECRETS

By JUNE THOMSON

Yesterday I went to my sister Naomi's funeral. It was a sad little ceremony, attended by only a few people, mostly acquaintances whom she had made in Rochester, where she had lived for the past fifteen years since her second divorce. I had the feeling none of them were close friends. Naomi had never possessed the gift of intimacy, not with either of her husbands and certainly not with me, her younger brother.

As a child, I had both envied and admired her. Thin and long-legged, she could outrun almost any boy of her own age and knew how to bowl overarm like a professional. Nothing frightened her, not even Father. At the same time, I was intimidated by her self-assurance and the intensity of her determination.

It was largely for this reason that we had grown apart, but not entirely.

As her coffin was lowered into the grave, I thought: It's too late now to ask her what really happened all those years ago on the clifftop in Cornwall.

It was towards the end of August 1939, shortly before the outbreak of the war, when Naomi was thirteen and I was seven; one of those perfect summers of long, hot days and impeccable skies which one remembers all one's life as part of a vanished childhood. The fear of war seemed only to add an extra dangerous glitter to the sea.

As we did every year, we spent that summer at the small, white-washed house our parents owned in the fishing village of Portmerron on the north Cornish coast. From its windows, we could look out at the sea and the surrounding cliffs, towering above the little harbour. At night, we went to sleep to the sound of waves slapping up against the rocks or sucking at the sand and, in the morning, we were wakened by the screams of the gulls.

But that summer, there were two changes to our usual holiday routine. For the first time that I could remember, my father wasn't able to join us. Because of the crisis, all leave had been cancelled at the Foreign Office where he worked.

And Edward Wilson came to stay.

"Why does he have to?" Naomi demanded when Mother broke the news to us one morning over breakfast.

Mother laid down the letter from Mrs. Wilson she had been reading.

"Because his father's been called up into the air force and his mother wants Edward to stay with us while she finds somewhere to live near to where he's been posted," she explained in that reasonable voice she often adopted with Naomi, rarely with me. It was only years later, when I heard myself using the same tone, that I realised it was her way of avoiding a confrontation.

"But he's stupid!"

Mother came close to losing her patience.

"I won't have you saying that, Naomi! And please remember you're to be nice to him. He's going to feel lonely here at first without his parents. I want you and Tom to make friends with him."

"I don't care what she says, he is stupid," Naomi asserted when, breakfast over, we walked down to the beach.

I nodded, knowing better than to disagree with her, although I secretly thought that anyone whose father was in the air force couldn't be entirely contemptible. I imagined Mr. Wilson in a leather helmet, like Biggles, flying over vast continents laid out below him and coloured red as they were in my school atlas. As for Edward, I had no clear recollection of him. His mother and mine were old childhood friends who had kept in touch, although they rarely met after the Wilsons moved to Reading. The last time I had seen him had been two years before at a Christmas circus in London, but it was the clowns I remembered more vividly than him.

He arrived two days later, accompanied by his mother, who left the same evening to return to Reading.

Even now my memories of him are far from clear for I have difficulty in distinguishing my childhood image of him from my sister's.

To her, he was merely a nuisance, a fat lump of a child who tagged along after us, spoiling our games, who couldn't swim and was hopeless at beach cricket. As if through her eyes, I saw him toiling after us across the sand, his face moist under his linen sunhat, calling out in a constant wail, "Wait for me!" Her private nickname for him was the Vest, because of the white singlet he always wore under his shirt. With her talent for mockery, she made up a song about him to the tune of Bobby Shaftoe:

Edward Wilson wears a vest,
He is nothing but a pest,
Let's lock him in a great big chest,
Soppy Edward Wilson.

When Mother was present, she would hum the tune under her breath or tap out its rhythm on the table until Mother, not understanding the joke but suspecting it was directed at Edward, told her to stop. After that, she only hummed or tapped in front of him, enticing me with a sideways smile to join in the fun.

My own memories of him, those not influenced by Naomi's attitude, are different. Because the house was small, we had to share a bedroom, which I resented at first until I came to enjoy his company. Generous with his possessions, he let me borrow his Rupert annuals or look through his stamp collection. But I remember him best sitting cross-legged on his bed, a round-faced, fair-haired boy of my own age, wearing blue and white striped pyjamas, his teddy bear, Benjy, perched on the pillow beside him, and discussing with me in his grave, adult manner those subjects, such as football and model trains, which small boys of seven find mutually absorbing.

He wanted to be a boffin when he grew up, like his father. At the time, I didn't know what the word meant.

"What's a boffin?" I asked.

Instead of laughing at me for my ignorance as Naomi would have done, he answered me quite seriously.

"It's someone who does research. Daddy's an expert in radio. That's why he's been called up into the air force."

"I thought your father was a pilot."

"Oh, no," he corrected me proudly, as if it was far better to be a boffin than to fly a plane. "He's part of a very special team that's been set up somewhere in Scotland to test out new equipment. Actually, it's terribly secret and I'm not supposed to say anything about it in case the Germans find out. So you must promise not to tell."

In giving him my word, I sealed a bond with him, the true nature of which I wasn't to understand until later.

It was largely on Edward's account that towards the end of the week Mother suggested that the three of us go on the bus that afternoon into Trewarth, the small seaside resort about six miles away.

"Do we have to go?" Naomi cried.

For once, Mother was adamant.

"It'll make a change and besides, Edward hasn't seen anything of Cornwall yet apart from the beach. Now, I've looked up the times of the buses. If you get the one straight after lunch, you'll have two hours to spend in Trewarth before catching the half-past four bus home."

"But there's nothing to do in Trewarth!"

"Nonsense! Of course there is," Mother said brightly. "There's the promenade and the donkeys and the Punch and Judy show on the beach."

Even Naomi realized that it was useless to argue, although she grumbled under her breath to me that it was all the Vest's fault as we went upstairs to get ready for the excursion.

"Silly idiot!" she muttered, slamming her bedroom door shut behind her.

As we left, Mother called out last instructions to us from the front steps.

"Keep together so you won't lose one another and hold hands when you cross the road. And don't miss the half-past four bus home. Naomi, did you hear me?"

If she did, Naomi made no sign. Her brow like thunder,

she stalked off down the road towards the bus stop outside the Portmerron Arms, her long brown legs flashing in and out under the skirt of the hated dress which Mother had made her wear for the occasion, while Edward and I trotted beside her, in clean shirts and shorts, our hair sleeked back with water.

The bus ride was enjoyable but Naomi was right about Trewarth. Once the temporary excitement of the shops and the holiday crowds had worn off, there was very little to do. Caged in between the breakwaters, the sea seemed tame after Portmerron as it lapped languidly up the beach. There were no rocks here to climb, no hidden pools to discover. There wasn't even room to run about, for the beach was strewn with deckchairs and the slumbering bodies of sunbathers.

There were, however, donkeys—a sullen line of them, heads hanging low in the heat, the sand around them stained with their droppings, on which the blowflies buzzed and feasted. Edward refused a ride on one of them, wrinkling up his nose in disgust at the smell.

As for the Punch and Judy show, we had missed most of the performance. Using this as an excuse, Naomi made us stand at the back among the grownups, although I suspected her pride wouldn't let her join the semicircle of little children seated on the sand in front of the booth. With her arms tightly folded across her chest, her disapproval made itself so apparent that neither Edward nor I dared to join in the laughter, not even when Punch seized the stick and beat the policeman over the head with it.

When the curtains closed and the Punch and Judy man emerged from the back to pass round the hat, she dragged us away.

"What are we going to do now?" Edward asked plaintively as we crunched up the beach towards the promenade.

"I don't know. I said the place was boring," Naomi replied in an I-told-you-so voice.

I was going to suggest that we go to the penny amusement arcade when Edward noticed a sign at the top of the steps, pointing to a museum.

"I want to go there," he said.

"You won't like it," Naomi warned him.

"Yes I will."

He came to a halt in the middle of the pavement and stood there facing her, plump legs set apart and an expression on his face not unlike Naomi's when she was determined to get her own way.

"I want to go," he repeated.

My sister sighed in the same way Mother did when faced with our intractability, usually Naomi's, but, to my surprise, she gave in. Perhaps she realized that she had gone too far in spoiling our afternoon and word might get back to Mother.

"Oh, all right then. Come on!"

Seizing us by the hands, she hurried us across the road at the traffic lights and into a side street where the museum was situated in a grey stone building, up three steps.

It was sixpence each to go in. Naomi clicked her tongue at this exorbitant amount, although I had the feeling that she secretly enjoyed the importance of paying over the half-crown which Mother had given to her for spending money and being handed the tickets by the lady in the kiosk from a big yellow roll.

"I'll look after them," she told us, putting them away, together with the change, into her navy-blue school purse which hung on a strap over the front of her dress and which Mother had made her take with her. She kept us waiting while she snapped the button fastener firmly shut before leading the way inside.

After the heat and glare of the town, the interior was as cool and as dim as a church. Long, cream-coloured blinds drawn down over the windows kept out the sun. As we entered, our footsteps rang out on the stone floor.

There were only two rooms, the first devoted to the wildlife of the area, almost entirely stuffed seabirds, perched on pieces of rock or squatting on meagre nests of twigs and pebbles. Their malevolent black eyes glared at us through the dusty glass of their cases.

Naomi made us stay together and we trailed after her

from one display to the next while she read out loud to us
from the explanatory cards fixed to the wall at the side of
each exhibit.

" 'The Great Black-Backed Gull, *Larus marinus*,' " she
intoned in a loud, clear voice, " 'is common along the
North Cornish coast where it nests singly or in colonies.
Larger than the Herring Gull, it is distinguished by its
heavy bill, its black wings, and pinkish legs. A predator, it
will steal the eggs and young of other seabirds.' "

Several people turned round to look, as if we really were
in church and ought to be silent, but Naomi only tossed
her head and went on with the readings until Edward and
I began to fidget and finally even she grew tired of the
game. When we moved into the second room, given over to
local history, she allowed us to go off on our own, Edward
hanging back to look at a case of Roman finds, mostly old
coins and bits of broken pottery, while I made straight for
one of two large exhibits set up in alcoves on each side at
the further end of the room.

It was a tableau depicting a smugglers' cave, lit by only
the yellow glow from two lanterns, standing on papier-
mâché rocks, which cast eerie shadows over the bearded
faces of three men, bending down over brandy casks and
large, oilskin-wrapped parcels, labeled "Tobacco" in case
there was any doubt about their contents. But I was puzzled by the treasure chest, open and carelessly spilling out
ropes of pearls, jewelled coronets, and great handfuls of
gold coins which, taken with the black eye-patch one of
the figures was wearing, suggested pirates rather than
smugglers.

Unless, of course, they were meant to be wreckers as
well.

Father had told us about the wreckers, how they stood
on the cliffs with lanterns, luring ships onto the rocks, and
then plundered their cargoes.

I started to walk towards Naomi in order to ask her
opinion.

She was standing, totally absorbed, in front of the other
tableau, although I caught only a glimpse of it before she
whirled about as I approached.

Behind her, I could see the interior of a darkened room
—a hut, perhaps, or a primitive cottage. Curious objects,
bundles of dried herbs, leather bottles and crude earthen-
ware jars, hung down from the low, beamed ceiling or
were scattered about the floor beside an open fire over
which a big, black pot was suspended from a chain. In the
lurid glow from a red bulb, not quite concealed under the
logs and the scarlet crepe-paper flames, I could dimly dis-
cern the silhouette of a woman, crouching beside the
hearth, a black cat at her side and a broom made out of
sticks propped up in a corner.

There was something sinister about the setting but before I could examine it more closely, Naomi had whisked
me round so that I had my back to it.

"What do you want?" she demanded fiercely.

"Nothing," I stammered. "I was only going to ask you
about the smugglers."

"There isn't time," she retorted, looking at the boy's
watch strapped to her wrist. "We have to go now."

Pushing me in front of her by the shoulder, she collected
up Edward and swept the pair of us out of the museum
and along the street to the promenade.

We were almost a quarter of an hour too early for the
bus. There would have been time for us to go to the penny
arcade and to have had a turn on the crane or one of the
pin-tables or, better still, the mechanical model of the
death of Mary Queen of Scots and to have made the little
figures jerk into action, especially the executioner who
brought his axe crashing down to send the poor Queen's
head tumbling from her shoulders.

Naomi wouldn't let us. We might miss the bus and then
Mother would be cross.

But she relented far enough to buy Edward and me each
a triangular stick of orange ice cream from the Wall's
Stop-Me-And-Buy-One tricycle on the sea-front and then
left us by the bus stop, sucking at the sweet, frozen juice
which made our teeth ache and which tasted of the cardboard container while she disappeared inside Boot's the
Chemist, a little way up the street.

She was back within minutes, the pocket of her dress

bulging with something in a white paper bag which she refused to show us.

"It's none of your business," she said briskly, just like Mother and then, spitting on her handkerchief, began to scrub our faces clean for the journey home.

We were silent on the bus, too dazed by the sun and the heat to talk. Edward and I sat together, Naomi occupying a seat by herself on the other side of the aisle, as if she had nothing to do with us.

"I think a bath and early bed tonight," Mother said over tea, seeing our flushed faces.

"I'm not tired," Naomi said. Indeed, she looked bursting with energy and purpose. "I was thinking of walking up to the cliff-top with Tom. We haven't been there yet this holiday. Edward needn't come if he doesn't want to."

He took up the challenge as I think he was meant to.

"But I'd like to go, too. I haven't been there either."

Mother looked doubtful.

"I don't know, Edward. It's a long walk and you've had a very busy day."

"I'm not a bit tired, honestly," he assured her, his face stricken. "Oh, please, Mrs. Mortimer!"

Mother capitulated.

"Very well then, you may go, but only if you promise to keep to the path and not go near the edge."

"I promise," he said solemnly. "Cross my heart."

Mother turned to address Naomi, who had been watching this exchange with her head on one side and a little smile on her face, oddly triumphant.

"You heard that, Naomi?"

Naomi nodded, tossing back her hair as she got up from the table.

"I'm going upstairs to take off this stupid dress," she announced.

But she didn't, not straightaway, for I heard the back door close behind her and it was several minutes after Edward and I had gone up to our room to change our clothes as well that she finally came upstairs.

Mother must have heard her, too, for she went out into the hall to call up to her.

"Naomi, what are you doing in my bedroom?"

Naomi's voice was raised in reply.

"I'm looking for the nail scissors."

"What do you want them for?"

There followed one of those silences which children use with such effect to draw attention to an adult's obtuseness.

"To cut my nails with."

Of course, silly, was the unspoken rider.

"Then put them back when you've finished with them," Mother said sharply.

Even so, Naomi was ready before us and came banging on our door, calling out impatiently, "Come on, you two! Hurry up!"

The path started at a stile only a few yards from the house and, after crossing a small field of rough grass, began the long, slow climb upwards round the side of the cliff.

Naomi went first, striding ahead of us in her boy's khaki shorts and her white aertex blouse, as vigorous and intrepid as an explorer leading an expedition into unknown territory. Scrambling after her, I could see her sharp elbows pumping in and out and her long dark hair, held back by an elastic band, bouncing purposefully between her shoulder blades.

Behind me, Edward, puffing up the slope, kept calling out every few yards, "Wait for me!"

I stopped unwillingly for him, torn between a reluctance to abandon him and an eagerness to catch up with my sister, remembering her assertion as we had started off that the last one at the top would be a sissy.

At last, the path rounded the shoulder of the cliff and the view burst upon us in a sudden, dazzling revelation of sky and sea. It was like entering into another world where all the familiar dimensions, seen at ground level, were expanded to new and dizzying proportions. The sky was a vast, circular, blue immensity, extending around us on all sides, unobstructed by rooftops or masts or chimney pots.

As for the sea, it lay below us, almost motionless at that height, its silvery surface, faintly crinkled, stretching out for miles and miles to a far-off smudged purple line which was the horizon.

We could look down not only on the sea but on the gulls, circling beneath or suspended, pinned and screaming, against the wind.

And how it blew up there! It met us head-on as Edward and I came panting round the last bend in the path to find Naomi already on the headland, straining forward into its blast like the figurehead on a sailing ship. It had snatched the band from her hair, which was tossing in wild gusts about her head.

It even tore the words from her mouth as she turned to speak to us until, laughing with exhilaration, she flung herself down on the grass, out of its grasp.

We joined her, I lying prone beside her, Edward sitting more decorously with his legs crossed as he did on his bed at home.

"I said, Isn't it wonderful up here?" Naomi repeated. "Better than horrible old Trewarth and the soppy museum. Aren't you glad you came?"

She was looking directly at Edward who, still breathless from the climb, nodded dumbly.

There was a brilliance about her which had nothing to do with the sunlight or the sea.

And then, as if already bored with sitting still, she leapt to her feet and the wind reclaimed her, whipping at the legs of her shorts and her shirtsleeves so that they cracked like flags.

"Don't you wish you could fly?" she shouted, raising her arms above her head. "I do! I'd fly all over the world, to Africa and Asia and China."

"China's in Asia," Edward pointed out.

He was watching her uneasily, dazzled by her glitter and yet wary of it.

"I know that, stupid!"

Swooping down, she seized him by the shoulders and lugged him to his knees.

"Come on! Let's try!"

"Don't be silly," he said, squirming under her grip. "People can't fly."

"Your father does."

Proud though he was of his father, Edward didn't contradict her and I realised then how seriously he regarded the secret he had confided in me; too precious to be told even to Naomi. It was the first time in my life I had ever shared a secret with anyone other than her.

But he was too honest, or perhaps too naive, to lie and instead, he replied obliquely, "That's in an airplane with an engine."

"You don't need an airplane. There's gliders and hot-air balloons. They don't have engines," Naomi retorted.

Even I knew she was right. As for Edward, he was reduced to silence.

Feeling in the pocket of her shorts, she took out a small white jar with a blue lid, its sides still patched with little bits of paper where the label had been scraped off.

"Or there's this," she added.

"What is it?" Edward asked.

"It's flying ointment."

Edward looked at her sceptically.

"There isn't such a thing."

"Yes, there is."

"Where did you get it from then?"

"Never you mind. It's a secret, isn't it, Tom?" she said, inviting me to join in the conspiracy even though I didn't understand it. "Smell it."

Taking off the lid, she thrust the jar under Edward's nose. He drew back, pulling a face.

"It's horrible."

"It's meant to be. It's a very special ointment made from magic herbs which only grow in jungles or on the top of high mountains."

"Can I have a smell?" I pleaded.

She waved the opened jar in front of my face, long enough for me to see that it contained a thick, white substance, with exactly the same appearance and scent as the cold cream Mother used, except it was flecked with green morsels of what looked like leaves, snipped up small, which gave off the sharp, distinct aroma of mint.

For the first time, I began dimly to make the connection

between the tableau in the museum and Naomi's visit to the chemist's and the back garden at home. The incident with Mother's nail scissors also fell into place together with scraps of half-remembered knowledge from the children's encyclopedia.

"Didn't witches use flying ointment?" I asked.

Naomi glanced at me approvingly, as if I had said the right thing for once.

"Of course they did. They used to rub it into themselves, like this."

Dipping two fingers into the jar, she smeared the cream onto Edward's bare legs and arms below his shorts and shirt sleeves, rubbing it hard into his skin.

"It tingles," he complained.

"It's meant to," Naomi told him. "That means the magic's working. Now stand up and see if you can fly."

He scrambled reluctantly to his feet, his knees and elbows glistening, stained here and there with the green juice from the little bits of leaves.

"Go on!" Naomi ordered. "Don't just stand there like a ninny. Wave your arms up and down, like me."

Kneeling upright, she began to flap her own arms. As if mesmerised, Edward mimicked her, slowly at first and then more eagerly as the rhythm seized him.

"Harder!" she shouted into the wind. "Harder! That's better. And now run!"

He ran, beating his arms up and down, his legs working like pistons as the wind claimed him and, as if it were a huge hand thrusting against his back, propelled him faster and faster down the slopes.

"Don't go near the edge!" Naomi shrieked.

But the warning came too late.

As the wind caught her words and whirled them away, he, too, arms flailing, went spinning off into space.

I must have jumped to my feet although I wasn't aware of doing so, only of Naomi clutching me by the ankle in so fierce a grip that her fingers burned through my socks down to the skin. I couldn't see her face for the tears that were pouring down mine and a terrible blankness of vision at the horror of it all. But I heard her voice quite distinctly.

"Walk! Don't run!"

I obeyed her numbly, following her across the cliff and copying her when she dropped down to wriggle forwards on her stomach for the last few yards.

Lying side by side, we peered down over the edge.

Far, far below was the beach we played on, so diminished in size that it seemed nothing more than a tiny, pale crescent of sand. To the left, something else pale lay on its face in the water, gently lifting and falling in the waves like a piece of flotsam.

"It wasn't our fault," Naomi said. "He tripped."

"Did he?" I asked. I couldn't remember that, only his feet in his brown Clark's sandals slithering frantically over the short, slippery grass.

"Yes, he did. He was running when he tripped and fell. I told him not to go near the edge."

That part at least was true.

"It wasn't our fault," Naomi repeated. "He was stupid. He wouldn't do what he was told. That's what we have to tell Mummy. But you're not to say anything about this," she added. She was holding in her hand the white jar of flying ointment. Getting carefully to her feet, she flung it far out to sea with that powerful overarm action which I so much envied.

"Why not?" I asked, watching as it made a wide arc through the air before disappearing into the dazzle of the sea.

"Because it was a joke," she explained, dropping down again beside me. "Just a joke. But Mummy wouldn't understand and she'd be terribly, terribly angry with both of us. So would Daddy."

And so I was drawn into the conspiracy after all, one of silence, compounded of the fear of adult anger and a sense of awful guilt which I couldn't understand myself and which, for that very reason, I could never have expressed to anyone else.

So the truth, whatever it might have been, never came

out, never even at the inquest at which, I learned later, a verdict of accidental death was returned.

Naomi and I didn't go to the funeral; only our parents attended. By that time, war had been declared and we had been sent away to stay with our grandparents in Wiltshire where we remained for the rest of the war, safe from the air raids on London.

Things were never the same again. That was the last summer we spent at the house in Cornwall. Later, it was requisitioned for evacuees from Southampton and, after the war, my parents sold it.

I have never returned to Portmerron; neither, as far as I know, had Naomi, although I can't be certain of that.

As I explained at the beginning, we drifted apart as we grew older, the gap which had always existed between us becoming wider over the years until finally we communicated with each other only out of a sense of duty, exchanging cards at birthdays or Christmas.

Watching as her coffin was lowered into the ground, I thought again of Edward, the first real friend I ever had. But it was too late to find the answer to the question I should have asked Naomi all those years ago on that Cornish cliff-top.

"Did you really mean him to die?"

THE BIG DANCE

By TOM VERDE

B ancroft sat on the porch of the Regency Cafe waiting
for his pot of tea to steep and fanning the flies away
with a small dessert menu. The aqua cement walls of the
cafe's terrace and the green potted ferns in the corners
made the place look cool, but provided little actual comfort
from the pervasive heat. On the lawn in front of him were
round, wooden tables surrounded by delicate, painted
cane chairs. Even though the tables were shielded by red-
and-white Cinzano umbrellas, no one was sitting at them.

The sky was clear and brilliantly blue, although Bancroft knew that at any minute it might cloud over and the
rain would fall in heavy, powerful sheets. This would last
for an hour or so and then suddenly stop, like a faucet
being snapped off. The rains had come early to Malawi
that year. Each morning, noon, and evening it rained and
this would go on for the long months that preceded the
summer. Although they were a predictable annoyance,
Bancroft didn't mind them much. They were fairly punc-
tual and Bancroft admired punctuality, even that of rain-
storms.

Waiters in dark trousers and stiff white shirts stood at
the doorway to the cafe holding round brown trays and
lazily chatting among themselves. Bancroft kept glancing
over at them, hoping to intimidate his waiter into bringing the plate of scones and jam that he had ordered. He
continued to be mystified by how long everything took in
this country, especially something as simple as cutting a
scone in half and placing it on a plate. Although he hated
to wait, he got a sense of pleasure out of snapping at waiters, tailors, street vendors—anyone at all in the city who
caused him irritation. "Get away from me, you dogs—
choka, choka, iwe," he would snarl, employing one of the
few Chichewan phrases he had bothered to learn.

"You there," he now said to the small black man who

was his waiter. "What the devil is taking so long here? A man could starve to death."

"Yes, sir," said the waiter with a short bow. He hurried into the cafe but returned empty-handed, promising Bancroft that he would soon have his food.

Bancroft huffed and poured his tea. "Well, make it fast."

He loosened his tie and placed his hat on the chair next to him. The stiff collar of his shirt had crumpled around the top and he pulled his handkerchief from his breast pocket to wipe the back of his neck.

"Damned heat," he said out loud.

A tall blonde woman and her young daughter stepped up on the porch and sat down at one of the tables. Bancroft eyed her carefully as she put her bags down on the floor and crossed her long legs. Her daughter plopped down in the chair opposite her and asked for ice cream; the woman ordered tea and unfolded a map on the table. Bancroft didn't recognize her and he believed he knew every white person in Blantyre, for he had been there fifteen years. A tourist, he thought to himself. Why anyone would want to come on holiday to Malawi was beyond him. The safari was better in Zimbabwe and the only decent beaches were on the shores of Lake Malawi, far north of the city. He decided that she must have been visiting with her husband who, like himself, worked for one of the British-owned companies in the city.

Bancroft's scones arrived and he covered them with butter and jam as he watched the blonde woman drink her tea. Bits of the scone clung to his mustache as he chewed and thought of the different ways he might enjoy having sex with her. The bottom of her skirt had risen a little, exposing part of her thigh, which was white and round. He paid close attention to the thigh as he poured himself more tea and swirled a generous helping of sugar into the cup.

He was in the habit of keeping a Malawian girl about as a mistress, yet he remained very lustful for women of his own race—often those who were married because he greatly enjoyed the detachment of making love to a married woman. It meant that he could not possibly be placed in a position of responsibility for the woman or her desires, save those of her sexuality.

Bancroft had been married himself once, many years ago, when he lived in London. His two-year bride came with him to Malawi when Britchard & Peck, the tea export company for which Bancroft worked, sent him to Blantyre to take over the position of chief fields inspector. Although Bancroft considered the job an excellent opportunity, his wife, Adela, was much less than enthusiastic. She hated it there, and she began to hate him as well. Eighteen months barely went by before she packed her bags and returned to England for what she told Bancroft and everyone else was a holiday.

"It's this oppressive heat," she said, "and this ghastly country. I simply must experience a cool, wet British September again before I die."

She let out that she would be back in six weeks, but somehow both she and Bancroft knew that she would not return. He was hardly surprised then when her letter telling him of this arrived some weeks after her departure. In it, she wrote Bancroft that she could no longer tolerate his drinking, his gambling, his staying out until all hours, and above all what she termed his "infidelity," which he thought a rather gracious way of describing his habit of soliciting prostitutes. Bancroft had saved the letter until he moved into a small house in the center of town, when he found it in a box with some other items of correspondence, all of which he discarded.

The woman and her daughter stood up at the table and gathered their things to go. Bancroft fiddled with the idea of running after her and perhaps asking her to join him later for a drink, but thought better of it. He had to be in court that afternoon, so he paid his check, donned his hat, and made his way across the sun-bleached square, busy with heckling street vendors, towards the courthouse.

Bancroft's solicitor, Mr. Starkey, had told him to arrive an hour early so that the two of them could go over some aspects of Bancroft's case. He was being tried for the murder of a Malawian woman named Melissa Mkandawire whose body was discovered near a village just outside of

Blantyre. The murdered girl was a prostitute. Her parents said that she had been seeing Bancroft and that he was known to be violent with her. They were certain that it was he who killed their daughter. The sworn statement of a gardener who worked at the house next door to Bancroft's had led to his arrest. The gardener, when questioned by the police, said that he saw Melissa Mkandawire enter Bancroft's house on the night of the murder. He did not see her come back out. He stated that he also saw Bancroft's car leaving the property and that the car was not back at the house until the next day.

It was with great effort that Mr. Starkey secured Bancroft's release before the trial, and then only with the posting of a substantial bail put up by Britchard & Peck. The white community in Blantyre was shocked to hear the news, which they could not believe. Bancroft had the sympathy of his companions at the club and at the tea company; the Malawians with whom he had contact simply avoided mentioning the situation, although it was being spoken of in every village from Blantyre to the Zomba Plateau.

Bancroft was pleading not guilty and bore the accusation with phlegmatic disconcern. He carried on his business and left the defense work to Mr. Starkey, who truly believed in Bancroft's innocence. The evidence against his client was entirely insufficient, he contended. He was prepared to prove that Bancroft had been in the northern city of Lilongwe at the time of the murder. The prosecution had one witness, the gardener—an old man who had worked at the house next to Bancroft's less than a month. Mr. Starkey looked into this man's history and learned that he had a reputation as a shiftless drunkard. The solicitor was confident that this witness's testimony would be called highly into question when stacked up against the word of his client, a respectable businessman in the community.

Bancroft, of course, was guilty. He had beaten Melissa Mkandawire to death in his bedroom after the girl had asked him for more money. She was angry and had said that he had not paid her for the last two times. Bancroft simply laughed in her face. She grew hysterical and Bancroft hit her in the mouth, splitting open her lower lip. Sucking on her own blood, she began to scream at Bancroft, insulting him, telling him that he was a terrible, disgusting old man, an awful lover and a foolish *azungu,* or white man, who could pay her now or pay dearly later when she told her people what he had done to her. In a rage, Bancroft picked up a heavy stick from beside the fireplace and hit her on the shoulder. She raised her arms to protect her head and he began to swipe at her body with the stick, cornering her as she stumbled back across the room. She was screaming at him to stop when he dealt a final blow to her skull.

He then sat down in a chair on the other side of the room and looked at the girl's crumpled body on his bedroom floor. His mouth was dry and he was breathing terribly hard as his mind raced, absorbing what he had just done and formulating a plan to cover it up. The chair beside the fireplace was overturned, the small table in the corner had broken when she fell on it, there was blood all over the rug—he must get rid of that; the body must be disposed of quickly, before it got light. Bancroft went into the living room, his hands shaking, and poured himself a drink of whiskey. He poured another and then returned to the bedroom where he rolled the girl's body up in the rug. He went out and spread newspapers in the trunk of his car, then returned to the house for the body. He placed it in the trunk, drove down his driveway, and headed north.

When he was a few miles outside the city, he turned down a dirt road that led into the jungle, past the vast, open tea fields. He pulled his car over to the side of the road, took the body from the trunk, and dumped it in the woods. He got back in his car and drove toward Lilongwe until he saw a brush fire in a field several miles away from where he had dumped the girl's body. These fires burned day and night and were set by villagers to clear the land for planting. He stopped his car, dragged the bloodied rug, the newspapers, and the log with which he had bludgeoned the girl to the fire and tossed them in, watching the flames leap up and consume these last bits of evidence against him. His face was flushed from the fire and he rubbed the soot from his eyes, but he waited until it all had burned. All the while his mind was bent on getting to Lilongwe as soon as possible so that he could check into the hotel and spend the night away from Blantyre, hopefully creating for himself an alibi.

The following day, he visited the company's branch office and attended to some routine business there. His position allowed him to come and go as he pleased and no one questioned his unscheduled appearance. He stopped off at the club for lunch and a game of golf and was back in Blantyre that evening. The next morning, the police came to his house and put him under arrest for the murder of Melissa Mkandawire. He immediately contacted Mr. Starkey, who spent the day in the magistrate's office arranging Bancroft's release pending the trial. As there was no official coroner in the city, the police relied on the forensic report of one of the doctors from the city hospital to determine how the girl had been murdered. The cause of death had been simple enough to deduce—blood loss and the cracked skull. The doctor, an overworked government employee, could not precisely state when the victim died, however, and speculated that it had been between the hours of one and four A.M.; Bancroft had checked into his hotel by eleven o'clock the preceding night.

It was generally assumed among the white community that the girl had been murdered by one of her own people —a jealous boyfriend or perhaps members of the secret cult of the *Gule wa Mkulu,* or the Big Dance, also known as the *Nyau.* The *Nyau* was one of the few traditional cults left in Malawi and certainly its most dangerous. Its devotees met in graveyards at night arrayed in terrifying costumes resembling jungle creatures. They traveled the roads, performing fearsome dances and accosting any stranger they came upon, asking him a series of secret questions. If the person could not properly answer them, the *Nyaus* would pursue him and attack him with the ferocity of whatever beast they were impersonating. Not infrequently, these confrontations ended in death.

Although the government condemned these activities,

the Big Dance was still in practice in the outlying areas where the arm of the law was short and ineffectual. Incidents such as this were not spoken of by urban Malawians; the people in the villages, though, knew the *Nyau* well and most knew how to protect themselves against its horrible violence. Although the killing seemed arbitrary and senseless, Malawian tradition ran deep in the cult, and two hundred years of British occupancy had done virtually nothing to root it out.

The Blantyre courthouse was located in the government building in the center of town. The pale-yellow mudbrick structure had once been the *boma* or District Officer's headquarters. Outside the courtroom door was a low, two-tiered bench upon which witnesses were required to sit before being called in for testimony. On the door to the courtroom was a sign written in both Chichewa and English which read "All witnesses giving evidence must remain out of court."

Mr. Starkey's office was located in the same building, two doors down. As Bancroft walked along the porch surrounding the *boma,* he noticed the old gardener sitting quietly on the bench. The man wore tattered pants, an old soiled jersey, and a tired straw hat on his head. His chocolate-brown face was sprinkled with white stubble, and Bancroft observed that one of his eyes was filmed over with blindness. Looking down at the spindly figure, Bancroft also noticed that the man's right foot was twisted unnaturally in toward the left. So, this was the prosecution's star witness, he chuckled to himself. He went briskly past the old man, who bowed his head and softly clapped his hands together in greeting. As Bancroft walked on, the one good eye followed him down the porch.

"Hullo, Bancroft," said Mr. Starkey as his client entered the office. "Bloody hot one again today, eh?"

"Beastly," replied Bancroft, taking off his hat and sitting in a wooden chair.

"We're up for hearing at one, but I don't think it will last much into the afternoon. Should get us out for tea, anyway. How are you holding up, old man?"

"Fine," said Bancroft, lifting a cigarette from a case and lighting it. "I trust you've gotten everything all sewn up here."

"Not to worry, old boy. I have a sworn statement from the desk clerk at the Lilongwe Hotel saying that you were in your room well before the time of the victim's death, plus character witnesses lined up from here to Jo'berg. Your record with the company has been impeccable. The only thing the prosecution has going for them is the testimony of a half-crippled, purblind old man—a testimony it will be no great task to call into serious question. No, no, believe me, we'll have you out by teatime or I stake my reputation on it."

The trial went much as Mr. Starkey had predicted. Under cross-examination, he showed that the gardener was a known drunkard whose testimony could not be relied upon. Bancroft was acquitted of all charges and released that afternoon. Melissa's parents were in the courtroom and sat rigid as the magistrate announced his decision. They returned to their village that night and held the ceremony for the dead, the entire village sharing in their grief.

Bancroft spent the rest of the afternoon and evening at the club, standing rounds for his friends and celebrating his acquittal. The club closed at ten and Bancroft, quite drunk and lustful, thought he would drive north to a brothel he had once visited well outside the city. He drove along the highway several miles looking for the right road, but as he had only been once before, he was unsure of the way. He took his next left, down an open dirt road lined by tall acacia trees. The foliage grew thicker along the roadside as he began to realize that he had gone the wrong way. Uncoordinated from the drink, he awkwardly slammed his foot toward the brake pedal and hit the accelerator instead. The car lurched forward and he lost control of the wheel, causing him to drive headlong into a ditch by the side of the road. The engine died and though Bancroft tried starting it again, it wouldn't turn over. The headlights shone crookedly into the jungle before him and he stumbled out of the car, leaning on the dented hood and waving his hand through the steam hissing from the radiator. He felt a bruise starting on his forehead and kicked the side of the car.

"Damn!" he shouted. He had no idea where he was or how far he had driven from the city. The accident had sobered him a bit and he could think clearly enough to know that he had somehow to get back. He listened in the darkness for the sounds of other cars but heard nothing except the slow, dying hiss of the vehicle.

"I must be bleeding miles from the main road," he cursed to himself as he reached into his pocket for a cigarette. As he raised his face from the burning match, he thought he saw a light flicker in the jungle. It flickered again, this time a little closer. He stepped toward the edge of the trees and followed the light as it bobbed in and out of view.

"Is someone there?" he asked. There was no response. "Can you help me? My car is stuck."

He saw the light again and then it disappeared. He walked slowly along the edge of the trees and came upon an opening. There before him was a tall, thatched wall buttressed by a small embankment. He had never seen such an odd structure before and he stepped over the embankment for a closer look. Behind the wall he saw several oblong mounds on the jungle floor; each mound was covered with yellowed, dead wreaths. There was an unnatural strange silence in the place and the earth beneath his feet was soft and dank.

Suddenly, in the distance, he heard the baying of an animal. It could have been a dog, but then again it might have been a hyena. He listened for the howl again but heard nothing. Strange, he thought, that it should only howl the one time.

He stood still, looking around him in the darkness, and grew fearful. He thought that he had better spend the night in the car and wait until daylight when he could find his way back to the main road and perhaps hitch a ride to Blantyre. As he stumbled from behind the wall, he heard a soft, muffled growl somewhere behind him. Turning

slowly, his hand trembling as he brought his cigarette
from his lips, he looked in the direction of the growl but
couldn't tell what it was or where it was coming from. He
hurried out to the road and heard the growl again, this
time much closer. When he reached the road, his breath
stopped short. A hundred feet away in the pale moonlight
was some kind of tall, dark, quivering, four-legged creature. It looked like a wildebeest, but it had far too much
hair. Turning its quaking head, the creature suddenly noticed him and then he heard it howl.

Bancroft turned quickly on his heels and ran. He heard
the creature howl again and he turned back to see it chas-
ing him, long, black streams of hair flying behind it as it
ran. It shook angrily and dipped and bowed its massive
head to some silent rhythm as it thudded along, and Bancroft began to sob with fear when he heard the creature's
howl once more, this time very recognizably human. His
lungs began to ache and his heart drummed mercilessly.
He didn't need to look behind him again to know that the
creature was but a few feet away for he heard the thick
rustle of its body as he stumbled in a rut in the road and
fell face down in the dust. He turned over on his back and
saw the creature standing over him, furiously shaking its
ghastly body.

"G—get back," he stammered, "g—g—get away!"

He groped beside him as he edged his way in the dirt,
searching for something to strike at the beast with. Then
he felt a dry, dusty, twisted foot on his wrist. There were
men all around him now in long straw skirts and carved
wooden masks. In their hands they held clubs that were
thick and shiny. He heard cruel laughter echoing densely
behind the masks and the one who stood with his foot on
Bancroft's wrist leaned over and spoke to him in
Chichewa.

"Choka . . . choka iwe, eeh, azungu?"

Bancroft quickly pulled his arm out from under the
man's foot and tried scrambling upright. He heard the
man let out a cry and then felt the heavy weight of a club
on the back of his neck. He fell to the ground in pain and

saw the creature leaping in front of him. He saw four human legs underneath the hairy coat and put his hands over his head as he sobbed, "No, no, please!"

The blows then began to fall hard and fast.

JEREMY

By R. M. KINDER

More than anything else, the five-year-old boy wanted to be touched, but he didn't actually know that. He felt it, a longing that made him draw near to his mother whenever she stood or sat still, which was rarely. Then he would wait a few inches away and if she didn't seem tired or angry, which he recognized again by a sense he was too small to identify, he would eventually lean into her, or sit by her feet. Once, when he had been able to sit near her for a longer time than usual, while she spoke with a visiting neighbor, he had gently taken her hand and when she did not immediately pull it away, he had been so overcome with a pleasant feeling that he had kissed the back of the hand.

"For God's sake, Jeremy," she had said, "that's sickening."

He sometimes thought of that day, and felt her words, and it made him keep his distance as he knew he was supposed to do. He knew never to approach her when someone else was in the house. She was a busy woman and he understood busy very well.

He learned to cherish every gift she gave, and he thought they were many. "My mother makes me eat breakfast," he told another child at kindergarten, and then enumerated each item he had eaten for dinner the night before and for breakfast just that morning. He tested her sometimes, going outside without a coat, or leaving part of his milk, or not brushing his teeth, and he would hear, "Jeremy," and feel relief that she loved him enough to notice. He would turn back to complete his part of the communion, mimicking the angry walk of other boys.

She liked him to read, and he made a bond with her that when his father was home and Jeremy was not to watch the terrible shows on television, he could stay in the room if his eyes were down. He had a small reclining chair which she had herself upholstered, and he would rest his elbows on the arms and hold the book squarely before him, reading only enough to respond if she were to ask him what he read, and faithfully turning a page every few minutes.

Sometimes his father said, "Jeremy, want to . . ." and completed it with things Jeremy might have enjoyed, a trip to the store, a walk, an ice cream. Sometimes Jeremy did go with his father, but along came the uncomfortable awareness of her at home alone, impatient, announcing when they arrived how long they had taken. If she came, it was worse. He might at any moment do something terribly wrong, spill ice cream on his clothing or the floor, sit in a ridiculous way. He preferred the comfort of the little recliner, an arm on each side, his eyes focused on one world, his ears on another. Other children occasionally had babysitters, he knew, and he thought that strange, that parents would risk their child to just anyone, which his mother had never done and would never do.

He became very adept at looking at one place and being in another, at taking his love and pleasure from nooks and crannies no one else knew.

When he was eight, she doled out chores and freedoms, since he was a big boy now. He came home right after school and she would assign the next few minutes, to sweep the porch, carry out the trash, stack the week's newspapers in the garage. She never gave him too much to do, and when guests came she would introduce him and he would hear his name in their conversation, what he did, how well he did it. She urged him to play and named the boys she liked, and he would straggle down the street, stand in some yard, join in some game. He played the way she would have wanted him to, neatly, fairly. She bought him a watch so he wouldn't come home too early or too late.

When she touched or kissed his father, or just sat beside him, Jeremy would watch without looking, intensely, feeling himself there between them, in them, and fearing discovery so that he sat rigid until they separated.

"What's wrong with you," his father said once, and Jeremy couldn't speak because he wasn't back together yet.

As he grew older he learned what this was, this leaving of himself, and he practiced in his room at night. First, he tried only his hands. He closed his eyes and tried to withdraw his fingers as from a glove. When he succeeded, it was in a dream, and he woke panicked and sweaty because he had been unable to slide back in. But as he was whole, capable of touching the blanket and turning on the lamp, the fear eased and he flexed his hands to rest them. Each night then, unless he was tired, he withdrew more and more from himself. He never left his room though, even when he knew he could, that he could grip the doorknob and turn it and stand listening. He learned to do it even while he read, and then, much later, to let the other read. Sometimes they looked at one another, and he grew accustomed to that face shaped much like his father's, to the dour expression much like his mother's. "Can you talk?" he asked, and heard the simple, "Yes," with which he himself would have responded. He approved of the grace and restraint of the other.

They talked. Not often, but enough so that Jeremy understood their desires were not the same. Jeremy could see no reason to leave this place, though he admitted they would have to some day. Once he fell asleep with the light on and woke in complete darkness to hear, "I want to go now. I can't stay here any longer." The voice was so terribly sad that Jeremy threw back the covers and stumbled toward the sound. He felt his hand taken and himself drawn near, and was so touched that he stood there embracing the other till he realized they had joined again. "Come back out," he said, but nothing happened. "Please." He lay down and closed his eyes. "You don't have to be ashamed," he said. "Not with me."

Each night now he woke to sobbing and he whispered reassurances that they would leave.

"When?"

"Soon," he said. "I have to think where, how."

"We just leave. I could go now. No one would know."

"No. Don't. You can't go without me."

"But I can. I did."

Jeremy turned on the light. The other was seated across the room, heavier, a dark stubble on his cheeks. He glanced quickly at Jeremy and then at the floor.

"I went into the hall one night. Tonight I went outside."

"Out of the house?"

"Into the garage."

"You didn't."

"Your father backs the car in."

"Promise me you won't do it again. Promise."

"I won't."

"You won't go, or you won't promise?"

The other didn't answer. He stood, and his height surprised Jeremy, who watched himself move toward the bed slowly, and lean down close and fade inside. "Answer me," Jeremy said to the empty room.

Jeremy taped the door shut and fought sleep to hold the other in. But some mornings the tape was broken and he knew from his own exhaustion how far he must have gone.

"Are you slipping out at night?" his father asked. "You look like you've got a hangover."

"Don't be ridiculous. Of course he's not slipping out. He wouldn't do that. Would you?"

"No," he said. He woke that night to find his bedroom door open, and he rushed into the hallway whispering, "Get back here. Get back here now." His parents' door was open and he stepped inside, saw the shadow in the chair across the room. He didn't dare speak, didn't dare look toward the bed. He gestured, pleaded with his mind, backed out quietly when the other stood.

"What were you doing?" he said, when they were back in his room. "My God. In their bedroom. What if they had wakened?"

"Let them. Do them both good." He lay down where Jeremy usually lay. "I don't like them, you know."

Jeremy stood quietly a moment. Then he lay down, too. "I know," he said. "I wish you did, but I understand."

Jeremy could do nothing to keep him from his parents' room. He would wake, aware of danger, to hurry to the hallway so he could be nearby if they awoke. The other was coarser now to Jeremy, and seemed larger even than himself. He said terrible things, sometimes using Jeremy's own lips.

"I could kill them," he said once, in a soft voice. "And no one would know."

"I would."

The other laughed with Jeremy's voice.

Jeremy knew when it was going to happen. In the kitchen his eyes were caught by the glint of knives; outside, by stones. When he tied the newspapers in the garage, his hands braided the twine thicker, knotted it. "Oh don't," he whispered.

"I need to leave," he told his mother.

"What do you mean, leave? Dinner will be ready in ten minutes."

"I mean leave the house. Move away."

"When the right time comes, I'll help you do just that. But that's a year or two in the future."

He took hammer and nails from his father's tool chest, put the nails in his pocket, the hammer in his waistband. He put them in his dresser. "Shut up," he said.

When dinner was over and his parents sat in the living room before the television, he went to his room and closed the door. He pushed and tapped the nails in. Every now and then he would kick the door lightly to mask a final drive of the hammer. It still took a long time.

He had to leave, but he didn't know how.

He heard them go to bed. He didn't undress or turn out the light, but he got under the covers. He kept his eyes open, but it didn't work. He tried to hold the other in, then pull him back. He threw his arms around the thick chest and tugged, but was shaken off. The hammer was taken up, the nails jerked out wildly, and Jeremy raced down the hall, finally even yelling, "Stop, stop, for God's sake stop," but there was nothing he could do. He wasn't big enough or strong enough. He was thrown out of the room and the door shut in his face. When it opened again, he didn't need to see what was in there. He had heard it. He followed himself through the kitchen, into the garage.

"Come back," he said. "Come back." He stood there a long time. Then he went in the kitchen and wiped up the floor and folded the rag neatly on the washer. He took his father's keys from the wall hook and returned to the garage. He started the motor. He lay down in the seat to wait for the other to return.

THE JOURNEYER

By ROBERT CAMPBELL

Forty years had gone by since he'd been in the university city; Oxford was much changed. All the bustle and hustle, homeless lying about in the graveyard in the center of the town, right by the tottering church plastered with signs announcing this and that. Admission to the tower, appeals for contributions for a new roof, a new altarpiece, gave it the look of a commercial establishment with gaudy goods—spiritual awakening, masses for the dead, and quick beneficences on offer.

It was only when, after payment, admission was granted at the gates of the colleges and passage allowed into the walled gardens and lawns, quads and pathways, that anything like the easy grace and tranquility of these places of ancient learning was arrived at. There was much to be missed even then.

The girls wore jeans and running shoes instead of lisle stockings, pleated skirts, and sensible oxford shoes. Sweaters tied about the waist or worn about the shoulders, the sleeves looped once like a pair of thin embracing arms.

The boys looked less changed, trousers, sweaters, and anoraks being ageless male costumes.

There were very few young men or women batting around in sleeveless gowns, flying here and there along the paths with the intent look of those who were the keepers of the flame as they had once done.

Bicycles everywhere. So that was one thing, at least, not much changed.

There were groups of tourists being shown around by docents wearing their ribbons of office.

He felt aloof from them. He needed no guide, although he had to admit there was so much he'd forgotten after forty years. He remembered that he had not felt so much a stranger then, even when new to the university and city, even knowing far less than he knew now after years of casual reading.

That was a quality of youth, never to feel a stranger no matter where one might find oneself, he realized with a sense of discovery. He felt the insight notable. He would write it down when he returned in the evening to his bed and breakfast on a lane just off the Bodley Road, a two-mile walk away.

He'd never been a student at any of the Oxford colleges. He'd merely been a journeyer in England that year when he was twenty-three; in all of Europe but most memorably in England.

Twenty-three years old, temporarily relieved of the need to make a living because of a legacy left him by an expired aunt. A young man looking for adventures and finding them everywhere.

Adventure to some is braving the hardships of mountainsides and gorges; scaling the Himalayas. Or beating through bush and thorn on the way to the Nile's source. Or spending a season excavating the ruins of Karnak.

But adventure to a young man of twenty-three is finding a woman of a likely age and discovering of what she is made. The mind of her and the body—breasts and belly and tender core.

Oddly—or perhaps not so oddly—he remembered few of the names of the girls met and tasted during that adventuresome year; few of their faces. That is to say he remembered nearly all of them but somehow could not put name and face together, separating them one from another, fixing face to form and both to mind. So that they had become one in his mind, the several he'd embraced and enjoyed.

Perhaps it had been the openness of his desire for them, his smile, his tentative stammerings, the easy way his cheeks colored in pleasure or mild distress, making his blue eyes seem so much bluer, his even teeth so much whiter—everything that was fair and beautiful about him then so much more beautiful—that made him so successful with the girls and young women.

Whatever the catalyst might have been it was as though an attractive young woman waited for him everywhere. On the ship crossing the Atlantic. In Copenhagen, waiting for him in the Tivoli Gardens, the very first night ashore. In Oslo a young woman smiled at him as he counted the trees in Gustav Viegland's fountain, her body proving to be every bit as fine as that of the adolescent girl flying through the tree of bronze around the basin. In Stockholm there was the secretary with the face of a Botticelli angel met in the Riche Bar. In Paris, Rome, Hamburg, Brussels, there were young women waiting to embrace him.

And in Oxford there had been many.

Now, as he walked the quiet pathways and busy streets, he passed hundreds of young people, girls and young women even more comely and desirable than the girls and young women he remembered from the past. He turned his head one way and the other searching for a glance or smile. When he stood still in the middle of the walk, they parted and spilled around him with scarcely a beat of hesitation in their progress, as though he were a lamppost or a stone.

Stunningly, with a whelming feeling of disaster, it came to him that he was invisible to a large portion of the world.

Suddenly his bladder was giving him a great deal of distress. He popped into a tea shop. There were counters selling pots and packaged teas and cozies on the ground floor. A split stairway led to the rest rooms on one side and the tearoom on the other.

As he turned to the steps leading to the rest rooms, the young woman at the counter called out, "Sir. Sir?" and when he paused to look her way, went on to say with some reluctance, "The facilities are for customers only. The management makes me say that."

"Well, that's understandable," he said, smiling to put her at ease, "if not always practical. There comes an age when such matters are urgent and someone might easily find himself in town and in need without cash enough for a meal, having left his checkbook at home."

"Oh, dear," she said. "If that's the case, go ahead. I won't tell."

He continued on, noticing the sign saying much the same thing the salesgirl had said fixed to the beam above the stairway, went into the small lavatory, and relieved himself at the urinal, vaguely irritated that she'd been so quick to see the hypothesis he'd described as a probable description of his own predicament.

He zipped up, washed and dried his hands, surveyed himself in the mirror, unconsciously posing, stretching his neck so that the incipient turkey wattles wouldn't show, then went out and back up the short flight of stairs, turning sharply left at the top, throwing what he thought was a wickedly flirtatious smile over his shoulder at the girl, who'd forgotten all about him, and went down the double flight into the small tearoom at the bottom.

There was a woman, a morning shopper judging from the bag and bundles on the chair beside her and at her feet, sitting in the corner having her tea, and two young women, in their late twenties or early thirties, with that air of insistent modernity cultivated by executive females, having a conversation over small bowls of soup at another table tucked under the staircase.

He chose a table against the wall, steps away from a glass case that presented a variety of cakes and flans, close enough to the bill of fare chalked on a board behind the counter to be read without resorting to his glasses.

There was a doorway at one end of the counter space leading into a kitchen of sorts, equipped with a microwave oven and a refrigerator set into the wall, sinks and counter space where the simple fare on offer was prepared. What he could see of it was visible because of one of those large convex mirrors useful to householders backing their cars into busy streets or cashiers trying to keep an eye on inaccessible places in their shops. It left him with the odd feeling that he could observe the girls working there but that he could not be seen, though of course their seeing the customers was the whole purpose of the mirror.

Three girls were standing and sitting in the kitchen. Two too many, he thought, judging from the size of the place and the number of its customers here in the very middle of teatime.

One girl was perched on a stool, a bowl caught between her knees, peeling away at potatoes.

Another was standing at the sink washing dishes.

The third, a young woman of about eighteen or nineteen, presented a saucy face and a saucy manner, even doing nothing more than she was doing, standing there leaning against a counter, arms folded beneath her breasts, one arm crooked so that she might reach a curl falling from her tilted head with one hand, playing with it, legs crossed at the knee and one foot poised on the toe of her boot.

They all wore mob-caps such as actresses wear in Victorian comedies on stage, screen, and television. The sort that was even sometimes worn when he'd been twenty-three.

It was the girl with folded arms, doing nothing, who glanced up into the mirror and saw his reflection as he sat there glancing at the menu with one eye. She launched herself forward with a thrust of her buttock and made her way unhurriedly to his table.

"I don't know how hungry I am," he said.

"Just a pot of tea, then?"

"Well, it's been a long time since I've visited Oxford or the area and perhaps I should have a go at the local fare."

He expected her to remark upon his American accent but she didn't, she just stood there as though perfectly willing to wait there instead of elsewhere until he made up his mind, but never mind the chat.

"Will I have a cream tea, then?" he said, trying to phrase it as an Englishman might. "What sort of jam?"

"It comes with an assortment," she said.

"I could use a treat," he said, and looked at her in that certain shy, ingenuous way that had once been so attractive to girls and women when he'd been a young man. A little tease. A little overture. Hoping that she would make some pert, clever remark in return, opening up the way to familiarity, the exchange of small information that might lead to something.

She walked away without comment.

He tried to find a place to put his eyes. The executive

woman facing him looked over her companion's shoulder. Her eyes looked into his and passed by. She hadn't seen him.

When the hot water and teapot arrived, he chose from a basket of foil packets a blend he'd never heard of before called Four Red Fruits. He was allowed two bags, which he placed in the heated pot and drenched with hot water, securing them as they steeped with the lid capturing their strings and tags.

There were three warm scones, a small bowl of Devonshire double cream as thick as the butter served in separate silver packets. Three tiny jars, the size called sample or introductory, one each of strawberry jam, orange marmalade, and plum jelly, made up the assortment. There was a small pitcher of ordinary cream for the tea alongside a silver bowl of castor sugar and a spoon.

He sat there over the light meal, his head down, paying attention to the precision with which he knifed cream and jelly on each piece of scone broken off from the whole. There was a bad moment when a strawberry seed insinuated itself under his denture. He had to execute some very tricky, subtle maneuvers of plate and tongue in order to remove it without giving anything away.

He wanted to cry.

By this stage of the game, when he'd been twenty-three, a young American abroad, he would have been in conversation with the two businesswomen, perhaps making plans to meet them both that evening, perhaps having them both together before the night was out, as had happened once in Stockholm and once again in Paris. He would have enchanted the waitress and perhaps even lured the other two out of the scullery to pass remarks with him so that he might have had a chance to look them all over and take his pick.

"Is everything all right?" the waitress asked.

He looked up with an expression of wild gratitude on his face because to her, at least, it seemed that he had not altogether disappeared. But before he could do more than swallow and nod, she was off to tender the bill to the shopper in the back and give back change to the businesswoman, doing her job, asking the questions concerning service and customer satisfaction according to the book.

A wave of hatred against her rose in his chest and he choked.

Through his watering eyes, he could see she'd stopped and was watching him.

No doubt fearing that the old bastard would have a heart attack or choke to death on her shift, he thought. As soon as he took a swallow of tea and nodded his head as though answering the question of everyone still in the establishment, she continued on her way, showing a pair of newcomers who had just appeared at the foot of the steps to a table.

He glanced their way. They were a middle-aged couple with the air of visitors determined to drink up every moment of their holiday so they'd have stories to tell when back at home.

He went slowly on with his own meal as they ordered tea and sandwiches.

He eavesdropped on their conversation when their meal was served.

Now listen to that, he thought. Those two are going on about the publican's wife somewhere cutting off the crusts.

"It was ever so nice, cutting off the crusts."

"Reminds me of the pub we stopped in over to Land's End. Did the same thing. Cut off the crusts and loaded it full of prawns."

"Lovely that."

A young woman came in and ordered a bun and a container of milk at the counter, a student catching her lunch on the run, too busy with her life even to sit down and have a meal in a civilized manner. She looked right and left while she waited, her eyes bouncing over him with a skip and a jump.

Did you see? Her eyes slipped past me like I wasn't even here, he thought, anger spilling into his stomach, turning his cream tea sour. If I took me teef out and gummed her a smile she'd fink I was adorable. She'd want to take me home and put me on the shelf. Give me a little cuddle every now and then. I know the type. Notice the jeans? So tight you can see the crack. When she takes a step the denim rides right along her quim. Lovely that. Always in a state of high excitation she is. He watched her go to the stairs and mount the first flight. He thought of following her. He thought of following her without her ever knowing. Following her everywhere, even to her most private places. Confronting her when they were alone, when there was no one else around, nowhere else to put her eyes, nothing else to see but him.

"Anything else?"

"What?"

The waitress was standing there as though she'd read his thoughts about the student. Unless he was very much mistaken, there was a sly little smile at the corner of her mouth. For the first time he noticed she wore a small ceramic nametag pinning a handkerchief to her uniform blouse.

"What else do you have to offer, Hillary?" he asked, letting his tongue linger over her name as though savoring it.

"You mean something sweet?" she said, letting the smile grow.

"Well, perhaps something sweet with just a touch of tart."

Was he being too subtle for her, he wondered, all this playing about with words.

"We've got a nice slice of apple flan which is nice and sweet and a gooseberry tart with some tang to the sweetness."

So she'd got it after all. There was more to her than met the eye.

"Which would you recommend?"

"I'd say the tart though it's a trifle dearer."

"Well, money's of no consequence."

"Then it'll be the gooseberry tart? With a nice spoonful of Devon cream on top?"

"So much cholesterol," he said, tapping his chest. "I don't know if I should."

"A man your age shouldn't be worrying about clogged arteries and heart attacks," she said.

"I'll have it with cream then."

He watched her hips, swaying more than they had before when there had been others in the tearoom, all the way through the kitchen doorway and then lifted his eyes to watch her prepare his treat. There was only the girl at the sink left. It was the end of teatime and the other girl had already gone.

He watched Hillary's lips moving and heard the girl washing dishes laugh. Hillary lifted her eyes to the mirror and to his reflection as she turned to get the cream from the fridge.

Being very accommodating, very flirtatious, she was. All of a sudden, end of shift, flirting with the elderly tourist, stroking him, even being a bit suggestive, in hopes of a substantial tip. He might be hopeful but he was no fool. The looks, or lack of them, he'd received all day from the young people about him had taught him a harsh lesson and he didn't need telling twice.

The girl at the sink did the last dish and dried her hands, removed her apron, and reached for her coat. He heard them say tomorrow and g'day and she was out the back door leaving them alone, Hillary and himself and the gooseberry tart which she was bringing to him.

"Have a taste and tell me what you think," she said, putting down the plate and a clean fork, thrusting her hips slightly forward.

Teasing the animals, he thought.

He cut a piece of the tart from the whole with the side of the fork, took up a smear of cream and speared the morsel, brought it to his mouth, leaning over the dish a bit as though protecting his lap against accident, but staring at the dip of her skirt at her crotch. He chewed slowly, as though judging the excellence of the tart, pursing his lips, thrusting out his tongue to lick at them from corner to corner.

"Oh, yes," he said, "any man would give a great deal for a taste of your gooseberry tart."

"When you finish the one you have, you can order some to take along with you," she said.

Wasn't she clever, he thought, bandying the old innuendo, the old double entendre, back and forth, working the old fool for everything he was worth just for the exercise in it, the test of her allure. Well, he thought, I wonder just how far I can take it, just how far would she be willing to go?

"Have you a minute?" he asked.

"Beg pardon?"

"Well, I notice everyone's gone. It's past teatime and we're quite alone, so no one would be the wiser if you sat down for a moment, would they?"

"I suppose I could sit down if I liked," she said. "I'm the manageress here. But I've still got some cleaning up to do before I close up."

"What cleaning up?"

"Well, your pot and plates. This and that. Wipe the tables. You know."

"I thought you might give me just a moment." He saw her frown a little, obviously wondering where the banter had flown, asking herself why the old fool was becoming so serious and soft-voiced, and if that boded no good. "You see, I've come back to Oxford on a sort of sentimental journey," he went on. "It was here I found my life's love and lost her nearly forty years ago."

He sipped his tea as though surprised and embarrassed at revealing so intimate a secret to a stranger. She sat down. He'd caught her interest and why not, the fiction had worked often enough before through the travels of his middle age, in Brussels and Bath and Vienna and Rome.

It was a lovely, tragic, inventive story he told, with just enough false starts and stops of memory, digressions and elaborations of no particular consequence to anyone except the one who'd lived the experience, to lend an air of authenticity that glibness and perfect progression would never have given it.

There'd been a young student from France, who wore black stockings, pleated skirts, white blouses, berets, and a bat-winged gown of silk. She'd had one brown eye and one blue eye so solemn and innocent and disquieted—but unafraid—that the mere sight of them had always brought sympathetic tears to his eyes. They'd slept together in the bed-sitter he'd rented for the two months. Lying in bed they'd planned her return to Paris when summer came and his traveling with her, to meet her parents and make the plans for marriage. She'd been taken ill a week before their planned departure, a congestion of the chest, and she'd been dead within seven days.

He wiped a tear away. It had been one of his finest performances. Hillary reached out to touch his hand.

"Well," he said, with a sharp taking in of breath, indicating a rededication to that old resolve, following the great tragedy, that he must get on with his life—even though it turned out that he'd had to get on with it all alone—and leaning back and slapping his knees lightly with his palms, he went on to offer his apologies for being so long telling his story and could he help her somehow. "Wipe the tables or wash my dishes. I'm not too old a dog to learn those tricks." The inference being that he'd done such chores for himself so often over the years that they were no trick at all.

"You sit and finish your tea," she said, getting to her feet. "I'll fill the pot with hot if you like."

"That's very kind of you, I've had a sufficiency. But if I could sit here just a moment longer." He laughed with a little catch to it as though there were unshed tears bravely controlled. "I have the terrible feeling that when I walk up those stairs and out the door, there will be no one on the streets. No one in the town. I'll be all alone out there."

"Ah, luv," she murmured and left him to do her closing up chores.

What must it be like outside, he wondered. Was the sun out picking shadows from the students going here and there in the parks and quads, from the citizens on the shopping streets, and casting them across the roadways and the buildings? Was the river turned to molten silver or had the day turned grey as it so often did here in the

English midlands as the setting of the sun approached
and turned the river and canals into turgid lead.

He'd walked down a flight of steps beside a bridge along
Bodley Road on the way to his bed and breakfast the day
before and found a path that followed the canal, past some
small factory yards, a coal tip, some blocks of flats, a pub
announcing itself with a sign painted on its brick flank,
and on to a park below a heath, where everything was
silent and only three white swans on the water beneath a
footbridge gave evidence of life anywhere.

That's when the first great surge of loneliness of a sort
he'd never felt before had nearly overcome him. It was the
loneliness of age, the realization that there was no more
time to mend the fabric of his life, that he'd cast its pattern or had had a pattern imposed upon him, and here he
was past it, with nowhere to go and no one to go to.

"Well, I'm off," she said, startling him.

He glanced up from his cold tea and saw her standing
there, quite another young woman than the one who'd
served him.

She still wore her knee-length boots but now she wore a
dark-blue leather skirt so much shorter than the conceal-
ing cotton skirt she'd worn before that he was suddenly
conscious of what could only be called her demanding
thighs. A broad red fake-patent-leather belt circled her
waist, cinching in that which already was scarcely evi-
dent. A white turtleneck jersey that clung to her breasts
and belly, a school scarf wound round her neck once, the
long end trailing, and a knitted watch cap completed her
ensemble.

But that wasn't all. The makeup she'd put on her face
was the cause of the most dramatic aspect of her transfor-
mation. The lipstick was boldly applied, the lips outlined
in a red so dark it was almost maroon and then filled in
with cherry. There were artificial blush marks slanting
along the tops of her cheekbones and eye liner accenting
her eyes heavily, top and bottom.

She looked sluttish and available. It gave him a new
confidence.

He stood up and settled the topcoat he'd never removed

more carefully on his shoulders, standing taller than he had before, holding one half of the skirt back with one hand while searching for his billfold with the other.

"I haven't paid for my cream tea and sweet," he said.

"The tart," she said. "That'll be two pounds twenty."

He handed her three pounds.

"I'll get your change," she said and going to the cash drawer, quickly rang up the last sale of the day and came back with his eighty pence.

He held his hand cupped to receive it, looking at her. She counted the coins out carefully, placing her thumb on the last one she placed in his palm, pressing down a bit, looking right back at him.

"I wonder," he said.

She smiled and said, "I thought you might. I wonder what you wonder."

"I wonder if I might be bold on such short acquaintance."

"You want to take me out?"

"I thought a meal."

"You've just had a meal."

"I mean I'd like to buy you supper. Take you to the cinema or the theater."

"Make a night of it?" she said, insinuatingly.

"If you like. We can do anything you've a mind to do. I'm simply in great need of company and don't have a clue what I can do about it."

"Except ask strange girls for dates."

He smiled disarmingly, trying to look old but not decrepit, worldly-wise and interesting, the kind of man who could show a girl a fascinating time for an evening, no matter the difference in their ages.

"That's just it. I don't feel we're strangers. Perhaps it was the good advice you gave me about the tart."

She cocked her head a bit. Vivien Leigh in "Waterloo Bridge." He wondered if she'd ever seen the film in some rerun house or on the television. She had the same gamine quality of the amateur whore that Vivien had managed to convey.

He thrust the eighty pence at her. "Look here. That was

unforgivable of me, telling you my sad story and then asking you to share an evening with me."

She didn't put out her hand for the money. "Well, I don't know about that," she said. "Give me some time to think about it."

"What shall I do while you think about it?"

"You can walk me home. It's only about a mile along the Bodley Road."

"I'm living just off the road myself."

"How far along?"

"The owner of the bed and breakfast said two miles. I walked it yesterday and the day before and it seemed about right."

"I live about a mile along, just down the road from the little wooden church. Do you remember passing it?"

He nodded, grinning. "Would you say our meeting was fated?"

"Here, here," she said, as though warning him not to read too much into the accident of their meeting. "There's thousands live along Bodley Road and hundreds of them stop in here for tea."

"Well, if you won't believe in destiny and miracles," he said, taking her arm as though they were old friends, "please allow me to do so."

They left through the back door, she locking it behind her, both in very high spirits, gaining the high street and walking over to Bodley Road, she tucking her arm in his now, matching her stride to his.

He remembered vaguely seeing the wooden church. If he was correct, it stood not more than a hundred yards back from the path beside the canal on the side he'd not walked before.

The air was becoming just crisp enough as the sun slipped down the sky to cloud the breath and exhilarate his spirit. It was a fine day for doing what they were doing, for what they were, he hoped, about to do.

At the bridge over the canal he said, "There's the church, right there, isn't it?"

"My digs are just back of it a quarter mile or so along the side road."

"Could we come up on the back side of it from the path along the canal or is there much else intervening?"

"I was just going to say. I often go that way," she said, and without saying more, as if in perfect agreement without the need for speech, they turned off the sidewalk and went down the stairs leading to the canal and path.

The quarter mile along the canal was unattractive. The junkyards of the city were gathered there. But then there was a narrow empty plot and, stopping there, she pointed up the slightly sloping wasteland to a small block of flats set well back from the scarcely moving stream.

"I tell everyone I live in the country," she said.

"Does it get better further on?" he asked.

"How do you mean better?"

"Quieter. More tranquil."

"More desolate?" she asked, the word somehow sounding strange coming from her mouth, as though she'd already guessed the purpose that was only then growing in him.

"More peaceful," he said. "The whole city of Oxford seemed peaceful forty years ago. But that seems past."

"So, it's peace you want," she said. She clasped her hands in the crook of his arm and hugged it to her. "If you're in the mood for a walk, I'll show you quiet places you'd think were picture postcards."

It took a long time getting there. They passed a solitary fisherman and were once overtaken by a man with a briefcase.

He tired but neither faltered nor complained.

She informed him that she'd decided to spend the evening with him. So they talked about which restaurant, which club or cabaret they should try.

At last she said, "We'd better be starting back or we'll be caught out in the dark."

Dusk was falling, turning a tranquil setting even more tranquil. There were swans—the same swans or other swans—in a wide spot overhung with willows. There was a broad heath with a bench at the verge up a short rise beneath a copse of trees. When he begged a moment's rest, they climbed the little hill. At the top there was another footpath crossing the heath toward a distant suburb of the town and another running down the center parallel to their view. A jogger trotted along perhaps two hundred yards away and at the very end, no more than toy figures, someone pushed a baby in a pram.

He sat down with a grateful sigh and rueful smile, making much of his age again, angry with her because she didn't sit down at once but stood looking all around.

"I'm not used to walking so much at home," he said.

"Home?" she said, finally sitting down beside him.

"New York," he said.

"It's a dream of mine, visiting New York."

"It's become a hateful place," he said.

"Well, there are opportunities there. A lot to do. Excitement. Challenges."

"Hard to make a living in the big cities," he said.

She cut her eyes at him; a sluttish glance. "Oh, I'd have no trouble. I'd find a way."

"It's more expensive than you think," he said, hating her youthful optimism and self-assurance.

"Well, then, I'd find someone to pay my bills for me, wouldn't I?"

His heart began to beat faster. She was suggesting things to him. She was saying that she would find a man to keep her. An older man like himself?

"Your family wouldn't like it if you went so far away."

"I've got no family here. My mum and dad live up in Birmingham, don't you know. They said good riddance to bad rubbish when I left home to go to London and if they heard I was going so far away as New York they'd be happier still. Less chance of my body being delivered on their doorstep for burial."

There it was again. A remark that seemed meant to tease him with the thought that she knew the rage in him, knew what means he had to use to put the demons to rest.

His eyes were on her mouth—her red, writhing mouth —as she spoke. He dropped his eyes a fraction. She'd placed a beauty mark just there above her chin, a whore's advertisement.

"Well, your friends would miss you," he said.

"Not likely. I share a flat with two of the girls in the shop. I see enough of them all day. I can't wait to get away from that at night."

"Is that why you decided to accept my invitation?"

"Now, don't get touchy. What difference does it make. It's just that you want the company of a girl, isn't it?"

"Everyone would rather spend an evening with someone than alone."

"But you wanted a young woman—a girl—to laugh and joke with. Maybe have a little cuddle? I mean you wouldn't be so anxious to spend the evening with another man like yourself, a traveler on his own. The pubs and tea shops are full of them. Or some old biddy who'd be glad of the chance to have a meal and a chat and perhaps even a little slap and tickle," she said with a certain aggression in her manner.

"You're getting a little bold, here, aren't you?"

"I don't mean to be insulting. I'd just like to put it on the table with the teapot and the scones, so to speak. You're a man who's come back to a place where you'd had some lovely adventures when you were young and it's not at all like you remembered it."

His eyes fell another fraction or two. He could still see her mouth moving like some scarlet sea creature, a little tongue flicking out now and then, but his vision was centered on the hollow of her throat.

"The young women look right through you, don't they? Oh, I've heard it all before. Do you think you're the only one to discover he's grown old? That's the way it is. It comes to every one of us."

He wanted to shut her up. He didn't want to know.

"You should've seen my mum when she was my age," she went on. "I've seen photos. She was even prettier than me. You should see her now. So, my eyes are wide open. I know I'll grow old one day and look much like she does now. So, what's the answer? To live life while you can. Oh, oh, don't look like that. Are you going to cry? I'm not trying to hurt your feelings. I'm trying to tell you I understand and I can make it better for you. It'll cost you. Everything has a price, doesn't it? But, I promise you a square deal, value for money."

"What are you talking about?" he murmured, the blood running as heavily as a freezing river in his ears.

"I mean you've got a wad of money and I've got youth. It's quiet here, just like you wanted. Go on up to the heath if you want and have a look around. It's grown too dark for joggers or mums wheeling their prams across the paths. We're all alone here. We don't have to bother with a restaurant or a movie house or a cabaret. I can give you what you really want right here, right now."

She opened her coat. She reached out for his hands and placed them on her hard breasts outside her jumper.

He was about to raise his hands to her throat, to place the thumbs just so, but she drew him closer and he gave way, hoping that there might be magic in the moment and that her kiss would unburden him of the years.

She placed her red mouth on his. He seemed to feel her lips curved up into a knowing smile. He felt her tongue like a bit of fire.

He didn't see or feel her reach down into her boot with her right hand. He never noticed the thin blade, no thicker than an old-fashioned hatpin, poised at his neck between scarf and jaw. He was about to break the kiss— her mouth offensive all at once, tasting of grease—and raise his hands to her throat. He was about to punish her for being young and understanding him so well. And while he thought the thoughts required to complete those simple acts, still held in thrall by her young mouth, greasy taste and all, he felt an icy sensation below his ear, a point of pain that was not quite a pain, and then a savage agony spread into a blackness into which he fell.

Hillary gave way slowly, sliding back along the bench until the man was bent in the middle, his legs tilted a little at a slant, his head and torso on the bench, cheek against the slats, his hat falling off and rolling away along the ground.

She went quickly through his pockets, putting his wallet filled with credit cards, money clip, and small change into her own pockets. She arranged the scarf so that the puncture wound and slight trickle of blood was concealed.

He looked like some old gentleman who'd been strolling along the canal and, sitting down to rest for a moment to enjoy the peace and quiet and appreciate the swans, was suddenly taken with a heart attack and had died peacefully there in the twilight.

"There, luv," she said, "just as I promised. You'll never grow a day older."

THE 9:13

By MARTIN NAPARSTECK

A fist slammed into the back of the head of the man wearing the dark-blue uniform, and he muttered incoherently as his legs weakened and he crumbled to his knees and slumped backward. His head hit the concrete floor, impacting only inches from where the fist had hit.

The man standing wondered briefly if the one in the uniform was dead, but he didn't know how to tell if anyone was dead, and in truth, he knew, he really didn't care. He had more important things to concern himself with: how to get out of the building, how to get off of the grounds, how to get out of the city.

Only four eastbound passenger trains a day pass through Rochester. Years ago there were up to a dozen. Of the four still running, three pick up, on a typical run, about two dozen passengers. The fourth, which originates in Toronto and goes through Syracuse and Albany on its way to Boston, is scheduled to arrive in Rochester at 9:13 P.M., but it is often delayed at the border at Buffalo by customs officials. Not many years ago the customs officials took only ten or fifteen minutes to question the passengers and make a few spot checks—haphazard checks really—of luggage. But now there are drugs and international terrorists and God knows what else, and the customs people are more thorough, more questioning, more suspicious. Amtrak builds twenty minutes into the schedule for the customs delay. It has taken up to three hours.

People in Rochester familiar with the unpredictability of the delays avoid the 9:13. On a bitter January night, with a foot or more of powdery snow, there were just two passengers—both men—in the Rochester Amtrak station waiting for the 9:13. The Gulf War was two weeks old and the front pages of the three newspapers that could be purchased from vending machines in the station were domi-

185

nated by news of the war: a demonstration in downtown Rochester protesting President Bush's decision to go to war was met by another larger turnout of his supporters. The 15,000th sortie had been flown; parts of the Gulf were covered with an oil slick. In the afternoon *Times-Union* there was also, on page one, just below the war, a follow-up on the two-day-old Super Bowl. The only nonwar news on the front page of the *Democrat & Chronicle* was an interview with a defensive safety who played fifty-seven seconds in the game. The *New York Times* had no Rochester news at all. No wonder the story about the escape was on page six of the second section of the *D&C* and not in either of the other papers.

One of the men in the station picked up a copy of the morning paper that someone had left on one of the back-and-backside-shaped chairs. The chair was a soft blue, almost a noncolor. The man sat in it, facing a large window that separated him from the dark, invisible tracks. He saw his own reflection and that of the other man, who was in a seat that faced away from the window, although it was in the same row as his. He flipped carelessly through the paper. He had a vague sense of searching for the crossword puzzle, but he wasn't certain he would do it if he found it. He saw the story about the escape on the bottom of a page. The headline said, "Possible Escape From Home for Disturbed." The story was only about four inches long, and at first the man wasn't going to read it, but then he realized that he wasn't interested, not really, in the crossword puzzle, and that he was tired of reading about the war, of hearing about it on TV and radio. He had no idea how long he would have to wait for the 9:13, and so he read it. It was an act of acceptance, nothing more. The article said:

An incident late last night at the Western New York Residence for Adults in Need of Supervision may have resulted in the escape of one or more individuals, according to city police.

The home, known until a decade ago as the Rochester Institute for the Criminally Insane, refused through a spokeswoman to acknowledge that the incident occurred.

City police, however, did confirm that they were investigating a fight between staff members and some residents of the home and said that a count of residents showed that at least one resident was unaccounted for. The spokeswoman said that that information was incorrect and that the count was not yet complete.

The home is known to house at least several persons found not-guilty of murder charges because of insanity.

The man did not make conscious note of the story, but its details did lodge themselves in his subconscious. He was a large man, big enough to be an offensive lineman on a college football team. His hands were enormous; once he had held six baseballs in one of them. His face was broad, with a mouth that seemed to extend its full width, but his teeth were small, and that bothered him, so he seldom smiled. He still had his first set of teeth; he was the victim, a dentist once told him, of a defective gene, and he was required to brush his teeth five times a day and visit a dentist every third month. The plan had so far worked, for he was in his forties and had not yet lost his baby teeth.

"Who are you?" the other man said. His tone was sharp, uninviting, almost demanding.

"What? You talking to me?"

"Nobody else to talk to, is there? Who are you? What's your name?"

"Why do you want to know?"

"Just asking. Just trying to be friendly. Don't you like to be friendly?"

"Why don't you leave me alone."

There was about fifteen feet between the two men.

"My name is Thunder. They call me Thunder."

"Thunder? Like in the wind and stuff?"

"That's right, Thunder. What's your name?"

The man with the big hands and small teeth did not answer for several seconds, for a length of time that to him seemed enormous, and he didn't know if he wanted to answer or not. But without really making a decision, he said, "Joe." He said it softly; loud enough to hear at fifteen feet, but soft enough to expose his timidity.

"Joe? Oh." Then the man who had started the conversation turned away and looked at the window, toward the tracks that were hidden by the darkness beyond the windows. The clock on the wall opposite the window said 9:47.

A squealing, a few clicks, then a disinterested voice from the ceiling: "The nine-thirteen from Toronto to Syracuse, Albany, Boston, and points in between has been delayed; expected estimated time of arrival now ten-nineteen."

"Shoot," said Thunder. He stood and walked to the counter but couldn't see anyone behind it. He tipped his head in an unsuccessful attempt to see into an office, but the door was open less than two inches. Thunder walked to the group of vending machines near the station's entrance. He took a dollar bill from his pocket and put it into a dollar-changing machine, but the machine refused to accept it. It pulled the dollar in three-quarters of the way, paused, then pushed it out. Thunder put the bill on top of the machine, ironed it with his fingertips, and reinserted it, but the machine rejected it again. "Shoot," he said; he spoke loudly but with an air of glee. "You got change?" he asked, still looking at the machine. When he didn't get an answer he turned quickly, his full body swiveling in near-military fashion, and spoke the sentence again—"You got change?"—but this time there was a clear demand in the tone, and a hint of annoyance. A third time, this time snapping, almost threatening: "You got change?"

Joe turned his head, but his body remained almost rigid. "No, no, I don't have any change. I don't, I really don't."

Thunder snickered softly. "No need to get hyper, mister. I was just asking. Look, tell you what, you got some change I can buy you a soda. Pepsi. That's what they got. No Coke. Got orange and root beer and Diet Pepsi. I can put the dollar in the soda machine and get change, but I got to buy a soda, and I don't want soda. I want a pack of peanuts and that's sixty cents and the candy machine don't take dollar bills, so if you give me—" he paused for a moment "—you give me thirty-five cents I can get my peanuts and you get yourself a soda, any flavor you want. Okay? What do you think?"

"But I do not desire to have a soda."

"You do not desire to have a soda?" Thunder spoke the words slowly, as if trying to figure out their meaning, as if confused by something about them, perhaps their tone. "Look, Mister, Joe, I'll buy you a soda." He walked to the soda machine, put his dollar bill in it, and that machine also rejected the bill. "Shoot." He walked over to Joe, sat in the chair next to him, so their elbows touched. "You got a neat, ironed dollar bill?"

"No, no, I do not." Joe stood, at first tentatively, so he almost paused as he rose, but then quickly and with a small air of defiance. He moved three seats away and sat down, looking at Thunder from the corners of his eyes.

Thunder stared at Joe. His stare lasted more than a minute, but neither man spoke. Then the ceiling spoke again. "Estimated arrival time of the nine-thirteen has been revised; the estimated arrival time is now ten twenty-two. Ten twenty-two." Both Joe and Thunder turned to look at the clock on the wall alongside the vending machines. It said 10:04. Thunder continued to stare at Joe; Joe looked back, seeing an emotion he could not recognize in Thunder's eyes, but quickly averted his eyes, glancing at the darkness beyond the window, at the emptiness of the rest of the room, at the vacancy behind the counter.

"Why are you looking at me?" he said softly, almost pleadingly. But Thunder did not answer. 10:09. Thunder continued to stare. Joe stood and walked to the door that would take him to the tracks, but he decided not to go out. He didn't want to be outside alone with Thunder. If they had to be alone together he wanted to be inside. Suddenly he blurted out something he just realized: "You don't have any luggage. Are you traveling without any luggage?"

Thunder said, "Don't need none. You ain't got none either." He snickered for a few seconds, as if enjoying his observation. But then he became quiet and continued to stare. 10:16.

Joe went to the candy machine. He wanted to do something, but he decided he couldn't use the change he had in his pocket, because that might annoy Thunder. And for the same reason he couldn't take out an unwrinkled bill. He wasn't even certain he had a bill that wasn't wrinkled. He hoped he did not, because if Thunder found out about it, there might be a confrontation. Above everything else in life right now, Joe wanted to avoid a confrontation.

10:19. A long silence; Joe believed his forehead was perspiring, but he wasn't certain. He stood near the candy machine, but looked toward the blackness of the window. Still, he saw Thunder staring at him. The blackness beyond the window and the silence of the room and the insistence of Thunder's stare blended into a single entity. Joe now knew for certain that his forehead was heavy with perspiration. He refused to touch it, but he knew; he knew.

10:23. A rumbling from outside the window. The ceiling: "The nine-thirteen for Syracuse, Albany, Boston, and points in between, and for transfer at Albany to Montreal and to New York City and points south is now arriving; only passengers with tickets may board the train. Thank you for traveling Amtrak."

Joe took a tentative step toward the door, but he stopped when he saw Thunder rise. Thunder stood and extended himself as tall as he could, as if he were stretching without lifting his arms. He said, "My name ain't Thunder."

"What?"

"My name ain't Thunder."

"No?"

"No, it ain't."

"Oh."

"Ain't you curious what it is?"

Joe stammered a bit. Not a word, just an eh-eh-eh sound.

"It's Eddie."

"I—I see."

"Ain't you curious why I told ya it was Thunder?"

"Yes, I suppose so. Why?"

"Why what?"

"Why did you tell me your name was Thunder?"

"I ain't gonna tell ya." Eddie snickered. He seemed to Joe to be very pleased with himself.

Joe walked quickly through the doors to the trackside, and he knew Eddie was only a few steps behind him. A train was slowing, and a conductor stood on a train step and stepped to the platform a second or two before there was a complete stop. Joe felt a sense of panic. He wanted to know which car Eddie would get on, so he could get on another one, but he didn't want to turn and look. Eddie was about ten feet behind him, smiling blandly, his eyes vacant. Joe turned quickly to the conductor: "Can I get on a car near the front?"

"This is the only car we have open; once you're on you can relocate if you wish."

"Please."

The conductor looked mildly confused, as if he didn't know how to respond. "I'm sorry, sir, but this is the only entrance to the train at the moment; once you are on you can move to any car you wish. All seats are unreserved."

Joe handed his ticket to the conductor; his hand shook.

"Someone will take the ticket after you in-board, sir."

"In-board?"

"Yes, sir."

Joe got on the train. The car he entered had no passengers. He sat near its middle, at a window seat on the south side, the side near the station, because for the moment there was more light there. He knew the light from the platform would disappear as soon as the train pulled out, but for now it was something. Some grasp at comfort.

Eddie stood three seats in front of Joe. Then he walked slowly by him, never removing his eyes from Joe's face, and sat three rows in back of him, directly in back of him, so Joe couldn't see him even when he turned, because the backs of the seats were even with the top of Eddie's head. The train lurched an inch or two, then again, then it chugged and seemed to skip, and then it was rolling, slowly for a few seconds, but quickly the speed increased, and Joe realized he now had to ride the train for at least an hour and fifteen minutes before the next stop, Syracuse, and that he was alone in the car with a man who made him as frightened as he had ever been in his life. The man had done nothing, and Joe had done nothing to antagonize him, but Joe was certain in his gut that he was in great and immediate danger.

The interior walls of the car were silver; the seats alternated between red and blue, and each had a white cloth draped across the headrest. Two seats, a three-foot-wide aisle, and two more seats for the width; twenty or thirty rows for the length; neither Joe nor Eddie counted. Above each set of two seats, on the aisle side, were two small lights on the bottom of the luggage racks. About half of the lights were on. Coke and Pepsi cans, empty bags of potato chips, discarded newspapers, some crumpled Kleenex, a kid's red and green muff—the remains of passengers past—littered the empty seats and the empty aisle and the empty luggage racks. At the rear end of the car were two rest rooms, one with a sign that said Women, the other without a sign but with two screw holes indicating where a sign had once been. A conductor came in from the front door, walked down the aisle, glancing around as he approached the two passengers, and stopped in front of Joe. Joe looked up at him but didn't know what the conductor wanted.

"Your ticket, sir."

Joe took the ticket out of his jacket side pocket and handed it to the conductor.

"Thank you."

"You're welcome," Joe said firmly, as if obeying a mother's elbow in his side.

The conductor ignored the response. Despite the Thank You and the Sir, he clearly had no interest in being polite and certainly not in being friendly. His tone was more disinterested than formal. He tore part of the ticket off, handed the rest back to Joe, and wrote something on a piece of cardboard and stuck it into a slot on the edge of the luggage rack. Then the conductor went on to Eddie and repeated the same routine, but Eddie said, "How long before we get to the next stop?"

"Estimated arrival time in Syracuse is now twelve-oh-four, sir." The conductor turned and walked toward the front of the car; as he did, he said into the air in front of him, "The dining car closed at nine."

Joe leaned over to see what the conductor had written, but he couldn't see it clearly, so he stood. "NYC" in thick black letters was on the top of a one-by-five white card. He wanted to turn to look at the card above Eddie but thought that if he did he would attract Eddie's attention, so he sat down.

"That's your destination," Eddie said. "They write your destination on the card, so if you're asleep when they get there, they know to wake you up." After a pause, he added, "Ain't you ever been on a train before?"

Joe did not turn around to answer. "I've been a passenger on a train many times in my life." It was a lie; this was his first time on a train, but he didn't want Eddie to know that; that might make Eddie think he was naive, or a novice, or in some other way vulnerable.

Joe sat in the window seat and looked out the window. He saw his own reflection and occasional glimpses of passing buildings. He tried to angle his glance to see Eddie, but he couldn't. Gradually he became aware of a series of soft, almost inaudible clicks and a growing sense of darkness. The darkness grew ever so slightly as the clicks continued. Then Eddie was alongside of him, walking forward, reaching up and clicking out all of the lights that were on. He clicked out the one shining on the empty seat next to Joe. Joe felt a small sense of panic, an emptying of his gut, a quick throb in his chest. He half stood and reached up quickly and turned on both of the lights for his pair of seats.

Eddie didn't turn around, but as he continued forward, clicking out more lights, he said, "You ain't reading."

"I like light," Joe said softly. He hoped he didn't sound timid.

"You need a night light," Eddie said with a false squeakiness in his voice.

"If I want the light on I can have the light on," Joe said, and for a moment he feared he would cry. God, he didn't want to cry.

"Ain't you heard there's an energy crisis?" Eddie was finished turning out all the lights, and he returned to his seat, three rows behind Joe. He repeated his question: "Ain't you heard there's an energy crisis? I said. I don't like being ignored like I ain't here. I am here and I asked you a civil question and I'm entitled to a civil answer. Ain't you heard there's an energy crisis? What do you think our boys are getting killed for in the Middle East?"

"Boys and girls," Joe said.

"What?"

"Boys and girls. There are girls fighting in this war, too."

"No they ain't."

"Yes they are. That information is readily available in the better newspapers and on the better quality news programs on television and radio. It was on National Public Radio."

"No they ain't."

"I read it in the paper and heard it on television. And on National Public Radio."

"There may be girls there but they ain't fighting. They don't let girls be in fighting outfits. They're what you call your support troops."

Joe paused for a few moments. He felt his face flush. "Yes, of course, you are correct. I was careless." He felt very embarrassed. He wanted to be alone, in a room all by himself, sitting or lying down, to allow the shame to go away. He felt his lips stretch and quiver a bit, as they always did when he felt shame.

Eddie thought of himself as a slight man. Certainly he was much smaller than Joe. He was five or six inches shorter, probably weighed fifty or sixty pounds less, had shoulders notably less wide, a neck obviously less thick, and a general appearance of being considerably weaker. He did not have the extra girth above the waist that Joe did, but he had a pot belly. The girth on Joe added to the sense of size and strength that goes with size; the small mound on Eddie only emphasized the slenderness of the rest of his body. Still, Eddie did not think of himself as physically inferior to anyone. He considered himself tough. The army rejected him when he applied in the sixties because it didn't recognize that toughness, and he lost his chance to go to Vietnam. He was on his way now to Boston to join up there. The army or the navy or the air force or the marines or the coast guard; the service didn't matter. He would tell them he was ready to go to the Persian Gulf. Not to serve his country, not to prove anything to himself, not to come back a hero, not to do any of a thousand things an enlistment might do. But just to go; that's what guys like him were meant to do, and that's what, Jesus Christ almighty, he would do. The police department in Cleveland told him to go away, and when he wrote to the French Embassy in Washington for an application for the Foreign Legion, he never received a reply. The letter he sent to the French Embassy in Ottawa must have been misrouted, because two weeks after he sent it he received brochures on the Riviera and Paris and the French Alps. Christ, those were sissy places. He wasn't going to go to any of them. For now, he was going to Boston to join up. Then he would go overseas.

Joe annoyed him. Joe was too big, the type of man who makes other men back down in a bar. Damn it, Eddie wasn't going to back down, not from Joe, not from nobody.

"The dark bother you, Joe?" Soft lights illuminated the space between the luggage racks and the ceiling, and other softer lights lit a walking path down the aisle, but the spaces between the fronts and backs of seats, the spaces where people sat, were dark. Outlines of bodies could be seen, but nothing more, unless the reading lights were on. Eddie could see the light at Joe's seat, but not Joe; the backs of the seats were too high. "I said, does the dark bother you?"

"No, the dark is not a disturbance to me. I am a fully grown adult and I am long beyond the point in my life that would result in my being disturbed by the darkness."

"Shoot, man."

The conductor came in the front door and walked through the car. A walkie-talkie hanging from his belt and bouncing on his hip pocket squawked. No one was speaking on it. The noises were electronic, brief, and frequent, as if someone on the other end was playing with a button. The conductor left the car through the rear door.

"Know what happens next?" Eddie said.

"No." Joe's voice vibrated with timidity.

"In a few minutes, that conductor guy will come back. He just walks to the end of the train and then walks to the front. Dumb job. Dumb, man, dumb. You wouldn't catch me having a dumb job like that."

"His work is respectable, I am certain. A man, or a woman for that matter, should not be called derogatory names for performing respectable assignments."

"Shoot, man."

Then they were both quiet. After a few minutes, the conductor came through the rear door, walked through the car without speaking, and left through the front door.

"Dumb," Eddie said. "Dumb."

"I believe in the dignity of the working man," Joe said. "And the working woman."

"The working woman? You mean like streetwalkers? Whores? Where's the dignity in that? Shoot, man."

Joe did not answer. Eddie wanted Joe to say something; he wanted to have an argument with him. But he decided to wait. For what, he didn't know. But he would wait until it came.

Eddie watched the back of the seat Joe sat in. Joe looked at the reflection in the window, trying but unable to see Eddie.

The front door of the car slid open, and the conductor stepped inside, then paused and looked at the two men. After a few moments, he took two or three tentative steps further into the car, then walked very quickly past them and exited through the rear. "Looks like he don't want to spend no time with us," Eddie said. Joe didn't reply. He studied the reflection. Eddie stared at the back of the seat Joe sat in.

The back door to the car slid open. The conductor came

in, stood at the door as it slid shut, and watched the two men. Eddie turned to watch him. Joe still looked at the reflection. The conductor turned quickly, took something from his pocket, did something with it to the door, placed it back in his pocket, and walked hurriedly—watching carefully to see what the two men were doing—to the front of the car. He exited quickly, but then there were some noises, like metal on metal, barely audible above the clanging and roaring of the train moving rapidly over the tracks.

"Shoot," Eddie said, and he stood quickly and ran down the aisle, bumping off the sides of several seats, until he was at the front door. He pushed the black panel marked Push, but the door wouldn't open. He banged it several times with his fist, and he kicked another panel at the bottom of the door. He turned and ran to the back of the train, muttering loud enough for Joe to hear, "The shoot-head locked us in here, the shoot-head."

He pushed and kicked at the rear door, but that one wouldn't open either. "Why the shoot would the shoot-head lock us in here?" He walked up to Joe's seat, took another step so he could see Joe's face. Joe turned from the window to face Eddie. Eddie said, "Why the shoot would he lock us in here? What did you do? Who the shoot are you?" He backed away, two steps, three, four steps, but then he stopped. "Who are you?" He was confident there was no fear in his voice, only demand; he wanted that to be there.

"My name is Joe. I've already informed you of that fact."

Eddie stuck his tongue out and licked his lower lip. He sat in the seat two rows in front of Joe and across the aisle, and he kept his body twisted to look at Joe.

Joe moved to the aisle seat and stared at Eddie.

Joe had no idea how much time had passed before he spoke. He wanted to be certain that his memory was correct, and that required that he take time to sort out the things that were flooding his mind. When he was certain of his memory, he said, "I know who you are. You're the man I read about in the newspaper in the station. You escaped from the home for adults who are in need of care. Aren't you?"

"What the shoot are you talking about?"

"I know who you are. You are a severely disturbed adult who requires institutionalization for the protection of society."

"You're crazy." Eddie wanted to sound threatening, and he was certain he did when he saw Joe's facial muscles tighten.

"No, sir, I am not," Joe said firmly, like a child determined to prove his point with the force of his voice. "You are not correct when you refer to me as crazy. I am not." After a few seconds, he added, "I am not."

"You're bonkers, looney, cuckoo, crazy, disturbed; you're a bean head."

"I am not, sir. I am not."

Then they were quiet and continued to stare at one another.

Occasionally the train passed a small village with a few streetlights, and that caused shadows to move rapidly across the interior of the car. Joe watched as Eddie's face briefly disappeared and suddenly reappeared, dim and incomplete, but still visible. At one point Eddie smiled; his teeth were uneven, one upper tooth between the front and the corner of the mouth was missing; the teeth were yellowish. Joe refused to smile; he did not want to reveal his baby teeth. He thought that maybe he should go to the men's room and brush his teeth. He wasn't certain there was a sink and running water there, but he decided not to go for a different reason: he didn't realize he would be able to lock the rest room door, and he thought Eddie might follow him in and watch, that Eddie might see that he still had his baby teeth, and he didn't want Eddie to see that. Not Eddie.

The front door to the car opened slowly. The conductor who had been in the car earlier came in, but this time he had another man with him. The second man wore bib overalls that were greyish, like old-time train engineers in cowboy movies. They talked briefly and almost silently to each other. Standing at the open door they surveyed the car. The conductor waved with his fingers—his hand held inches in front of his chest—to Eddie. "Sir, may I speak to you, please."

Eddie pointed to his own chest. "Me? You wanna speak to me?"

"Yes, sir, if you don't mind."

"What about?"

"Would you smile for me, sir?"

"Smile? What for?"

"Please humor me, sir."

Eddie smiled quickly and briefly, as if mocking happiness.

The conductor then spoke to Joe. "Sir, would you smile for me, please."

"I would rather not, if you don't mind."

"Please, sir."

"Am I required to do so as a condition of being a passenger on this mode of transportation?"

"Shoot," Eddie muttered.

The conductor said something softly to the man in the overalls. Then he turned to Joe. "Yes, sir. That is a condition of being a passenger on Amtrak."

"Shoot," Eddie said.

"Very well; if you insist," Joe said. He smiled broadly and held his smile for five or six seconds. Then he made it disappear.

"Thank you, sir."

The conductor turned to Eddie. "Sir, please come with me. It is very important."

"Is my smile better than his?" He had glanced at Joe's smile and had seen the smallness of his teeth. He didn't know why they were small. "My teeth ain't so good, but that ain't no reason for you to make me come up there."

The man in the overalls said something very softly to the conductor. The conductor said loudly enough for Joe and Eddie to hear, "Hell, no. You do that."

The man in the overalls didn't say anything, and for a few moments he just stood next to the conductor. He looked very nervous, but then he walked forward, at first slowly but then at a normal speed. He stopped a foot or two in front of Eddie and leaned over and whispered, "We believe this other man is dangerous and that for your own safety you should leave this car." He backed down the aisle quickly, bumping into the back of one seat, but managing to reach the conductor in a few seconds.

Eddie waited until the man in the overalls was next to the conductor. Then he stood and turned to Joe: "Bye-bye, looney bird." He walked to the front of the car, and with the two other men he left. The conductor quickly took a device out of his pocket and locked the door behind them. The three men stood in the crowded area between two cars. The shaking of the train was far greater there than it had been in the middle of the car.

"What's going on?" Eddie said, not trying to hide his annoyance.

"We think that man in there," the conductor said, "is an escapee from a mental institution. We got a radioed report from the Rochester police. Syracuse police will get on board at our next stop and take him in, but he might be dangerous. I'm sorry I locked you in there with him. When I got the report I had to do something to protect the other passengers on the train, so I locked both doors quickly. Then I realized that you could be in danger, so Mel came with me to get you out."

"Lucky you have rotten teeth," Mel said.

"What the shoot does that mean?"

"We were told the guy they want is big," Mel said, "but to make positive identification we were told to look for perfect baby teeth. Grown man but he still has his baby teeth. Soon as I saw your yellow teeth, ragged, one missing, I knew you were not the one they want."

"Ain't nothing wrong with my teeth."

"I didn't say there was."

"You sure as shoot did. You pretty much said the same thing as I'm ugly."

"Sir," the conductor said, sensing Eddie's growing anger, "let's get a seat in this car. Me and Mel will stand guard here."

"I ain't ugly and ain't nothin' wrong with my teeth."

"Oh, Christ," Mel said. "We have enough trouble without you starting an argument."

Suddenly Eddie had produced a knife from somewhere; not a knife, a bayonet, and he slashed it across the front of Mel's neck. As Mel's jaw vibrated and blood flowed out in little spurts, Eddie turned and shoved the knife into the conductor's chest. The whole sequence took less than four seconds. Eddie was proud of his quickness. If the army recruiters knew of his quickness with a bayonet, they would welcome him with enthusiasm, and that jerk of a sergeant who said he couldn't join to go to Vietnam because of the way he used a knife on that kid in high school, he would be embarrassed passing up such talent.

Both the conductor and Mel were down on the floor. Mel's head was on top of the back of the conductor's neck; the conductor's left hand was open at his own chest. Eddie thought of pushing them out the door, but then he thought that the train might come to a halt if a door opened while it was in motion. He yanked the bayonet from out of the conductor's chest. It wasn't an easy task because of the angle. He had to reach under both men and had little room to maneuver. He wiped the blade on the conductor's jacket. Then he took some Kleenex from his pocket and wrapped it around the blade. Holding the tissue, he wiped the handle back and forth on Mel's overalls. The knife was now clean, and still holding it in the tissue, he used the conductor's key to let himself back into the car. The door slid shut behind him. He walked toward Joe, who was looking at the reflection in the window until he heard the door shut. Joe looked up at Eddie, who walked up to him, right up to him, so his belt was just inches from his face.

"Here, take this." He held the bayonet out for Joe to take by the handle.

At first, Joe did not move. He said, "Why?"

"Because I can see you're afraid of me. And I thought if you had a weapon, you wouldn't be afraid anymore."

Joe reached hesitantly for the weapon; his hand paused with his fingers circled around but not touching the handle for a second. Then he grasped it.

"See ya," Eddie said. He walked to the front of the car,

watching as Joe watched him. "See ya," he called. He stepped around the two dead men and went into the next car. He took a seat across the aisle from a pretty, college-age girl who seemed to be asleep, although she wore headphones from a Walkman, and Eddie could clearly hear the beat of an acid-rock song. He liked the name Thunder, he decided, and he would use it again. He was becoming good at deception; the army would like that, if he could figure out a way to prove it to them. They wouldn't let him join in San Francisco, or in Kansas City, or in Indianapolis. And not in Rochester. Maybe in Boston they had more sense. He dozed off, watching the breast of the young girl rise and fall.

In the other car, Joe turned to look out the window, to watch his own reflection. He didn't feel happy thinking about Eddie. When he'd looked to the front of the car a few minutes earlier, Eddie was gone and the door was closed. Joe wondered why the two men had come in to take Eddie out with them. But he didn't wonder too much or too hard. So many things had happened to him so many times in his life that he could not understand, that he had developed the useful habit and ability of denying himself the right to wonder.

When the train stopped in Syracuse, policemen came into the car from the rear door and the front door at the same time. There were four of them, and they all held pistols. "Put down that knife," one of them said sternly. Joe had long ago, at the institution, learned to obey sternness immediately, so he did what he was told. He placed the bayonet on the floor alongside his seat. They placed his hands behind his back and put handcuffs on them and led him out the rear door. He did not know anything about the two bodies between his car and the one in front of it. He would not learn about them until he was back in the institution in Rochester the next morning. By then, nobody believed him about a man named Eddie or Thunder. Just like before he left; they so seldom believed him.

A SALESMAN'S TALE

By DAVID DEAN

They're back. The woman and the girl. I keep pretending I haven't noticed them, but I have. I certainly have.

They don't seem to be looking for me, though I must be
the reason they've returned. Why else do the dead come
back but to haunt their killers?

So far, they appear dazed and lethargic. They just sit
very still, facing the altar, as if gathering strength. They
remind me of moths that have just crawled from their
cocoons, weak and quivering, not quite recognizable until
they've dried and spread their wings. Maybe that's how
they've gotten so close without me noticing, and more im-
portantly, remembering. They've been taking shape and
mass for so long that it's been almost imperceptible.

To think that it was only a few weeks ago that I first
noticed the woman at all! Even then I didn't recognize her.
She crept in unannounced.

Now, I can hardly keep my eyes off them. Each Sunday,
as Barb and the kids and I enter the church, I look for
them. They're never there when we arrive. I always spot
them later, already sitting amongst the other parishion-
ers, as if they'd never left the church. I never see them
enter. That wouldn't be their way. This is far more un-
nerving. The woman knows I have to show up each Sunday. What excuse would I give Barb or the Monsignor?
After all, I'm a family man. I'm not about to let the two of
them disrupt my life just by occupying a pew! They tried
once before and look where it got them! I admit, I'm a
little curious, too.

She was always demanding . . . in more ways than
one, if you know what I mean. She wanted me to be part of
her, and the girl's, life. And I was . . . for a while. I was
still in the sales department and spent a lot of time on the
road and away from home. Naturally, I was not averse to
a little feminine companionship. In fact, the city she lived

in was one that my company did a lot of business in, so it was convenient. For both of us.

She was one of those recently divorced young mothers whose husband's whereabouts are unknown. No child support, no family, no skills, and no future. I was a godsend. She was appreciative. The girl was quiet. I never made any promises!

I did not, however, tell her that I had a wife and kids two states away. She didn't even know my real name. Each time I'd roll into town I'd make sure I tossed my wallet and wedding ring into my briefcase, which I'd leave in the car. I knew I was being eyed for promotion and I couldn't afford a scandal. I had my sights on the main office.

I always made a point of showing up after dark and leaving before light. The neighbors never really saw me or my car. It was a different company car each week, in any case.

Everything was just fine. I liked the woman. The woman was crazy about me. The little girl was a problem. She was too quiet. She reminded me of her father, whom I never met. I seemed to find her around every corner. Never smiling, never speaking. She watched me a lot. I knew she didn't like me. I even mentioned it to her mother a few times. She would always find a way to take my mind off the girl though, at least for a while. I took to thumping her when her mother wasn't around. Not hard, just enough to make her stay clear. I knew the woman would find out, but what could she do?

Then I got the promotion. I would not be returning to that town on any regular basis. I decided to tell them. Why? I'm not sure. If I had just walked out, like any other time, and not come back, that would have been the end of it. They could never have traced me. They didn't even know my name. The woman believed I worked for my company's biggest rival! That was one of my little jokes.

Maybe I wanted to see how much I meant to the woman. A few tears shed on my behalf seemed appropriate. I also wanted a shot at the little girl. I had decided to make her the reason for my leaving. Something for her mother to mull over in my absence. It would have made for a neat wrap-up except for one thing. My timing was bad.

Instead of waiting till the next morning when I was preparing to leave to break the news, I told them the night before. I had looked forward to an evening of tearful pleas and enticing promises and that's exactly what I got. I fell asleep, with a good meal in my belly, to the pleasing sounds of the woman lashing out at the daughter.

When I woke the next morning I found mother and daughter waiting for me at the kitchen table. They had my briefcase open and my driver's license and company cards spread out before them. They sat side by side and looked at me. They had closed ranks. I knew this was the girl's doing. She had been suspicious of me all along and after last night had decided to do something about it.

They both sat there without saying a word. They looked pale and dark around the eyes. They looked as if they had sat there all night waiting for me. Just like they do in church now. They never looked more like mother and daughter. I was afraid. They had power over me.

Looking into their eyes, I only took a moment to decide. Along with my papers and ID, they had brought in my samples. My samples are surgical instruments and a neatly wrapped package of them lay right inside the brief-case. I reached in, unwrapped them, and went to work.

That was many long years ago and I haven't given it much thought since. They were dead. Now they're back. But they're weak. Just like before. Laughably weak. I'm not easily frightened.

The woman and child are sitting four rows directly in front of my family and me when suddenly the priest raises his voice and points at them. I don't know what he's say-ing as I'm a little distracted, understandably. I glance up just in time to see him single them out as if they're an example or proof of his sermon. A number of people in the congregation turn to look at them. I'm not sure, but I think one or two glance in my direction also.

As if animated by the priest's gesture, the woman be-gins to slowly, almost mechanically turn her head to the left. I know instantly that she is scanning the church for me. The effort seems to cost her dearly. Her skin is pale and has a sickly, feverish glow. Her head stops turning just short of looking over her shoulder. She gazes for a few moments into the pews on her left. Then, without turning her head or body any further, her eyes, or should I say eye, as I can only see the one, begins to shift further yet to the left. It reminds me of an animal that is too sick or wounded to move, trying to see its executioner walking up behind it. The eye travels with painstaking slowness to the outer corner of the socket and stops, straining. On her full lips is just the slightest smile. I shift a few inches to my right, nudging Austin over. He kicks me. At this moment I'm glad to be behind her.

She holds that pose for just a few moments longer and then turns slowly forward. She didn't see me but she knows I'm here. The girl never moves. She's like a large doll propped up front as a good example to other children.

I've decided against taking communion today. The idea of walking into her field of vision makes my palms sweat. Not that I'm afraid, but she may call out something. They are gathering strength.

It's next Sunday already, and here we are back at Mass again. All of us. I didn't really want to come. Not because of them, they can't hurt me, I know that, but because I haven't been sleeping well. It's not unusual for a man who carries a lot of responsibility.

Barbara nudges me to stand for prayer, as I've been daydreaming. I notice as I do that the woman and girl are standing also. I hadn't seen them do that before now. They usually remain seated. I also notice they're only three rows in front of us now. They've crept up!

As I watch, the little girl snakes her spindly arm around the woman's waist. The arm seems grubby or bruised. I imagine my fingerprints etched in purple on her pale flesh. The woman raises her head, squares her shoulders and begins slowly to turn in my direction. I cannot look away.

Her face is vacant and unanimated as her gaze sweeps across the worshipers. When she reaches about three-quarters profile, she stops. I realize that I'm holding my breath. With what I imagine as an almost audible click the head swivels an inch more to the right and stops again. I am in her line of vision. She sees me.

The eyes quicken and focus. They are large and almond-shaped, the blue so brilliant that they seem lit from within. The skin is like milk, with high spots of color at the cheeks. The lips are full and moist and slightly parted. The woman's face is framed by dark, humid tendrils of hair, giving the impression that she has just risen from a warm and active bed. She looks exactly as she did the last night I saw her. I'm suddenly weak with longing. I feel tears welling up. She smiles. As if acknowledging the distress she has caused, the corners of her mouth turn up. Just the hint of a smile. A smirk, really. She's letting me know that she's not so weak anymore. I hear myself speak her name and then bite down hard on my lip, wishing I could call it back. I taste my blood, warm and salty in my mouth.

Barbara has me by the arm and is whispering something urgent in my ear. A number of people are staring at me. I turn away with an effort and begin up the aisle. I feel her eyes burning into my back and the only thing that keeps me from running is the weakness in my knees.

I step out into a brilliant, cold day and think of her parted lips revealing small, yellowing teeth. As I bring my handkerchief to my mouth, I picture those same teeth crushing my bones and faint.

It's Sunday morning again and I'm lying here wondering what they want and what I'm going to do. I can guess what they want. I think I know. What do all ghosts want? They want their murderer known. A sordid disclosure of his hidden past! Isn't that the way these stories go? The killer exposed like something poisonous found under a rock, pleading for forgiveness from a horrified world?

They won't find me that easily. I was always smarter than the woman; she knows that. She even told me so on occasion. I wouldn't be where I am today if I weren't. And they wouldn't be where they are if they hadn't tried to outsmart me! They must have felt pretty smug sitting there with my future spread out over their kitchen table. I wonder how smug they felt when I unwrapped my little present?

That's it, isn't it? Initiative. I must take action. It's no good lying about the house, pretending to be ill and waiting for God only knows what! Barbara knows something isn't right. We haven't had sex for a week. Since last Sunday, I just can't do it. And the children. Every time they're around I start to get weepy. I can't explain it, and they just stare at me as if I were a stranger. So I must do something . . . and I think I know what. I'm going to beat them to the punch!

Probably, in cases like this, it's the remorse and regret that eventually wear a person down and make him do something stupid. But what if that person were to rid himself of the so-called guilt by confession, and I don't mean to the authorities? They suggested the answer themselves by appearing at Mass. I'll be first in line for the confessional! The church has to forgive, and after that, what power could they have over me?

The church is almost empty upon our arrival, which is no surprise as we're nearly thirty minutes early. I've convinced Barb that I must attend confession prior to Mass. She wants to ask questions but is afraid, I think. I scan the interior quickly as we enter, just to make sure. They're not here. I would have been very surprised if they were. Everything is going as I'd hoped.

I get Barb and the children situated in our usual spot, which is on the opposite side of the church and somewhat forward of the confessional. I genuflect, turn, and cross the aisles to the booth. I can see that there's no one ahead of me by virtue of a small light fixture attached to the side of the booth. A red light is illuminated when the confessional is in use, and a green when it is vacant and a priest is on duty within. The green lamp is on. I kneel at the nearest pew to say a quick prayer before entering, in case a priest is watching, and glance underneath the half-curtain shrouding the entrance as I do so.

In the dimly lit interior I see small, white legs ending in a scruffy pair of Mary Janes. The feet are on the floor pointing in my direction and I see, even in this dim light, that the legs are lacerated in many places, forming a crisscross pattern. The wounds are not bleeding, having dried without healing. The child on the other side of this curtain is clearly not kneeling for confession. Suddenly I'm aware of the priest at the front of the church, attending the altar. I realize now that there is no one to hear her confession. That's not why she's there. She is waiting for me to pull back that curtain and join her there in the darkness.

I stand up, swaying, and begin walking away. My legs will barely support me and I grab at several people on my way, who must think I'm drunk. I can't stop looking over my shoulder for fear that she'll come out of that box behind me. I don't want to see her face! Barb is clutching a child in each arm and staring at me white-faced as I stumble towards the door. She doesn't see the woman kneeling not ten feet from them stand and slowly begin that awful turn. I shout a warning as I rush out through the doorway.

It's Sunday again! No matter. I'm not going to Mass today. A simple solution to a complex problem. They can have the church. I'll stay right here at home. Not that it makes much difference.

Barbara took the kids and left last Sunday, right after my little episode at confession. She's frightened. Austin and Vivian, picking up on their mother's mood, just stared at me while Barb packed. That made me very uncomfortable. They ran when I tried to hold them. I was in no condition to make them stay.

Barb's suspicious, too, I think. She says I shouted out the word "murder" as I fled church last week. I know I didn't say that, I was trying to warn her of the woman. It's funny under the circumstances that she should hear that, though I can't recall what I did say.

I haven't been in to work all this week, either. The office has phoned several times and left messages on my answering machine, but with Barb gone I just can't seem to find the energy to lie about being ill. Barb used to do that for me sometimes. In fact, I can't seem to summon up any energy at all. Perhaps they're draining me. Maybe that's how they've grown in strength. By sucking out my strength and resolve, they leave behind a vacuum that draws in all the weaker emotions, like guilt and remorse. I can almost feel them forming a lump in my chest. Something hard yet brittle. If I press down on my rib cage I can feel it crack and slide from underneath the pressure of my palm. Tears spring to my eyes, and my muscles become weak and flaccid, unable to support me. It's a sickening feeling. Mostly, I just lie here and pretend not to notice.

It's a bright, sunny day out, though it rained most of last night. The rain made me wakeful as I kept thinking that I could hear voices just beneath my bedroom window. The gurgling of water through the gutters was the cause. Still, I was expectant. Several times the sound of the rain blowing through the shrubbery put me in mind of women in long dresses strolling through the yard. Dresses that would trail across the grass as they walked, rustling slightly. It was a peculiar thought and I guess that's why I dreamt so strangely afterwards.

I must have fallen asleep close to dawn. In my dream, the sun was rising above the drenched earth. My house had that clean, windswept but slightly drowned look that it probably has this very moment. I was lying in my bed, dreaming, when there was just the slightest of sounds. The soft scrape of a tiny shoe on the walkway leading to my front door. Barely audible, yet instantly recognized.

I felt myself trying desperately to wake up, but I couldn't seem to open my eyes! Even though I was dreaming, I couldn't see! Somehow, I managed to sit up in bed and I began to force my eyelids apart with my fingers. Then I could see again.

My room was flooded with the morning sun and I could see that I was alone, but as sometimes happens with dreams, I could see outside my house as well. As if I were floating, disembodied, above my home looking down at the vacant scene. There was no one there, only an empty, concrete pathway leading to my front door, which was standing wide open!

I wanted desperately to rejoin my body, which was hidden beneath the roof now, and warn myself! There was someone in the house with me! Then, as is the nature of dreams, I was there. Sitting up in bed, staring at my bedroom doorway. Waiting for them to step into my vision. There was a loud bang in the hallway, followed by silence. I choked off a scream. Then the whispering began. Just outside of my line of vision. Hushed, conspiratorial tones, as if a course of action was being discussed. Finally, the conversation ended and I could hear small female laughter drifting away.

I awoke sitting up in bed, staring at my bedroom doorway. I could feel a cool, fresh breeze blowing into my room. I slept with all windows and doors closed and locked.

When I went into the hall, I could see small patches of damp leading to my room and returning to the front door, which stood open. I noticed the hall closet was also open and a shambles. An old briefcase lay on the bare floor in front of it. I recognized it. This was what had made the loud bang in my dream. It had been flung from its shelf. It would contain my samples.

I picked it up, carried it into the kitchen, and set it on the table. I didn't need to look inside. They were still there. I had never bothered to remove them. The police would never connect me with the scene and even if they did, I had thoroughly cleaned the instruments. Even so, I don't know why I've kept them. Easier than getting rid of them, I suppose.

I walked into the living room and closed the front door. Oddly enough, I didn't feel so much frightened as disappointed. I was weak, after all. They could now come and go in my life as they pleased and I was powerless to stop them. I knew what they were waiting for. My wife and children were gone, my career as good as finished. Only one thing was left and they were waiting for it. Confession. Humiliation. But I think I know something that they don't want me to.

Confession only occurs if there's guilt and conscience

and they are drawing mine out and nurturing it. It's become a cancer that I can't ignore or trust, yet it's mine! That's the key! Ultimately, I can remove it. They may have underestimated me, after all.

I have a few shots to steady my nerves and take the parcel from the briefcase. Originally, I was studying to be a doctor, but financial hardships diverted me to business. Even so, I remained on the fringes and still take great pride in the instruments we manufacture. As I unwrap them, I can see they gleam as if new.

Something strikes the windowpane in the kitchen door, startling me, and I drop a surgical knife with a clatter. The door is locked and I'm not foolish enough to open it. Standing off to one side, I tease back the curtain and put my eye to the glass. A cardinal, bright as a splash of blood, lies broken on my rear stoop. My eyes are drawn in the direction it came from. That's what they've been waiting for.

The two of them are standing close together under a barren maple tree, facing the door. The woman's eyes are riveted on mine. The child's face remains an accusing shadow. As if on cue, the woman begins moving across the lawn toward me, her face a mask of rage, flecked with spittle. Somehow, she knows what I intend to do. I can see her mouth working grotesquely, grinding without sound. Her stride is impossibly long and she covers the distance with a nightmarish speed. I can't take my eyes from her and it's only an involuntary reaction that makes me fall back, releasing the curtain just as she reaches the door. I see her silhouette on the other side of the material. I expect her face to thrust through the glass! But the glass does not break and the door does not burst open. She remains as she is, a frozen outline on the fabric, radiating hatred. I watch, unable to move, and understand how strong they have become. By the end of the day they will not have to wait for me to sleep to enter this house. No barrier will stop them. Now is my only chance to act! Knowing this, I can turn my back on my guardian and begin to work. I reach for a scalpel.

* * *

Suicide is never a pretty sight and this one was particularly gruesome. The detective-lieutenant surveyed the carnage and grimaced. How, he asked himself, could a person open himself from sternum to pelvis? Surely there were easier, less agonizing ways to kill oneself? He would have to wait for the medical examiner's report, but he felt certain that this old boy had done some digging around while he was at it. What in the world for?

As the wrecked body was being carried out and the scene-of-crime officers began their exhaustive cataloguing, the lieutenant held a scrap of paper up to his eyes. He clasped it with a pair of tweezers and reread its contents. It should have pleased him but it didn't. On this piece of paper was both the explanation for the suicide and quite probably the solution to a ten-year-old double slaying. In other words, a confession. It must have been written by the eviscerated man, as all the doors were dead-bolted from the inside, but his experience told him that it was in a distinctly feminine hand.

HE WHO WAITS FOR YOU

By DAVID C. HALL

You are standing in front of the dark window, as if looking out.

A window should never be left like that at night. The blinds should be drawn or curtains closed. From out there in the dark they can see you, but you can't see them. You look out, but you don't see anything, nothing more than the dark on the other side of the glass and the murky reflection of the room on its surface.

I am sitting here in an armchair, not far from where you are, but I feel the distance between us. I have felt it many times, but I have never managed to understand it.

I could speak to you, but I know it wouldn't change anything. I did speak to you in fact, a few months ago. You gave no indication of having heard me. I muttered, it's true. I told you you ought to pull the curtains, that someone might see you. Maybe you didn't hear me.

There is nothing for me to do except wait. Eventually you will turn to me. I cross my legs. I contemplate the crease on my trousers, the shine on my brown shoes. I'm used to waiting.

Your face, when you turn, is pale. Your skin has always been pale, but now the light has gone out of it. It has gone slack and colorless. It occurs to me that maybe you have been putting on rouge for years, and only now, for the first time, you have forgotten to do it. That amuses me, in a sad sort of way. Your reddish blonde hair is still lovely. Perhaps there are streaks of grey in it, and you dye them. Hairdressers are very clever at that sort of thing these days, I understand. My barber has even offered to do it for me.

It doesn't matter. I have gone too far now to turn back just because you dye your hair or use cosmetics to restore the glow that your skin has lost. I will always remember your face as it was before you needed these things. I am constant, if nothing else.

"Who?" you ask finally, when I have almost forgotten what I said to you.

I make a vague gesture. I smile. You put your hands in the pockets of your long grey skirt. You are coming toward me now. Your expression is not particularly welcoming, but you are coming closer. The distance is going. I motion to the chair beside me. It is your chair actually, both of yours, his really, not mine to offer at all.

"Do you think they are watching me?" you say and stop there in the middle of the big living room, full of furniture and other things that you have picked out, accumulated in the course of the years. I was with you when you bought some of them. I don't know if you remember. I don't really know what you remember.

"I think you should draw the curtains," I say. I am calm and serious, since the situation calls for seriousness. You look at me. I nod. I smile again, an intimate, reassuring smile. You turn, you go back to the window and pull the cord that draws the curtain. I derive a certain satisfaction from that. You will obey me, you will recognize my right to decide things for you. It is nothing in itself really, no more than when you would accept without hesitation my choice of a table when we walked into a restaurant together. But now the stakes are higher. You don't know that, perhaps, but I know it. That is enough.

You sit down finally, leaning your head against the back of the chair. Your hand, on the arm of the chair, is not far from mine. I notice the nails are painted a bright red which is, I believe, the fashion this year. I could reach out my hand to cover yours. It would be a gesture of friendship, of sympathy. But no. It's too soon, there wouldn't be any point.

"I suppose I should call the police," you say.

"You have to compose yourself."

I offer you my pack of cigarettes. You look at it and hesitate for a moment. I believe you almost smile when you take the cigarette. I lean toward you to light it, and I study your eyes that look down at the tip of the cigarette, the soft, vague curve your breasts make under the silk blouse. How many times have I done this? You lean back and slowly blow out the smoke. I like watching you smoke. It's a long time since you gave it up, and our best times were before that, I think. Nothing shows on my face of all of this, I am sure. I am cold, impassive. That is what they think of me. I know that. Now at least I can turn it to some use.

"Leave it to me," I say.

You look at me again with those pale eyes, which are not at all stupid, not easily fooled. You know me very well. I flinch, inwardly, I hope. You know me well enough to catch the significance of the flutter of an eyelid. I lift my glass. I remember my part. I am cool and responsible. I am a man. I know what has to be done.

"I know people who can handle this," I say. "Perhaps you should have some cognac."

You are no longer looking at me. You have gone down into your sorrow, your anxiety, and closed me out. But you accept the idea that I will take care of everything. You assume that I will serve you. It does not even occur to you to doubt it. I am, after all, your friend, your dearest friend.

"Call them," you say, without looking at me. Your face, which I see in profile, has assumed in sorrow some of the dignity of tragedy. It is a kind of loveliness I have never seen in you before. It frightens me a little, but then you have always been able to frighten me, all these years. There has always been something you could give, or take away.

"Not from here," I say.

That startles you, and with a look I let you know that it is possible that your phone is tapped and that I have thought about that, I understand this kind of thing. Don't think that I don't enjoy all this a little. Maybe in the end I am a bit of a clown. It never occurred to me until now.

"You have to understand," I say calmly, "that for one wrong move on our part they could kill him."

I wonder if you have realized that with all this your husband the second-rate politician is at last going to become famous, which I suppose has always been his ambition. And you too, although a little less so. Not me.

But you are not thinking about that, of course. You put your hands to your face, cover your eyes. Like all your gestures it is graceful, as if you had studied how to do it a long time ago, with the nuns.

"You have to realize," I say, in the same monotonous, patient voice, "that this is not going to be easy."

I didn't know that I was going to enjoy making you suffer. I should have known, but I never thought about it.

I drain my glass and set it down on the coaster on the table. Suddenly I feel shaken, as if in spite of all my plans I had made some terrible, unforeseeable mistake. I have always felt like this with you, even at the best times, when the night was finished and you left me with a brush of your lips over mine. I had always made some mistake. Or maybe it was always the same one: that I was not someone else.

You walk with me to the door. We do not kiss. I could hug you, show you a kind of friendly warmth, share your sorrow in a touch of your skin. Another man would. I stick to my role. I wait. There will be time.

You know I hate to drive, I hate the ugliness of the tollways with their urine-colored lights, gas stations and restaurants that serve fast, disgusting food. When I arrive I am tired and my throat is sore from too many cigarettes. It's late, and in the village there is that silence which is only to be found in villages at night, so quiet that you think there is nobody left still alive.

When I get out of the car I can smell the manure on the fields around. I take out the big iron key and unlock the wooden door. Inside it smells of stone and damp. I turn on the main switch and the lights on the ground floor. Something moves toward the back of the house, where old furniture and junk is stacked. A cat, I suppose. Mice make hardly any noise, rats, I don't know.

I open the door to the room and turn on the lightbulb hanging from the ceiling. He is still asleep where I left him, on the floor, tied, with a chloroform-soaked gag in his mouth. The room is full of the smell of chloroform, and when I take the gag off I can smell urine, because he has pissed himself. In his sleep, I suppose.

I wish you could see him now, I wish you could smell him. He was handsome in his day, I admit, and later he was distinguished, but he isn't now. He had enough intelligence to know what his masters wanted done, and to do it. Most of all—and I suppose that is what you liked about him—he had that masculine vitality that is so typical of second-rate politicians like him, always patting people on the back and putting their arms around others' shoulders. He put his arms around my shoulders enough times. You know that. He meant no harm. As far as I know he has never meant any harm to anyone. He has never needed to.

I slap him awake. When he sees me he tries to talk but only manages to slobber. His lips are numb from the chloroform. With his teary eyes and drooping lips there is something simian in his face that I have never seen there before. I take a couple of photos, closeups, just for myself.

Then I sit him up on the chair, put the white screen behind him so that the wall won't show up in the picture, and prop the newspaper against his chest. I take several shots, although all that matters is that he is recognizable and the newspaper headline legible, to establish the date. I know that this kind of thing is done this way. I follow the rules.

And also I have to admit that I like the idea that you will see him for the last time like this, in the photos, dirty and stupefied. He can almost speak now. He stammers. He begs me to tell him what's going on, to untie him. He's so simpleminded he still hasn't grasped what should really be obvious, that if I have let him see me it's because I am going to kill him.

It's a shame I'll never be able to tell you how stupid he looks now, drooling from the corners of his mouth, how stupid he really is, and always has been.

Perhaps some day when we are old, after many years together, I'll tell you about it, and we'll both have a good laugh.

No. I know I will never tell you about it. But it's nice to imagine, even if only for a moment.

He is beginning to understand, I think, however slowly. I can wait. It would be too cruel to let him die without understanding the reason. I have waited for you—how many years now? Fifteen? Twenty? I can wait a few minutes more.

People will be surprised that they have kidnapped, and then killed, a politician as insignificant as he is. But terrorism, as everyone knows, is irrational.

ACCOMMODATION VACANT

By CELIA FREMLIN

"I'm sorry . . ." The woman's eyes slithered expertly down Linda's loose, figure-concealing coat, and her voice hardened. "No, I'm sorry, the room's been taken. . . . No, I've nothing left at all, I'm afraid. . . . Good afternoon. . . ."

Familiar enough words, by now. Goodness knows we ought to be used to it, thought Linda bitterly, as she and David trailed together down the grimy steps. She dared not even look up at him for comfort, lest he should see the tears stinging and glittering in her eyes.

But he had seen them anyway. His arm came round her thin shoulders, and for a moment they leaned together, speechless, in the grey, mean street, engulfed by a disappointment so intense, so totally shared, that one day, when they were old, old people, they might remember it as an extraordinary joy. . . .

"Lin—Lin, darling, don't cry! It'll be all right, I swear it will be all right! I promise you it will, Lin . . . !"

The despairing note in his young voice, the pressure of his arms round her, destroyed the last remnants of Linda's self-control. Burying her face against the worn leather of his jacket, she sobbed, helplessly and hopelessly.

"It's my fault, David, it's all my fault!" she gulped, her voice muffled amid the luxuriance of his dark, shoulder-length hair. "It was my fault, it was me who talked you into it. You said all along we shouldn't start a baby yet, not until you've got a proper job. . . ."

At this, David jerked her sharply round to face him.

"Lin!" he said, "never, never say that again! I want this baby as much as you do, and if I ever said different, then forget it! He's *our* baby, yours and mine! I'm his father, and I want him! Get it? I *want* him! And I'm going to provide a home for him! A smashing home, too," he pro-

221

claimed defiantly into the dingy, uncaring street. "—A home fit for my son! Fit for my wife and son . . . !" His voice trailed off as he glared through the gathering November dusk at the closed doors, the tightly curtained windows, rank on rank, as far as they could see. "My God, if I could only get a decent job!" he muttered; and grabbing Linda's hand in a harsh, almost savage grip, he hurried her away—back to the main road, back to the lighted buses, back "home."

That's what they still called it anyway, though they both knew it wasn't home anymore. How could it be, when they had to steal in through the front door like burglars, closing it in a whisper behind them, going up the creaking stairs on tiptoe in the vain hope of avoiding Mrs. Moles, the landlady, with her guarded eyes and her twice-daily inquisitions: "Found anywhere yet? Oh. Oh, I see. Yes, well, I'm sorry, but I'm afraid I can't give you any more extension. Six months you've had (to the day, actually; Linda remembered in every detail that May morning when she had come back from the doctor's bubbling over with her glorious news, spilling it out, in reckless triumph, to everyone in the house). Six months, and I could have got you out in a week if I'd been minded! A week's notice, that's all I'd have to've given, it's not like you're on a regular tenancy! Six months I've given you, it's not everyone'd be that patient, I can tell you! But I've had enough! I'm giving you till Monday, understand? Not a day longer! I need that room. . . ."

Sometimes, during these tirades, David would answer back. Standing in front of Linda on the dark stairs, protecting her with his broad shoulders and his mass of tangled, caveman hair, he would storm at Mrs. Moles face-to-face, giving as good as he got; and Linda never told him that it only made matters worse for her afterwards. His male pride needed these shows of strength, she knew, especially now, when his temporary job at the Rating Office had come to an end, and the only money he could count on was from his part-time job at the cafeteria—three or four afternoons at most.

If only he had finished his course and got his engineer-

ing degree instead of dropping out half way!—Linda silenced the little stir of resentment, because what was the
use? No good needling him *now* about his irresponsible
past. Poor Dave, responsibility had caught up with him
now, all right, and he was doing his best—his unpractised
best—to shoulder it. Doing it for *her*. For her, and for the
baby . . . recriminations don't help a man who is already
stretched to his limit. Besides, she loved him.

Monday, though! Mrs. Moles really meant it this time!
Monday—only four days away! That night, Linda cried
herself to sleep, with David's arms around her and his
voice, still shakily confident, whispering into her ear:
"Don't you worry, Lin! It'll be all right. I promise you it'll
be all right. . . ."

It wouldn't, though. How could it? They had been
searching for months now, in all their free time and at
weekends, lowering their standards week by week as the
hopelessness of the search was gradually borne in on
them. From a three-room flat to a two-room one . . . from
one room with use of kitchen to anything, anything at all.
. . . If all these weeks of unflagging effort had produced
nothing, then what could possibly be hoped from four
more days . . . ?

The next morning, for the first time since their search
began, David set off for the estate agent's alone. After her
near-sleepless night, Linda had woken feeling so sick, and
looking so white and fragile, that David had insisted on
her staying in bed—just as, a couple of weeks earlier, he
had insisted on her giving up her job. Before he left, he
brought her a cup of tea and kissed her goodbye.

"Don't worry, love, I'll come up with something *this*
time, just you see!" And Linda, white and weak against
the pillows, smiled and tried to look as if she didn't know
that he was lying.

After he had gone, she must have dozed off, for the next
thing she knew, it was past eleven o'clock, pale November
sunshine was glittering on the wet windows, and the telephone down in the hall was ringing . . . ringing . . .
ringing . . .

No one seemed to be answering. They must all be out.

With a curious sense of foreboding (curious, because what bad news could there possibly be for a couple as near rock-bottom as herself and David?), Linda scrambled into dressing gown and slippers and hurried down the three flights of stairs.

"Darling! I thought you were never coming. . . ." It was Dave's voice all right, but for a moment she hadn't recognised it, so long was it since it had sounded buoyant and carefree like that— "Darling, listen! Just *listen*—you'll never believe it. . . ."

And she didn't. Not at first, anyway; it was just too fantastic; a stroke of luck beyond their wildest dreams! In those first moments, with the telephone pressed to her unbelieving ear, she couldn't seem even to take it in.

What had happened, she at last gathered, was this: David had been coming gloomily out of the estate agent's with the familiar "Nothing today, I'm afraid" still ringing in his ears, when a young man, red-haired and strikingly tall, had stepped across the pavement and accosted him.

"Looking for somewhere to live, buddy?" he'd asked; and before David had got over his surprise, the stranger was well and thoroughly launched on his amazing, incredible proposition.

A three-room flat, self-contained, with a balcony, and big windows facing south—all for five pounds a week!

"And he'd like us to move in *today!*" David gabbled joyously on, "Just think of it, Lin! *Today!* Not even one more night in that dump! No more grovelling to the old Mole! God, am I looking forward to telling her what she can do with that miserable garret. . . ."

"But . . . but, darling . . . !" Linda could not help breaking in at this point. "Darling, it sounds fantastic, of course it does! But . . . but, Dave, are you sure it's *all right?* I mean, why should this—whoever he is—why should he be letting the flat at such a ridiculously low rent? And—"

"Just what *I* wanted to know!" David's voice came clear and exultant down the line. "But it's quite simple really— he explained everything! You see, he's just broken up with his girl, she's gone off with another man, and he just can't

stand staying on in the place without her. He's not thinking about the money, he just wants OUT—and you can
understand it, can't you? I mean, he was nuts about this
girl, they'd been together for over a year, and he thought
she was just as happy as he was. The shock was just more
than he could take. . . ."

"Yes . . . Yes, of course . . ." Linda's excitement was
laced with unease. "But—David—I still don't quite understand. Why *us?* Why isn't he putting it in the hands of the
agents . . . ?"

"Darling!"—there was just the tiniest edge of impatience in David's voice now—"Darling, don't be like that!
Don't spoil it all! Anyway, it's all quite understandable,
really. Just think for a minute. A chap in that sort of
emotional crisis—the bottom just knocked out of his life—
the last thing he needs is a lot of malarky about leases
and tenancy agreements and date of transfer and all the
rest of it. So he decided to bypass the whole estate agent
racket and simply—"

"So what was he doing, then, just outside an estate
agent's?"

The words had snapped out before Linda could check
them. She hated her own wariness, her inability to throw
herself with total abandon into David's mood of unques-
tioning exultation.

But this time David seemed to enjoy her hesitation: it
was as if she had played, unwittingly, the very card that
enabled him to lay down his ace.

"Aha!" he said—and already she could hear the smile in
his voice—the bold, cheeky, self-congratulatory smile with
which he used to relate the more outrageous exploits of
that bunch of tearaways he used to go around with—"*Aha,
that was cleverness! Real cleverness. Just the sort of
thing that I might have thought of.*" How wonderful it was
to hear his cocky, male arrogance coming alive again after
all these months of humiliation and defeat!—"He did just
the thing that *I* always do in a tricky situation—he asked
himself the right questions! Like, what's the quickest way
to clinch a deal—any deal? Why, find a chap who's desperate for what you've got to offer. And when the thing on

offer is a roof over the head—then where do such desperate chaps come thickest on the ground? Why, outside an
estate agent's, just after opening time! So that's what he
did—just hung about waiting for someone to come out the
door looking really sick. . . ."

It made sense. Sense of a sort, anyway. Linda felt her
doubts begin to melt. Joy hovered like a bright bird, ready
to swoop in.

"It—Oh, darling! It seems just too good to be true!" she
cried. "Oh, Dave, I'm so happy! And this young man—once
we're settled, and you've got another job, we must insist
on him taking more than five pounds—we mustn't take
advantage of his misery! Not when *we're* so happy . . . so
lucky . . . ! Oh, but we don't even know his name . . . !"

"We do! It's Fanshawe!" David countered exultantly.
"It's on the name-slip outside the door—R. Fanshawe. But
I've changed it, darling, I'm right here, and I've changed it
already! It says 'Graves' now! 'David and Linda Graves'!
Oh, Lin, darling, how soon can you get here . . . ?"

It was bigger even than she'd imagined, and much more
beautiful. It was on the fifth floor of a large modern block,
and even now, in winter, the big rooms were filled with
light. The sunshine hit you like a breaking wave as you
walked in, and through the wide windows, far away above
the roofs and spires of the city, you could see a blue line of
hills.

Linda and David could hardly speak for excitement.
They wandered from room to room as if in a trance, ex-
ploring, exclaiming, making rapturous little sounds that
were hardly like words at all; more like the twittering of
birds in springtime, the joyous nesting time.

Deep, roomy shelves. Built-in cupboards and ward-
robes. Bright, modern furniture—and not too much of it;
there would be plenty of room for their own few favourite
pieces.

"Your desk—it can go just here, Dave, under the window. It'll get all the light!" exclaimed Linda: and, "See,
Lin, this alcove—I can build his cot to exactly fit in! This
will be *his* room . . . !" and so on and so on, until at last,
exhausted with happiness, one of them—afterwards,

Linda could never remember which, and of course, at the time, it did not seem important—one of them suddenly noticed the time.

"Gosh, look, it's nearly two!" exclaimed whichever one it was; and there followed quite a little panic. For by two-thirty David was supposed to be at the cafeteria, slicing hard-boiled eggs, washing lettuces, sweeping up the mess left by the lunchtime customers. . . . It would never do for him to lose this job, too. Hand in hand they raced out of the flat . . . raced for the bus . . . and managed to reach home in time to get David out of his leather jacket and into a freshly ironed overall just in time to be not much more than ten minutes late for work. Kissing him goodbye, Linda was careful not to muss up his hastily smoothed hair—the curling, shoulder-length mane was a bone of contention at the cafeteria—as, indeed, it had been at all his other jobs—but *she* loved it.

At the door, he paused to urge her to rest while he was gone; to lie down and take things easy.

"You weren't too good this morning," he reminded her, "so whatever you do, don't start trying to do any packing —we'll do it this evening, together. Oh, darling, just imagine Mrs. M's face when she sees us bumping our suitcases down the stairs this very night! Monday, indeed! *I'll* give her Monday . . . !"

Obediently, after he'd gone, Linda pulled off her dress and shoes and climbed into bed. It was quite true, she *was* tired. For a few minutes she lay staring up at the ceiling, trying to realise that she was looking at those familiar cracks and stains for the very last time. She couldn't believe it, really; the change in their fortunes had been so swift, so dreamlike somehow, that she hadn't really taken it in.

"Rest," David had urged her, but it was impossible. Excitement was drumming in her veins; it was impossible to be still, with all this happiness surging about inside her. She must *do* something. Not the packing—she'd promised to wait for David before starting on that—but there'd be no harm in getting things sorted out a bit . . . get rid of some of the rubbish. Those torn-off pages of Accommodation to Let, for a start: they'd never need *those* again . . . !

Clumsily—for she was nearly eight months gone now— she heaved herself off the bed, and as she did so, David's leather jacket, hastily flung aside when he'd changed for work, cascaded off the bed onto the floor, with a little tinkling, metallic scutter of sound.

The keys, of course. The keys of the new flat: and as she picked them off the floor, Linda was filled with a surge of impatience to see again her beautiful new home—"home" already, as this place had never been. She ached to look once more out of the wide, beautiful windows, to gloat over the space, the light, and the precious feeling that it was *hers!* Hers and David's, and the new baby's as well! She wanted to examine, at leisure and in detail, every drawer and cupboard; to make plans about where the polished wooden salad bowl was to go, and the Israeli dancing girl . . . and the books . . . and the records . . .

Well, and why not? The whole afternoon stretched ahead of her—David wouldn't be home till nine at the earliest. What was she waiting for?

The flat did not seem, this time, quite the palace of light and space that it had seemed that morning, but it was still very wonderful. The rooms were dimmer now, and greyer, because, naturally, the sun had moved round since this morning, and left them in shadow.

But Linda did not mind. It was still marvellous. Humming to herself softly, she wandered, lapped in happiness, from room to room, peering into cupboards, scrutinizing shelves and alcoves, planning happily where everything was to go.

What space! What lovely, lovely space! Opening yet another set of empty, inviting drawers, it occurred to Linda that, for a man with a broken heart, their predecessor had left things quite extraordinarily clean and tidy. In the turmoil of shock and grief, how on earth had he forced himself to clean up so thoroughly—even to Hoover the carpets, and dust out the empty drawers? Or maybe the defecting girlfriend had done it for him? A sort of guilt-offering to assuage her conscience . . . ?

Musing thus, Linda came upon a cupboard she had not noticed before—it was half-hidden by a big, well-cushioned armchair pulled in front of it. It looked as if it might be big enough to store all the things for the new baby. . . . Linda took hold of the handle and pulled—and straightaway she knew that it was locked. This, then, must be where the ultra-tidy Mr. Fanshawe had stored away his things? Spurred by curiosity, Linda tried first one and then another of the keys on the bunch David had been given—and at the third attempt, the door gave under her hand. Gave too readily, somehow. It was as if it was being pushed from inside . . . a great weight seemed to be on the move . . . and just as the fear reached her stomach, making it lurch within her, the door swung fully open, and the body of a girl slumped out onto the floor. A blonde girl; probably pretty, but there was no knowing now, so pinched and sunken were the features, already mottled with death.

Linda stood absolutely still. Horror, yes. In her recollections afterwards, and in her dreams, horror was the emotion she remembered most clearly. And what could be more natural?

But not at the time. At the time, in those very first seconds, before she had had time to think at all, it was not horror that had overwhelmed her at all, it was fury. Sickening, stupefying fury and disappointment.

"Damn you, damn you, damn you!" she sobbed, crazily, at the silent figure on the floor. "I *knew* it was too good to be true! I *knew* there would be a snag . . . !" And it was the sound of her own voice, raised in such blind, self-centered misery, that brought her partially to her senses.

She must *do* something. Phone somebody. Scream "Murder!" out of the window. Get help.

Help with what? How can you help a girl who is already dead . . . ? With the strange, steely calm that comes with shock, Linda dropped to her knees and peered closely at the slumped, deathly figure. No breath stirred between the bluish lips; no pulse could be felt in the limp, icy wrist.

The girl lay there lifeless as a bundle of old clothes, ruining everything.

Because, of course, the flat was lost to them now. Had, in fact, never been theirs to lose. The whole thing had been a trick, right from the beginning. What they had walked into, so foolishly and trustingly, was not a flat at all, but a dreadful crime. Presently, the police would be here, cordoning everything off, hunting down the real owner of the flat, bringing him back for questioning. They would be questioning herself and David, too. . . . That, of course, had been the whole point of the trick! Linda could see it all now. They had been lured here deliberately by the phoney offer of a home, in order that they should leave their fingerprints all over the place and be found here when the police arrived. A pair of trespassers, roaming without permission or explanation around someone else's flat! Because that's how it would look: why should the police—or indeed any other sane person—believe such a cock-and-bull story as she and David would have to tell? A ridiculous, incredible tale about having been offered, by a total stranger, an attractive three-room flat in a pleasant neighbourhood for only five pounds a week. All that this Fanshawe man had to do now was to deny totally the encounter with David outside the estate agent's, and it would be his word against David's—with, to him, the overwhelming advantage that his denials would sound immeasurably more plausible than David's grotesque assertions!

Neat, really. *"Aha,* that was cleverness!" as David had so lightheartedly remarked, only a few hours ago!

At the thought of all that happiness—of David's pride, his triumph, all to be so short-lived—a cold fury of determination seized upon Linda's still-shocked brain, and she knew, suddenly, exactly what she must do.

The dead cannot suffer. They are beyond human aid, and beyond human injury, too; so it wasn't really so terrible, what she was going to do.

Cautiously, and without even any great distaste, so numbed was she with shock, Linda got hold of the limp figure by the thick poloneck of its woollen sweater and began to pull.

Luckily, at this dead hour of the afternoon, the long corridors were empty as a dream. The lift glided obediently, silently downwards with its terrible burden . . . down, down, past the entrance floor, past even the basement . . . down, down to the lowest depths of all . . . and there, in an icy, windowless cellar, stacked with old mattresses and shadowy lengths of piping, Linda left her terrible charge.

It would be found—of course it would be found—but now there would at least be a sporting chance that the clues—now so thoroughly scrambled—would no longer lead so inexorably to the fifth-floor flat into which the new tenants had just moved. It would be just one more of those unsolved murders. There were dozens of them every year, weren't there?

It would be all right. It *must* be all right. It must, it must . . .

All the same, Linda couldn't get out of the beautiful flat fast enough that afternoon. While the grey November day faded—she dared not switch on any lights for fear of advertising her presence here—she pushed the big chair back in front of the cupboard again, and set the room to rights. Then, still trembling, and feeling deathly sick, she set off for home. It was only five o'clock: four whole hours in which to recover her composure before David got back from work.

And recover it she must. At any cost, David must be protected from all knowledge of this new and terrible turn of events. She recalled his triumphant happiness this morning, the resurgence of his masculine pride. . . . She pictured how he would come bounding up the stairs this evening, three at a time, carrying a bottle of wine, probably, to celebrate. . . .

And celebrate they would, if it killed her! Not one word would she breathe of her fearful secret—not one flicker of anxiety would she allow to cross her face.

Celebrate! Celebrate! Candles; steak and mushrooms, even if it cost all the week's housekeeping! She would wash and set her hair, too, as soon as she got in, and change into the peacock-blue maternity smock with the Chinese-y neckline. . . . She thought of everything, hurrying home through the November dusk that evening, except the possibility that David would be in before her. . . .

She stood in the doorway clutching her parcels, speechless with surprise, and staring at him.

"Where the hell have you been?"

Never had she heard his voice sound so angry. How long had he been here? Why had he come back so early . . . ?

"I said you were to *rest!*" he was shouting at her. "You promised me you'd stay here and rest! Where have you *been?* I've been out of my mind with worry! And where are the keys? The keys of the flat? They were here . . . in my pocket . . . !"

He was sorry, though, a minute later; when she'd handed over the keys, and had explained to him about her excitement, about the sudden, irresistible impulse to go and look at the beautiful new flat once more. He seemed to understand.

"I'm sorry, darling, I've been a brute!" he apologized. "But you see it was so scary, somehow, coming in and finding the place all dark and empty! I was afraid something had happened. I thought, maybe, the baby . . ."

The reconciliation was sweet: and if he questioned her a little over-minutely about her exact movements that afternoon, and exactly how she had found things in the flat —well, what could be more natural in a man thrilled to bits about his new home, into which he is going to move that very night?

And move that very night they did.

No more Mrs. Moles! No more tiptoeing guiltily up and down dark stairs! Everywhere, light and space and privacy! And on top of this, a brand-new, modern kitchen, and a little sunny room exactly right for the baby—only a month away he was, now! For a day or so, Linda had feared that the birth might be coming on prematurely; she had been having odd, occasional pains since dragging that awful weight hither and thither along cement floors, through shadowy doorways. But after a few days it all seemed to settle down again—as also, amazingly, did her mind and spirits.

At first, she had been full of guilt and dread: it was all she could do not to let David notice how she started at every footfall in the corridor . . . every soft moan from the lift doors as they closed and opened. Sometimes, too, she was aware—or imagined she was aware—of David's eyes on her, speculative, unsmiling. At such times she would hastily find occasion to laugh shrilly . . . clatter saucepans . . . talk about the baby . . . Anything.

But presently, as the days went by, and nothing happened, her nerves began to quieten. Indeed, there were times when she almost wondered whether she hadn't imagined the whole thing. Because there was nothing in the papers, nothing on the radio—though she'd listened, during those first few days, like a maniac, like a creature obsessed, switching on every hour on the hour.

Nothing. Nothing at all. Had the body, conceivably, not been found yet? Surely it was *someone's* business—caretaker, nightwatchman, or someone—to go into that cellar now and again. Or—was it possible that the murderer himself had discovered where it had been moved to—had, perhaps, even watched her moving it, from some hidden vantage point . . . ? The lift, the corridors had all *seemed* to be totally deserted, but you never knew. . . .

To begin with, weighed down as she was by guilt and dread, Linda had tried as far as possible to avoid contact with the neighbours; but inevitably, as the days went by, she found herself becoming on speaking terms with first one and then another of them. The woman next door . . . the old man at the end of the corridor . . . the girl who always seemed to be watering the rubber plant on the second-floor landing. Bits of gossip came to her ears, of tenants past and present, including, of course, snippets of information about hers and David's predecessor in the flat. . . . And slowly, inexorably, it was borne in on her that practically none of it fitted with David's story in the very least degree. The previous tenant had been neither red-haired nor tall—hadn't, in fact, been a man at all, but a woman. A young, blond woman, Linda learned, who had rather kept herself to herself. . . . Oh, there's been goings-on, yes, but there, you have to live and let live, don't you? Quite a surprise, actually, when the young woman gave up the flat so suddenly, no one had heard a thing about it, but there you are, the young folk are very unpredictable these days. . . .

And it was now, for the very first time, that it dawned on Linda that she only had David's word for it that the bizarre and improbable encounter with "Mr. Fanshawe" had ever taken place at all. Or, indeed, that any "Mr. Fanshawe" had ever existed!

This terrible, traitorous thought slipped into her mind one early December evening as she sat sewing for her baby. And having slipped in, it seemed, instantly, to make itself horribly at home . . . as if, deep down in her brain, there had been a niche ready-prepared for it all along.

Because everything now slid hideously, inexorably into place: David's disproportionate anger when he found she had visited the flat by herself that first afternoon: his unexplained, mysteriously early return from work on that same occasion. Perhaps, instead of going to the cafeteria, he had slipped off that working overall the moment he was out of sight and gone rushing off to devise some means of disposing of the body: his preparations completed, he would have arrived at the flat, scared and breathless—to find that the body had already disappeared! What then? Bewildered and panic-stricken, he would have hurried home—only to find that she, Linda, had been to the flat ahead of him! Had he guessed that she must have found the body? And if so, what had he made of her silence all these days? What did he think she was thinking as she sat there, demure and smiling, evening after evening, sewing for the baby? No wonder he had been giving her dark, wary glances! What sort of a look would it be that he'd be giving her tonight, when he came in and saw the new, terrible fear in her eyes, the suspicion flickering in her face and in her voice?

Suspicion? No! No! She *didn't* suspect him—how could she? Not *David!* Not her own husband, the man she loved!

How *could* she, even for an instant, have imagined that he might be capable of . . . !

Well, and what *is* a man capable of? A proud, headstrong young man who not so long ago was the daredevil leader of the most venturesome teenage gang in his neighbourhood? To what sort of lengths *could* such a young man go, under the intolerable lash of humiliation? He, who had set out in proud and youthful arrogance to conquer the world, and now finds he cannot even provide any sort of home for his wife and child? Such a young man—*could* he, in such extremities of shattered pride and of self-respect destroyed—*could* he simply walk into a strange flat, murder the occupant, and coolly take possession . . . ?

And even if he couldn't—couldn't, and hadn't, and never would—what then? What about *her?* How could she, having once let the awful suspicion cross her mind, ever face him again? How was she to behave . . . look . . . when he came in from work tonight? What sort of supper should one cook for a suspected murderer . . . ?

And as she sat there, crouched in the beautiful flat, while outside the evening darkened into night, she heard the soft whine of the lift—the opening and closing of its doors.

And next—although it was only a little after five, and David shouldn't be home till nine—next there came, unmistakably, the sound of the key in the door.

Afterwards, Linda could never remember what exactly had been the sequence of her thoughts. *Why?* had been one of them, certainly—*Why* is he arriving home so early? —and then, swift upon the heels of this, had come the blind, unreasoning panic. . . . What is he *doing* out there? Why doesn't he come right in . . . shut the front door behind him? Why isn't he calling, "Lin, darling, I'm back," the way he always does? Why is he being so quiet, so furtive . . . ? Lurking out there . . . standing stock still, to judge by the silence . . .

But after that, in Linda's jumbled memory, all was confusion. Had she recognised the blonde girl at once—so different as she now looked—or had there been several minutes of stunned incomprehension as they gaped at one another in the little hall, all at cross-purposes in their questions and ejaculations?

Because, of course, this was the rightful tenant of the flat, Rosemary Fanshawe by name; as astounded (on her return from a stay in hospital and a fortnight's convalescence) to find a strange girl in possession of her flat as Linda was at this sudden invasion by a stranger. Linda could never remember, afterwards, who it was who finally made coffee for whom, or in what order each had explained herself to the other; but in the end—and certainly by the time David got back at nine o'clock—all had been made clear, and a sort of bewildered friendship was already in the making.

For this bright, well-groomed girl was indeed the same that Linda had found and taken for dead; and there had indeed been a terrible lovers' quarrel, just as the red-haired young man outside the estate agent's had affirmed. What he had told David hadn't been a lie, exactly; rather a sort of mirror image of the truth, with all the facts in reverse. Thus it had been he, not Rosemary, who had ended the relationship: it had been her heart, not his, that was broken. It was she, not he, who had declared that she couldn't bear to stay in the flat for so much as another day. Hysterically, she had flung her things into cases . . . ordered a car to take them to a friend's house . . . and then, in less than an hour, had returned, half-crazy with grief and fury, to storm at him for not having tried to prevent her going. There had been a final, terrible quarrel, at the climax of which Rosemary had threatened dramatically to take a whole bottle of sleeping pills. Enraged by this bit of melodramatic blackmail (as he judged it), the red-haired boyfriend—Martin by name—had slammed out of the flat; but later, growing scared, he had crept back, and found to his horror that she really *had* taken the pills, and was lying—dead, as he thought—on the floor. (Actually, as they'd explained to Rosemary in the hospital, she'd only been in a deep coma, but a layman could not be expected to realise this, as both breath and pulse would be too faint to be discerned.) Appalled—and terrified at the thought that he might be blamed—Martin had bundled the "body" out of sight in the nearest cupboard, and set himself frantically to cleaning up the flat and removing all traces of their joint lives. All night it had taken him; and while he packed and scrubbed, his brain had been afire with desperate schemes for shuffling off the responsibility—preferably onto some anonymous outsider —while he, Martin, got clean away. By the time morning came, and his task was finished, his plans were also ready; he washed, shaved, and off he went to the estate agent . . .

And in fact, it all worked out much as he had hoped— with the fortunate addition that, as it turned out, it was probably Linda's action in dragging the "body" down to the basement that had saved Rosemary's life—the jolting, the knocking-about, and the icy chill of the cellar had prevented the coma becoming so deep as to be irreversible. That same night, she had recovered consciousness sufficiently to stagger out into the deserted street and wander some way before being picked up and taken to hospital.

And David, when he came home and heard the whole story? He was unsurprised. David was no fool, and he had realised right from the start (despite his show of bravado) that there was something very phoney indeed about that offer outside the estate agent's, but had decided (being the kind of young man he was) to gamble on the chance of being able to cope with the tricksters, whatever it was they were up to, when the time came. However, with his mind full of the possible hazards of the venture, he had naturally been thrown into a complete panic by the discovery that Linda had gone off alone that first afternoon into what might well prove to be a trap of some kind; and even after his immediate fears had been set at rest, he had not failed to notice, in the succeeding days, that Linda was oppressed and ill-at-ease. He knew nothing, of course, about the "body," but he could see very well that there was something. . . .

Now, he shrugged. He'd gambled and lost before in his short life.

"Oh, well. It's back on the road for us, then, Linda my pet," he said, reaching out his hand towards her . . . but at that same moment Rosemary gave a squeal as if she'd been trodden on.

"Oh *no!* Not *yet!* Oh, *please!*" she cried. "I can't possibly stay on in the flat by myself, I *must* have someone to share, now that . . ."

Of course, it wasn't quite the same as having the place to themselves; but it was much, much better than living at Mrs. Moles's. And for Rosemary, likewise, it wasn't quite the same as having Martin there; but it was much, much better than having to pay the whole of the rent herself. She found, too, that she enjoyed the company; and when, soon after his son was born, David resumed his engineering studies and began bringing friends home from college, she found she enjoyed it even more.

"Wasn't it lucky that I took those pills just when I did?" she mused dreamily one evening, after the reluctant departure of one of the handsomer of the embryo engineers; and Linda, settling her baby back in his cot, had to agree that it was.

Indeed, when you thought of all the ways the thing *might* have ended, "lucky" seemed something of an understatement.

LIAR'S DICE

By BILL PRONZINI

"Excuse me. Do you play liar's dice?"

I looked over at the man two stools to my right. He was about my age, early forties; average height, average weight, brown hair, medium complexion—really a pretty nondescript sort except for a pleasant and disarming smile. Expensively dressed in an Armani suit and a silk jacquard tie. Drinking white wine. I had never seen him before. Or had I? There was something familiar about him, as if our paths *had* crossed somewhere or other, once or twice.

Not here in Tony's, though. Tony's is a suburban-mall bar that caters to the shopping trade from the big department and grocery stores surrounding it. I stopped in no more than a couple of times a month, usually when Connie asked me to pick up something at Safeway on my way home from San Francisco, occasionally when I had a Saturday errand to run. I knew the few regulars by sight, and it was never very crowded anyway. There were only four patrons at the moment: the nondescript gent and myself on stools, and a young couple in a booth at the rear.

"I do play, as a matter of fact," I said to the fellow. Fairly well too, though I wasn't about to admit that. Liar's dice and I were old acquaintances.

"Would you care to shake for a drink?"

"Well, my usual limit is one . . ."

"For a chit for your next visit, then."

"All right, why not? I feel lucky tonight."

"Do you? Good. I should warn you, I'm very good at the game."

"I'm not so bad myself."

"No, I mean I'm *very* good. I seldom lose."

It was the kind of remark that would have nettled me if it had been said with even a modicum of conceit. But he wasn't bragging; he was merely stating a fact, mentioning a special skill of which he felt justifiably proud. So instead of annoying me, his comment made me eager to test him.

We introduced ourselves; his name was Jones. Then I called to Tony for the dice cups. He brought them down, winked at me, said, "No gambling now," and went back to the other end of the bar. Strictly speaking, shaking dice for drinks and/or money is illegal in California. But nobody pays much attention to nuisance laws like that, and most bar owners keep dice cups on hand for their customers. The game stimulates business. I know because I've been involved in some spirited liar's dice tournaments in my time.

Like all good games, liar's dice is fairly simple—at least in its rules. Each player has a cup containing five dice, which he shakes out but keeps covered so only he can see what is showing face up. Then each makes a declaration or "call" in turn: one of a kind, two of a kind, three of a kind, and so on. Each call has to be higher than the previous one, and is based on what the player *knows* is in his hand and what he *thinks* is in the other fellow's—the combined total of the ten dice. He can lie or tell the truth, whichever suits him; but the better liar he is, the better his chances of winning. When one player decides the other is either lying or has simply exceeded the laws of probability, he says, "Come up," and then both reveal their hands. If he's right, he wins.

In addition to being a clever liar, you also need a good grasp of mathematical odds and the ability to "read" your opponent's facial expressions, the inflection in his voice, his body language. The same skills an experienced poker player has to have, which is one reason the game is also called liar's poker.

Jones and I each rolled one die to determine who would go first; mine was the highest. Then we shook all five dice in our cups, banged them down on the bar. What I had showing was four treys and a deuce.

"Your call, Mr. Quint."

"One five," I said.

"One six."

"Two deuces."

"Two fives."

"Three treys."

"Three sixes."

I considered calling him up, since I had no sixes and he would need three showing to win. But I didn't know his methods and I couldn't read him at all. I decided to keep playing.

"Four treys."

"Five treys."

"Six treys."

Jones smiled and said, "Come up." And he had just one trey (and no sixes). I'd called six treys and there were only five in our combined hands; he was the winner.

"So much for feeling lucky," I said, and signaled Tony to bring another white wine for Mr. Jones. On impulse I decided a second Manhattan wouldn't hurt me and ordered that too.

Jones said, "Shall we play again?"

"Two drinks is definitely my limit."

"For dimes, then? Nickels or pennies, if you prefer."

"Oh, I don't know . . ."

"You're a good player, Mr. Quint, and I don't often find someone who can challenge me. Besides, I have a passion as well as an affinity for liar's dice. Won't you indulge me?"

I didn't see any harm in it. If he'd wanted to play for larger stakes, even a dollar a hand, I might have taken him for a hustler despite his Armani suit and silk tie. But how much could you win or lose playing for a nickel or a dime a hand? So I said, "Your call first this time," and picked up my dice cup.

We played for better than half an hour. And Jones wasn't just good; he was uncanny. Out of nearly twenty-five hands, I won two—*two*. You could chalk up some of the disparity to luck, but not enough to change the fact that his skill was remarkable. Certainly he was the best I'd ever locked horns with. I would have backed him in a tournament anywhere, anytime.

He was a good winner, too: no gloating or chiding. And a good listener, the sort who seems genuinely (if superficially) interested in other people. I'm not often gregarious, especially with strangers, but I found myself opening up to Jones—and this in spite of him beating the pants off me the whole time.

I told him about Connie, how we met and the second honeymoon trip we'd taken to Lake Louise three years ago and what we were planning for our twentieth wedding anniversary in August. I told him about Lisa, who was eighteen and a freshman studying film at UCLA. I told him about Kevin, sixteen now and captain of his high-school baseball team, and the five-hit, two home run game he'd had last week. I told him what it was like working as a design engineer for one of the largest engineering firms in the country, the nagging dissatisfaction and the desire to be my own boss someday, when I had enough money saved so I could afford to take the risk. I told him about remodeling our home, the boat I was thinking of buying, the fact that I'd always wanted to try hang-gliding but never had the courage.

Lord knows what else I might have told him if I hadn't noticed the polite but faintly bored expression on his face, as if I were imparting facts he already knew. It made me realize just how much I'd been nattering on, and embarrassed me a bit. I've never liked people who talk incessantly about themselves, as though they're the focal point of the entire universe. I can be a good listener myself; and for all I knew, Jones was a lot more interesting than bland Jeff Quint.

I said, "Well, that's more than enough about me. It's your turn, Jones. Tell me about yourself."

"If you like, Mr. Quint." Still very formal. I'd told him a couple of times to call me Jeff but he wouldn't do it. Now that I thought about it, he hadn't mentioned his own first name.

"What is it you do?"

He laid his dice cup to one side. I was relieved to see that; I'd had enough of losing but I hadn't wanted to be the one to quit. And it was getting late—dark outside already—and Connie would be wondering where I was. A few minutes of listening to the story of his life, I thought, just to be polite, and then—

"To begin with," Jones was saying, "I travel."

"Sales job?"

"No. I travel because I enjoy traveling. And because I can afford it. I have independent means."

"Lucky you. In more ways than one."

"Yes."

"Europe, the South Pacific—all the exotic places?"

"Actually, no. I prefer the U.S."

"Any particular part?"

"Wherever my fancy leads me."

"Hard to imagine anyone's fancy leading him to Bayport," I said. "You have friends or relatives here?"

"No, I have business in Bayport."

"Business? I thought you said you didn't need to work. . . ."

"Independent means, Mr. Quint. That doesn't preclude a purpose, a direction in one's life."

"You do have a profession, then?"

"You might say that. A profession and a hobby combined."

"Lucky you," I said again. "What is it?"

"I kill people," he said.

I thought I'd misheard him. "You . . . what?"

"I kill people."

"Good God. Is that supposed to be a joke?"

"Not at all. I'm quite serious."

"What do you mean, you *kill* people?"

"Just what I said."

"Are you trying to tell me you're . . . some kind of paid assassin?"

"Not at all. I've never killed anyone for money."

"Then why . . . ?"

"Can't you guess?"

"No, I can't guess. I don't want to guess."

"Call it personal satisfaction," he said.

"What people? Who?"

"No one in particular," Jones said. "My selection process is completely random. I'm very good at it too. I've been killing people for . . . let's see, nine and a half years now. Eighteen victims in thirteen states. And, oh yes, Puerto Rico—one in Puerto Rico. I don't mind saying that I've never even come close to being caught."

I stared at him. My mouth was open; I knew it but I couldn't seem to unlock my jaw. I felt as if reality had suddenly slipped away from me, as if Tony had dropped some sort of mind-altering drug into my second Manhattan and it was just now taking effect. Jones and I were still sitting companionably, on adjacent stools now, he smiling and speaking in the same low, friendly voice. At the other end of the bar Tony was slicing lemons and limes into wedges. Three of the booths were occupied now, with people laughing and enjoying themselves. Everything was just as it had been two minutes ago, except that instead of me telling Jones about being a dissatisfied design engineer, he was calmly telling me he was a serial murderer.

I got my mouth shut finally, just long enough to swallow into a dry throat. Then I said, "You're crazy, Jones. You must be insane."

"Hardly, Mr. Quint. I'm as sane as you are."

"I don't believe you killed eighteen people."

"Nineteen," he said. "Soon to be twenty."

"Twenty? You mean . . . someone in Bayport?"

"Right here in Bayport."

"You expect me to believe you intend to pick somebody at random and just . . . murder him in cold blood?"

"Oh no, there's more to it than that. Much more."

"More?" I said blankly.

"I choose a person at random, yes, but carefully. Very carefully. I study my target, follow him as he goes about his daily business, learn everything I can about him down to the minutest detail. Then the cat and mouse begins. I don't murder him right away; that wouldn't give suffi- cient, ah, satisfaction. I wait . . . observe . . . plan. Per- haps, for added spice, I reveal myself to him. I might even be so bold as to tell him to his face that he's my next victim."

My scalp began to crawl.

"Days, weeks . . . then, when the victim least expects

it, a gunshot, a push out of nowhere in front of an oncoming car, a hypodermic filled with digitalin and jabbed into the body on a crowded street, simulating heart failure. There are many ways to kill a man. Did you ever stop to consider just how many different ways there are?"

"You . . . you're not saying—"

"What, Mr. Quint? That I've chosen *you?*"

"Jones, for God's sake!"

"But I have," he said. "You are to be number twenty."

One of my hands jerked upward, struck his arm. Involuntary spasm; I'm not a violent man. He didn't even flinch. I pulled my hand back, saw that it was shaking, and clutched the fingers tight around the beveled edge of the bar.

Jones took a sip of wine. Then he smiled—and winked at me.

"Or then again," he said, "I might be lying."

". . . What?"

"Everything I've just told you might be a lie. I might not have killed nineteen people over the past nine and a half years; I might not have killed anyone, ever."

"I don't . . . I don't know what you—"

"Or I might have told you part of the truth . . . that's another possibility, isn't it? Part fact, part fiction. But in that case, which is which? And to what degree? Am I a deadly threat to you, or am I nothing more than a man in a bar playing a game?"

"Game? What kind of sick—"

"The same one we've been playing all along. Liar's dice."

"Liar's dice?"

"My own special version," he said, "developed and refined through years of practice. The perfect form of the game, if I do say so myself—exciting, unpredictable, filled with intrigue and mortal danger for myself as well as my opponent."

I shook my head. My mind was a seething muddle; I couldn't seem to fully grasp what he was saying.

"I don't know any more than you do at this moment how you'll play your part of the hand, Mr. Quint. That's where the excitement and the danger lies. Will you treat what

I've said as you would a bluff? Can you afford to take that risk? Or will you act on the assumption that I've told the monstrous truth, or at least part of it?"

"Damn you . . ." Weak and ineffectual words, even in my own ears.

"And if you do believe me," he said, "what course of action will you take? Attack me before I can harm you, attempt to kill me . . . here and now in this public place, perhaps, in front of witnesses who will swear the attack was unprovoked? Try to follow me when I leave, attack me elsewhere? I might well be armed, and an excellent shot with a handgun. Go to the police . . . with a wild-sounding and unsubstantiated story that they surely wouldn't believe? Hire a detective to track me down? Attempt to track me down yourself? Jones isn't my real name, of course, and I've taken precautions against anyone finding out my true identity. Arm yourself and remain on guard until, if and when, I make a move against you? How long could you live under such intense pressure without making a fatal mistake?"

He paused dramatically. "Or—and this is the most exciting prospect of all, the one I hope you choose—will you mount a clever counterattack, composed of lies and deceptions of your own devising? Can you actually hope to beat me at my own game? Do you dare to try?"

He adjusted the knot in his tie with quick, deft movements, smiling at me in the back-bar mirror—not the same pleasant smile as before. This one had shark's teeth in it. "Whatever you do, I'll know about it soon afterward. I'll be waiting . . . watching . . . and I'll know. And then it will be my turn again."

He slid off his stool, stood poised behind me. I just sat there; it was as if I were paralyzed.

"Your call, Mr. Quint," he said. And he was gone into the night.

THE MOMENT OF DECISION

By STANLEY ELLIN

Hugh Lozier was the exception to the rule that people who are completely sure of themselves cannot be likable. We have all met the sure ones, of course—those controlled but penetrating voices which cut through all others in a discussion, those hard forefingers jabbing home opinions on your chest, those living Final Words on all issues —and I imagine we all share the same amalgam of dislike and envy for them. Dislike, because no one likes to be shouted down or prodded in the chest, and envy, because everyone wishes he himself were so rich in self-assurance that he could do the shouting down and the prodding.

For myself, since my work took me regularly to certain places in this atomic world where the only state was confusion and the only steady employment that of splitting political hairs, I found absolute judgments harder and harder to come by. Hugh once observed of this that it was a good thing my superiors in the Department were not cut of the same cloth, because God knows what would happen to the country then. I didn't relish that, but—and there was my curse again—I had to grant him his right to say it.

Despite this, and despite the fact that Hugh was my brother-in-law—a curious relationship when you come to think of it—I liked him immensely, just as everyone else did who knew him. He was a big good-looking man, with clear blue eyes in a ruddy face, and with a quick, outgoing nature eager to appreciate whatever you had to offer. He was overwhelmingly generous, and his generosity was of that rare and excellent kind which makes you feel as if you are doing the donor a favor by accepting it.

I wouldn't say he had any great sense of humor, but plain good humor can sometimes be an adequate substitute for that, and in Hugh's case it was. His stormy side was largely reserved for those times when he thought you might have needed his help in something and failed to call

247

on him for it. Which meant that ten minutes after Hugh had met you and liked you, you were expected to ask him for anything he might be able to offer. A month or so after he married my sister Elizabeth, she mentioned to him my avid interest in a fine Copley he had hanging in his gallery at Hilltop, and I can still vividly recall my horror when it suddenly arrived, heavily crated and with his gift card attached, at my barren room-and-a-half. It took considerable effort, but I finally managed to return it to him by foregoing the argument that the picture was undoubtedly worth more than the entire building in which I lived and by complaining that it simply didn't show to advantage on my wall. I think he suspected I was lying, but being Hugh he would never dream of charging me with that in so many words.

Of course, Hilltop and the two hundred years of Lozier tradition that went into it did much to shape Hugh this way. The first Loziers had carved the estate from the heights overlooking the river, had worked hard and flourished exceedingly; in successive generations had invested their income so wisely that money and position eventually erected a towering wall between Hilltop and the world outside. Truth to tell, Hugh was very much a man of the Eighteenth Century who somehow found himself in the Twentieth and simply made the best of it.

Hilltop itself was almost a replica of the celebrated but long untenanted Dane house nearby and was striking enough to open anybody's eyes at a glance. The house was weathered stone, graceful despite its bulk, and the vast lawns reaching to the river's edge were tended with such fanatic devotion over the years that they had become carpets of purest green which magically changed luster under any breeze. Gardens ranged from the other side of the house down to the groves which half hid the stables and outbuildings, and past the far side of the groves ran the narrow road which led to town. The road was a courtesy road, each estate holder along it maintaining his share, and I think it safe to say that for all the crushed rock he laid in it Hugh made less use of it by far than any of his neighbors.

Hugh's life was bound up in Hilltop; he could be made to leave it only by dire necessity; and if you did meet him away from it you were made acutely aware that he was counting off the minutes until he could return. And if you weren't wary, you would more than likely find yourself going along with him when he did return, and totally unable to tear yourself away from the place while the precious weeks rolled by. I know. I believe I spent more time at Hilltop than at my own apartment after my sister brought Hugh into the family.

At one time I wondered how Elizabeth took to this marriage, considering that before she met Hugh she had been as restless and flighty as she was pretty. When I put the question to her directly, she said, "It's wonderful, darling. Just as wonderful as I knew it would be when I first met him."

It turned out that their first meeting had taken place at an art exhibition, a showing of some ultramodern stuff, and she had been intently studying one of the more bewildering creations on display when she became aware of this tall, good-looking man staring at her. And, as she put it, she had been about to set him properly in his place when he said abruptly, "Are you admiring that?"

This was so unlike what she had expected that she was taken completely aback. "I don't know," she said weakly. "Am I supposed to?"

"No," said the stranger, "it's damned nonsense. Come along now and I'll show you something which isn't a waste of time."

"And," Elizabeth said to me, "I came along like a pup at his heels, while he marched up and down and told me what was good and what was bad, and in a good loud voice, too, so that we collected quite a crowd along the way. Can you picture it, darling?"

"Yes," I said, "I can." By now I had shared similar occasions with Hugh and learned at first hand that nothing could dent his cast-iron assurance.

"Well," Elizabeth went on, "I must admit that at first I was a little put off, but then I began to see that he knew exactly what he was talking about, and that he was terribly sincere. Not a bit self-conscious about anything, but just eager for me to understand things the way he did. It's the same way with everything. Everybody else in the world is always fumbling and bumbling over deciding any-thing—what to order for dinner, or how to manage his job, or whom to vote for—but Hugh always *knows*. It's *not* knowing that makes for all those nerves and complexes and things you hear about, isn't that so? Well, I'll take Hugh, thank you, and leave everyone else to the psychia-trists."

So there it was. An Eden with flawless lawns and no awful nerves and complexes, and not even the glimmer of a serpent in the offing. That is, not a glimmer until the day Raymond made his entrance on the scene.

We were out on the terrace that day, Hugh and Elizabeth and I, slowly being melted into a sort of liquid torpor by the August sunshine, and all of us too far gone to make even a pretense at talk. I lay there with a linen cap over my face, listening to the summer noises around me and being perfectly happy.

There was the low steady hiss of the breeze through the aspens nearby, the plash and drip of oars on the river below, and now and then the melancholy *tink-tunk* of a sheep bell from one of the flock on the lawn. The flock was a fancy of Hugh's. He swore that nothing was better for a lawn than a few sheep grazing on it, and every summer five or six fat and sleepy ewes were turned out on the grass to serve this purpose and to add a pleasantly pas-toral note.

My first warning of something amiss came from the sheep—from the sudden sound of their bells clanging wildly and then a baa-ing which suggested an assault by a whole pack of wolves. I heard Hugh say, "Damn!" loudly and angrily, and I opened my eyes to see something more incongruous than wolves. It was a large black poodle in a full glory of a clownish haircut, a bright-red collar, and an ecstasy of high spirits as he chased the frightened sheep around the lawn. It was clear the poodle had no intention of hurting them—he probably found them the most won-

derful playmates imaginable—but it was just as clear that
the panicky ewes didn't understand this and would very
likely end up in the river before the fun was over.

In the bare second it took me to see all this, Hugh had
already leaped the low terrace wall and was among the
sheep, herding them away from the water's edge and
shouting commands at the dog, which had different ideas.
"Down, boy!" he yelled. "Down!" And then as he would to
one of his own hounds he sternly commanded, "Heel!"

He would have done better, I thought, to have picked up
a stick or stone and made a threatening gesture, since the
poodle paid no attention whatever to Hugh's words. Instead, continuing to bark happily, the poodle made for the
sheep again, this time with Hugh in futile pursuit. An
instant later, the dog was frozen into immobility by a
voice from among the aspens near the edge of the lawn.

"Asseyez!" the voice called breathlessly. "Asseyez-vous!"

Then the man appeared, a small dapper figure trotting
across the grass. Hugh stood waiting, his face darkening
as we watched.

Elizabeth squeezed my arm. "Let's get down there," she
whispered. "Hugh doesn't like being made a fool of."

We got there in time to hear Hugh open his big guns.
"Any man," he was saying, "who doesn't know how to
train an animal to its place shouldn't own one."

The man's face was all polite attention. It was a good
face, thin and intelligent, and webbed with tiny lines at
the corners of the eyes. There was also something behind
those eyes that couldn't quite be masked. A gentle mockery: A glint of wry perception turned on the world like a
camera lens. It was nothing anyone like Hugh would have
noticed, but it was there all the same, and I found myself
warming to it on the spot.

There was also something tantalizingly familiar about
the newcomer's face, his high forehead, and his thinning
grey hair, but much as I dug into my memory during
Hugh's long and solemn lecture I couldn't come up with an
answer. The lecture ended with a few remarks on the best
methods of dog training, and by then it was clear that
Hugh was working himself into a mood of forgiveness.

"As long as there's no harm done," he said, and paused.

The man nodded soberly. "Still, to get off on the wrong foot with one's new neighbors—"

Hugh looked startled. "Neighbors?" he said almost rudely. "You mean that you live around here?"

The man waved toward the aspens. "On the other side of those woods."

"The *Dane* house?" The Dane house was almost as sacred to Hugh as Hilltop, and he had once explained to me that if he were ever offered a chance to buy the place he would snap it up. His tone now was not so much wounded as incredulous. "I don't believe it!" he exclaimed.

"Oh, yes," the man assured him, "the Dane house. I performed there at a party many years ago and always hoped that someday I might own it."

It was the word *performed* which gave me my clue— that and the accent barely perceptible under the precise English. He had been born and raised in Marseilles—that would explain the accent—and long before my time he had already become a legend.

"You're Raymond, aren't you?" I said. "Charles Raymond."

"I prefer Raymond alone." He smiled in deprecation of his own small vanity. "And I am flattered that you recognize me."

I don't believe he really was. Raymond the Magician, Raymond the Great, would, if anything, expect to be recognized wherever he went. As the master of sleight of hand who had paled Thurston's star, as the escape artist who had almost outshone Houdini, Raymond would not be inclined to underestimate himself.

He had started with the standard box of tricks which makes up the repertoire of most professional magicians; he had gone far beyond that to those feats of escape which, I suppose, are known to us all by now. The lead casket sealed under a foot of lake ice, the welded-steel straitjackets, the vaults of the Bank of England, the exquisite suicide knot which noosed throat and doubled legs together so that the motion of a leg draws the noose tighter around the throat—all these Raymond had escaped from. And then at the pinnacle of fame he had dropped from sight and his name had become relegated to the past.

When I asked him why, he shrugged.

"A man works for money or for the love of his work," he said. "If he has all the wealth he needs and has no more love for his work, why go on?"

"But to give up a great career—" I protested.

"It was enough to know that the house was waiting here."

"You mean," Elizabeth said, "that you never intended to live anyplace but here?"

"Never—not once in all these years." He laid a finger along his nose and winked broadly at us. "Of course, I made no secret of this to the Dane estate, and when the time came for them to sell I was the first and only one approached."

"You don't give up an idea easily," Hugh said in an edged voice.

Raymond laughed. "Idea? It became an obsession, really. Over the years I traveled to many parts of the world, but no matter how fine the place, I knew it couldn't be as fine as that house on the edge of the woods there, with the river at its feet and the hills beyond. Someday, I would tell myself, when my travels are done, I will come here and, like Candide, cultivate my garden."

He ran his hand abstractedly over the poodle's head and looked around with an air of great satisfaction. "And now," he said, "here I am . . ."

Here he was, indeed, and it quickly became clear that his arrival was working a change on Hilltop. Or, since Hilltop was so completely a reflection of Hugh, it was clear that a change was being worked on Hugh. He became irritable and restless, and more aggressively sure of himself than ever. The warmth and good nature were still there— they were as much part of him as his arrogance—but he now had to work a little harder at them. He reminded me of a man who is bothered by a speck in the eye, but can't find it and must get along with it as best he can.

Raymond, of course, was the speck, and I got the impression at times that he rather enjoyed the role. It would have been easy enough for him to stay close to his own house and cultivate his garden, or paste up his album, or whatever retired performers do, but he evidently found that impossible. He had a way of drifting over to Hilltop at odd times, just as Hugh was led to find his way to the Dane house and spend long and troublesome sessions there.

Both of them must have known that they were so badly suited to each other that the easy and logical solution would have been to stay apart. But they had the affinity of negative and positive forces, and when they were in a room together the crackling of the antagonistic current between them was so strong you could almost see it in the air.

Any subject became a point of contention for them, and they would duel over it bitterly; Hugh armored and weaponed with his massive assurance, Raymond flicking away with a rapier, trying to find a chink in the armor. I think that what annoyed Raymond most was the discovery that there was no chink in Hugh's armor. As someone with an obvious passion for searching out all sides to all questions, and for going deep into motives and causes, Raymond was continually being outraged by Hugh's single-minded way of laying down the law.

He didn't hesitate to let Hugh know that. "You are positively medieval," he said. "And of all things men should have learned since that time, the biggest is that there are no easy answers, no solutions one can give with a snap of the fingers. I can only hope for you that someday you may be faced with the perfect dilemma, the unanswerable question. You would find that a revelation. You would learn more in that minute than you dreamed possible."

And Hugh did not make matters any better when he coldly answered, "And *I* say that for any man with a brain and the courage to use it there is no such thing as a perfect dilemma."

It may be that this was the sort of episode that led to the trouble that followed, or it may be that Raymond acted out of the most innocent and aesthetic motives possible. But, whatever the motives, the results were inevitable and dangerous.

They grew from the project Raymond outlined for us in great detail one afternoon. Now that he was living in the Dane house, he had discovered that it was too big, too overwhelming. "Like a museum," he explained. "I find myself wandering through it like a lost soul through endless galleries."

The grounds also needed landscaping. The ancient trees were handsome but, as Raymond put it, there were just too many of them. "Literally," he said, "I cannot see the river for the trees, and I am one devoted to the sight of running water."

Altogether there would be drastic changes. Two wings of the house would come down, the trees would be cleared away to make a broad aisle to the water, the whole place would be enlivened. It would no longer be a museum, but the perfect home he had envisioned over the years.

At the start of this recitative Hugh was slouched comfortably in his chair. Then, as Raymond drew the vivid picture of what was to be, Hugh sat up straighter and straighter until he was as rigid as a trooper in the saddle. His lips compressed. His face became blood-red. His hands clenched and unclenched in a slow, deadly rhythm. Only a miracle was restraining him from an open outburst, but it was not the kind of miracle to last. I saw from Elizabeth's expression that she understood this, too, but was as helpless as I to do anything about it. And when Raymond, after painting the last glowing strokes of his description, said complacently, "Well, now, what do you think?" there was no holding Hugh.

He leaned forward with deliberation and said, "Do you really want to know what I think?"

"Now, Hugh," Elizabeth said in alarm. "Please, Hugh—"

He brushed that aside.

"Do you really want to know?"

Raymond frowned. "Of course."

"Then I'll tell you," Hugh said. He took a deep breath. "I think that nobody but a damned iconoclast could even conceive the atrocity you're proposing. I think you're one of those people who takes pleasure in smashing apart anything that's stamped with tradition or stability. You'd kick the props from under the whole world if you could!"

"I beg your pardon," Raymond said. He was very pale and angry. "But I think you are confusing change with destruction. Surely you must comprehend that I don't intend to destroy anything but only wish to make some necessary changes."

"Necessary?" Hugh gibed. "Rooting up a fine stand of trees that's been there for centuries? Ripping apart a house that's as solid as a rock? *I* call it wanton destruction."

"I'm afraid I don't understand. To refresh a scene, to reshape it—"

"I have no intention of arguing," Hugh cut in. "I'm telling you straight out that you don't have the right to tamper with that property!"

They were on their feet now, facing each other truculently, and the only thing that kept me from being really frightened was the conviction that Hugh would not become violent, and that Raymond was far too level-headed to lose his temper. Then the threatening moment was magically past. Raymond's lips suddenly quirked in amusement and he studied Hugh with courteous interest.

"I see," he said. "I was quite stupid not to have understood at once. This property which I remarked was a little too much like a museum is to remain that way, and I am to be its custodian. A caretaker of the past, one might say, a curator of its relics."

He shook his head, smiling. "But I'm afraid I'm not quite suited to that role. I lift my hat to the past, it is true, but I prefer to court the present. For that reason I will go ahead with my plans, and hope they do not make an obstacle to our friendship."

I remember thinking, when I left next day for the city and a long hot week at my desk, that Raymond had carried off the affair very nicely and that, thank God, it had gone no further than it did. So I was completely unprepared for Elizabeth's call at the end of the week.

It was awful, she said. It was the business of Hugh and Raymond and the Dane house, but worse than ever. She was counting on my coming down to Hilltop the next day; there couldn't be any question about that. She had planned a way of clearing up the whole thing, but I simply had to be there to back her up. After all, I was one of the few people Hugh would listen to and she was depending on me.

"Depending on me for what?" I said. I didn't like the sound of it. "And as for Hugh's listening to me, Elizabeth, isn't that stretching it a good deal? I can't see him wanting my advice on his personal affairs."

"If you're going to be touchy about it—"

"I'm *not* touchy about it," I retorted. "I just don't like getting mixed up in this thing. Hugh's quite capable of taking care of himself."

"Maybe too capable."

"And what does that mean?"

"Oh, I can't explain now," she wailed. "I'll tell you everything tomorrow. And, darling, if you have any brotherly feelings you'll be here on the morning train. Believe me, it's serious."

I arrived on the morning train in a bad state. My imagination is one of the overactive kind that can build a cosmic disaster out of very little material, and by the time I arrived at the house I was prepared for almost anything.

But, on the surface at least, all was serene. Hugh greeted me warmly, Elizabeth was her cheerful self, and we had an amiable lunch and a long talk which never came near the subject of Raymond or the Dane house. I said nothing about Elizabeth's phone call, but thought of it with a steadily growing sense of outrage until I was alone with her.

"Now," I said, "I'd like an explanation of all this mystery. The Lord knows what I expected to find out here, but it certainly wasn't anything I've seen so far. And I'd like some accounting for the bad time you've given me since that call."

"All right," she said grimly, "and that's what you'll get. Come along."

She led the way on a long walk through the gardens and past the stables and outbuildings. Near the private road which lay beyond the last grove of trees she suddenly said, "When the car drove you up to the house, didn't you notice anything strange about this road?"

"No, I didn't."

"I suppose not. The driveway to the house turns off too far away from here. But now you'll have a chance to see for yourself."

I did see for myself. A chair was set squarely in the middle of the road and on the chair sat a stout man placidly reading a magazine. I recognized the man at once: he was one of Hugh's stablehands, and he had the patient look of someone who has been sitting for a long time and expects to sit a good deal longer. It took me only a second to realize what he was there for, but Elizabeth wasn't leaving anything to my deductive powers. When we walked over to him the man stood up and grinned at us.

"William," Elizabeth said, "would you mind telling my brother what instructions Mr. Lozier gave you?"

"Sure," the man said cheerfully. "Mr. Lozier told us there was always supposed to be one of us sitting right here, and any truck we saw that might be carrying construction stuff or suchlike for the Dane house was to be stopped and turned back. All we had to do is tell them it's private property and they were trespassing. If they laid a finger on us we just call in the police. That's the whole thing."

"Have you turned back any trucks?" Elizabeth asked for my benefit.

The man looked surprised. "Why, you know that, Mrs. Lozier," he said. "There was a couple of them the first day we were out here, and that was all. There wasn't any fuss, either," he explained to me. "None of those drivers wants to monkey with trespass."

When we were away from the road again, I clapped my

hand to my forehead. "It's incredible!" I said. "Hugh must know he can't get away with this. That road is the only one to the Dane place and it's been in public use so long that it isn't private any more!"

Elizabeth nodded. "And that's exactly what Raymond told Hugh a few days back. He came over here in a fury and they had quite an argument about it. And when Raymond said something about hauling Hugh off to court, Hugh answered that he'd be glad to spend the rest of his life in litigation over this business. But that wasn't the worst of it. The last thing Raymond said was that Hugh ought to know that force only invites force, and ever since then I've been expecting a war to break out here any minute. Don't you see? That man blocking the road is a constant provocation, and it scares me."

I could understand that. And the more I considered the matter, the more dangerous it looked.

"But I have a plan," Elizabeth said eagerly, "and that's why I wanted you here. I'm having a dinner party tonight, a very small, informal dinner party. It's to be a sort of peace conference. You'll be there, and Dr. Wynant—Hugh likes you both a great deal—and," she hesitated, "Raymond."

"No!" I said. "You mean he's actually coming?"

"I went over to see him yesterday and we had a long talk. I explained everything to him—about neighbors being able to sit down and come to an understanding, and about brotherly love and—oh, it must have sounded dreadfully inspirational and sticky, but it worked. He said he would be here."

I had a foreboding. "Does Hugh know about this?"

"About the dinner? Yes."

"I mean, about Raymond's being here."

"No, he doesn't." And then when she saw me looking hard at her she burst out defiantly with, "Well, *something* had to be done and I did it, that's all! Isn't it better than just sitting and waiting for God knows what?"

Until we were all seated around the dining-room table that evening I might have conceded the point. Hugh had been visibly shocked by Raymond's arrival, but then, apart from a sidelong glance at Elizabeth which had volumes written in it, he managed to conceal his feelings well enough. He had made the introductions gracefully, kept up his end of the conversation, and, all in all, did a creditable job of playing host.

Ironically, it was the presence of Dr. Wynant which made even this much of a triumph possible for Elizabeth, and which then turned it into disaster. The doctor was an eminent surgeon, stocky and grey-haired, with an abrupt, positive way about him. Despite his own position in the world, he seemed pleased as a schoolboy to meet Raymond, and in no time at all they were as thick as thieves.

It was when Hugh discovered during dinner that nearly all attention was fixed on Raymond and very little on himself that the mantle of good host started to slip and the fatal flaws in Elizabeth's plan showed through. There are people who enjoy entertaining lions and who take pleasure in reflected glory, but Hugh was not one of them. Besides, he regarded the doctor as one of his closest friends, and I have noticed that it is the most assured of men who can be the most jealous of their friendships. And when a prized friendship is being encroached on by the man one loathes more than anyone else in the world—! All in all, by simply imagining myself in Hugh's place and looking across the table at Raymond, who was gaily and unconcernedly holding forth, I was prepared for the worst.

The opportunity for it came to Hugh when Raymond was deep in a discussion of the devices used in effecting escapes. They were innumerable, he said. Almost anything one could seize on would serve as such a device. A wire, a scrap of metal, even a bit of paper—at one time or another, he had used them all.

"But of them all," he said with a sudden solemnity, "there is only one I would stake my life on. Strange, it is one you cannot see, cannot hold in your hand—in fact, for many people it doesn't even exist. Yet it is the one I have used most often and which has never failed me."

The doctor leaned forward, his eyes bright with interest. "And it is—?"

"It is a knowledge of people, my friend. Or, as it may be put, a knowledge of human nature. To me it is as vital an instrument as the scalpel is to you."

"Oh?" said Hugh, and his voice was so sharp that all eyes were instantly turned on him. "You make sleight of hand sound like a department of psychology."

"Perhaps," Raymond said, and I saw he was watching Hugh now, gauging him. "You see, there is no great mystery in the matter. My profession—my art, as I like to think of it—is no more than the art of misdirection, and I am but one of its many practitioners."

"I wouldn't say there were many escape artists around nowadays," the doctor remarked.

"True," Raymond said, "but you will observe I referred to the art of misdirection. The escape artist, the master of legerdemain—these are a handful who practice the most exotic form of that art. But what of those who engage in the work of politics, of advertising, of salesmanship?" He laid his finger along his nose in the familiar gesture and winked. "I'm afraid they have all made my art their business."

The doctor smiled. "Since you haven't dragged medicine into it, I'm willing to go along with you," he said. "But what I want to know is, exactly how does this knowledge of human nature work in your profession?"

"In this way," Raymond said. "One must judge a person carefully. Then, if he finds in that person certain weaknesses, he can state a false premise and it will be accepted without question. Once the false premise is swallowed, the rest is easy. The victim will then see only what the magician wants him to see, or will give his vote to that politician, or will buy merchandise because of that advertising." He shrugged. "And that's all there is to it."

"Is it?" Hugh said. "But what happens when you're with people who have some intelligence and won't swallow your false premise? How do you do your tricks then? Or do you keep them on the same level as selling beads to the savage?"

"Now, that's uncalled for, Hugh," the doctor said. "The

man's expressing his ideas. No reason to make an issue of them."

"Maybe there is," Hugh said, his eyes fixed on Raymond. "I have found he's full of interesting ideas. I was wondering how far he'd want to go in backing them up."

Raymond touched the napkin to his lips with a precise little flick, and then laid it carefully on the table before him. "In short," he said, addressing himself to Hugh, "you want a small demonstration of my art."

"It depends," Hugh said. "I don't want any trick cigarette cases or rabbits out of hats or any damn nonsense like that. I'd like to see something good."

"Something good," echoed Raymond reflectively. He looked around the room, studied it, and then turned to Hugh, pointing toward the huge oak door which was closed between the dining room and the living room, where we had gathered before dinner.

"That door is not locked, is it?"

"No," Hugh said, "it isn't. It hasn't been locked for years."

"But there is a key to it?"

Hugh pulled out his key chain and with an effort detached a heavy, old-fashioned key. "Yes, it's the same one we use for the butler's pantry." He was becoming interested despite himself.

"Good. No, don't give it to me. Give it to the doctor. You have faith in the doctor's honor, I am sure?"

"Yes," said Hugh drily, "I have."

"Very well. Now, Doctor, will you please go to that door and lock it."

The doctor marched to the door with his firm, decisive tread, thrust the key into the lock, and turned it. The click of the bolt snapping into place was loud in the silence of the room. The doctor returned to the table holding the key, but Raymond motioned it away. "It must not leave your hand or everything is lost," he warned.

"Now," he said, "for the finale I approach the door, I flick my handkerchief at it"—the handkerchief barely brushed the keyhole—"and, presto, the door is unlocked!"

The doctor went to it. He seized the doorknob, twisted it

dubiously, and then watched with genuine astonishment as the door swung silently open.

"Well, I'll be damned," he said.

"Somehow," Elizabeth laughed, "a false premise went down easy as an oyster."

Only Hugh reflected a sense of personal outrage. "All right," he demanded, "how was it done? How did you work it?"

"I?" Raymond said reproachfully and smiled at all of us with obvious enjoyment. "It was you who did it. I used only my knowledge of human nature to help you along the way."

I said, "I can guess part of it. That door was set in advance, and when the doctor thought he was locking it, he wasn't. He was really unlocking it. Isn't that the answer?"

Raymond nodded. "Very much the answer. The door *was* locked in advance. I made sure of that, because with a little forethought I suspected there would be such a challenge during the evening, and this was the simplest way of preparing for it. I merely made certain that I was the last one to enter this room, and when I did I used this." He held up his hand so that we could see the sliver of metal in it. "An ordinary skeleton key, of course, but sufficient for an old and primitive lock."

For a moment, Raymond looked grave, then he continued brightly. "It was our host himself who stated the false premise when he said the door was unlocked. He was so sure of himself that he wouldn't think to test anything so obvious. The doctor is also a man who is sure, and he fell into the same trap. It is, as you now see, a little dangerous always to be so sure."

"I'll go along with that," the doctor said ruefully, "even though it's heresy to admit it in my line of work." He playfully tossed the key he'd been holding across the table to Hugh, who let it fall in front of him and made no gesture toward it. "Well, Hugh, like it or not, you must admit the man has proved his point."

"Do I?" said Hugh softly. He sat there smiling a little now, and it was easy to see he was turning some thought over and over in his head.

"Oh, come on, man," the doctor said with some impatience. "You were taken in as much as we were. You know that."

"Of course you were, darling," Elizabeth agreed.

I think that she suddenly saw her opportunity to turn the proceedings into the peace conference she had aimed at, but I could have told her she was choosing her time badly. There was a look in Hugh's eye I didn't like—a veiled look not natural to him. Ordinarily when he was really angered, he would blow up a violent storm, and once the thunder and lightning had passed he would be honestly apologetic. But this present mood of his was different. There was a slumberous quality in it which alarmed me.

He hooked one arm over the back of his chair and rested the other on the table, sitting halfway around to fix his eyes on Raymond. "I seem to be a minority of one," he remarked, "but I'm sorry to say I found your little trick disappointing. Not that it wasn't cleverly done—I'll grant that, all right—but because it wasn't any more than you'd expect from a competent blacksmith."

"Now *there's* a large helping of sour grapes," the doctor jeered.

Hugh shook his head. "No, I'm simply saying that where there's a lock on a door and the key to it in your hand, it's no great trick to open it. Considering our friend's reputation, I thought we'd see more from him than that."

Raymond grimaced. "Since I had hoped to entertain," he said, "I must apologize for disappointing."

"Oh, as far as entertainment goes I have no complaints. But for a real test—"

"A real test?"

"Yes, something a little different. Let's say, a door without any locks or keys to tamper with. A closed door which can be opened with a fingertip, but which is nevertheless impossible to open. How does that sound to you?"

Raymond narrowed his eyes thoughtfully, as if he were considering the picture being presented to him. "It sounds most interesting," he said at last. "Tell me more about it."

"No," Hugh said, and from the sudden eagerness in his

voice I felt that this was the exact moment he had been looking for. "I'll do better than that. I'll *show* it to you."

He stood up brusquely and the rest of us followed suit— except Elizabeth, who remained in her seat. When I asked her if she wanted to come along, she only shook her head and sat there watching us hopelessly as we left the room.

We were bound for the cellars, I realized when Hugh picked up a flashlight along the way, but for a part of the cellars I had never seen before. On a few occasions, I had gone downstairs to help select a bottle of wine from the racks there, but now we walked past the wine vault and into a long, dimly lit chamber behind it. Our feet scraped loudly on the rough stone, the walls around us showed the stains of seepage, and, warm as the night was outside, I could feel the chill of dampness turning my chest to goose-flesh.

When the doctor shuddered and said hollowly, "These are the very tombs of Atlantis," I knew I wasn't alone in my feeling, and felt some relief at that.

We stopped at the very end of the chamber, before what I can best describe as a stone closet built from floor to ceiling in the farthest angle of the walls. It was about four feet wide and not quite twice that in length, and its open doorway showed impenetrable blackness inside. Hugh reached into the blackness and pulled a heavy door into place.

"That's it," he said abruptly. "Plain solid wood, four inches thick, fitted flush into the frame so that it's almost airtight. It's a beautiful piece of carpentry, too, the kind they practiced two hundred years ago. And no locks or bolts. Just a ring set into each side to use as a handle." He pushed the door gently and it swung open noiselessly at his touch. "See that? The whole thing is balanced so perfectly on the hinges that it moves like a feather."

"But what's it for?" I asked. "It must have been made for a reason."

Hugh laughed shortly. "It was. Back in the bad old days, when a servant committed a crime—and I don't suppose it had to be more of a crime than talking back to one of the ancient Loziers—he was put in here to repent. And since the air inside was good for only a few hours at the most, he either repented damn soon or not at all."

"And that door?" the doctor said cautiously. "That impressive door of yours which opens at a touch to provide all the air needed—what prevented the servant from opening it?"

"Look," Hugh said. He flashed his light inside the cell and we crowded behind him to peer in. The circle of light reached across the cell to its far wall and picked out a short heavy chain hanging a little above the head level with a U-shaped collar dangling from its bottom link.

"I see," Raymond said, and they were the first words I had heard him speak since we had left the dining room. "It is truly ingenious. The man stands with his back against the wall, facing the door. The collar is placed around his neck, and then—since it is cleverly not made for a lock—it is clamped there, hammered around his neck. The door is closed, and the man spends the next few hours like someone on an invisible rack, reaching out with his feet to catch the ring on the door which is just out of reach. If he's lucky, he may not strangle himself in his iron collar but may live until someone chooses to open the door for him."

"My God," the doctor said. "You make me feel as if I were living through it."

Raymond smiled faintly. "I have lived through many such experiences, and, believe me, the reality is always a little worse than the worst imaginings. There is always the ultimate moment of terror, of panic, when the heart pounds so madly you think it will burst through your ribs and the cold sweat soaks clear through you in the space of one breath. That is when you must take yourself in hand, must dispel all weakness, and remember all the lessons you have ever learned. If not—!"

He whisked the edge of his hand across his lean throat. "Unfortunately for the usual victim of such a device," he concluded sadly, "since he lacks the essential courage and knowledge to help himself, he succumbs."

"But *you* wouldn't," Hugh said.

"I have no reason to think so."

"You mean—" and the eagerness was creeping back into Hugh's voice, stronger than ever "—that under the very same conditions as someone chained in there two hundred years ago, you could get this door open?"

The challenging note was too strong to be brushed aside lightly. Raymond stood silent for a long minute, face strained with concentration, before he answered.

"Yes," he said. "It wouldn't be easy—the problem is made formidable by its very simplicity—but it could be solved."

"How long do you think it would take you?"

"An hour at the most."

Hugh had come a long way around to get to this point. He asked the question slowly, savoring it. "Would you want to bet on that?"

"Now, wait a minute," the doctor said. "I don't like any part of this."

"And *I* vote we adjourn for a drink," I put in. "Fun's fun, but we'll all wind up with pneumonia playing games down here."

Neither Hugh nor Raymond appeared to hear a word of this. They stood staring at each other—Hugh waiting on pins and needles, Raymond deliberating—until Raymond said, "What is this bet you offer?"

"This. If you lose, you get out of the Dane house inside of a month, and sell it to me."

"And if I win?"

It wasn't easy for Hugh to say it, but he finally got it out. "Then I'll be the one to get out. And if you don't want to buy Hilltop, I'll arrange to sell it to the first comer."

For anyone who knew Hugh, it was so fantastic, so staggering a statement to hear from him, that none of us could find words at first. It was the doctor who recovered most quickly.

"You're not speaking for yourself, Hugh," he warned. "You're a married man. Elizabeth's feelings have to be considered."

"Is it a bet?" Hugh demanded of Raymond. "Do you want to go through with it?"

"I think, before I answer that, there's something to be explained." Raymond paused, then went on slowly, "I'm afraid I gave the impression—out of false pride, perhaps—that when I retired from my work it was because of a boredom, a lack of interest in it. That was not altogether the truth. In reality, I was required to go to a doctor some years ago, the doctor listened to the heart, and suddenly my heart became the most important thing in the world. I tell you this because while your challenge strikes me as being a most unusual and interesting way of settling differences between neighbors, I must reject it for reasons of health."

"You were healthy enough a minute ago," Hugh said.

"Perhaps not as much as you would want to think, my friend."

"In other words," Hugh said bitterly, "there's no accomplice handy, no keys in your pocket to help out, and no way of tricking anyone into seeing what isn't there! So you have to admit you're beaten."

Raymond stiffened. "I admit no such thing. All the tools I would need even for such a test as this I have with me. Believe me, they would be enough."

Hugh laughed aloud, and the sound of it broke into small echoes all down the corridors behind us. It was that sound, I am sure—the living contempt in it rebounding from wall to wall around us—which sent Raymond into the cell.

Hugh wielded the hammer, a short-handled but heavy sledge, which tightened the collar into a circlet around Raymond's neck, hitting with hard, even strokes at the iron which was braced against the wall. When he was finished, I saw the pale glow of the radium-painted numbers on a watch as Raymond studied it in his pitch darkness.

"It is now eleven," he said calmly. "The wager is that by midnight this door must be opened, and it doesn't matter what means are used. Those are the conditions, and you gentlemen are the witnesses to them."

Then the door was closed—and the walking began.

Back and forth we walked, the three of us, as if we were being compelled to trace every possible geometric figure on that stony floor, the doctor with his quick, impatient step and I matching Hugh's long, nervous strides. A foolish, meaningless march, back and forth across our own shadows, each of us marking the time by counting off the passing seconds and each ashamed to be the first to look at his watch.

For a while there was a counterpoint to this scraping of feet from inside the cell. It was a barely perceptible clinking of chain coming at brief, regular intervals. Then there would be a long silence, followed by a renewal of the sound. When it stopped again, I couldn't restrain myself any longer. I held up my watch toward the dim yellowish light of the bulb overhead and saw with dismay that barely twenty minutes had passed.

After that there was no hesitancy in the others about looking at the time, and, if anything, this made it harder to bear than just wondering. I caught the doctor winding his watch with small brisk turns and then a few minutes later try to wind it again and suddenly drop his hand with disgust as he realized he had already done it. Hugh walked with his watch held up near his eyes, as if by concentration on it he could drag that crawling minute-hand faster around the dial.

Thirty minutes had passed.

Forty.

Forty-five.

I remember that when I looked at my watch and saw there were less than fifteen minutes to go I wondered if I could last out even that short time. The chill had sunk so deep into me that I ached with it. I was shocked when I saw that Hugh's face was dripping with sweat and that beads of it gathered while I watched.

It was while I was looking at him in fascination that it happened. The sound broke through the walls of the cell like a wail of agony heard from far away, and shivered over us as if it were spelling out the words.

"Doctor!" it cried. *"The air!"*

It was Raymond's voice, but the thickness of the wall

blocking it off turned it into a high thin sound. What was clearest in it was the note of pure terror, the plea growing out of that terror.

"*Air!*" it screamed, the word bubbling and dissolving into a long-drawn sound which made no sense at all.

And then it was silent.

We leaped for the door together, but Hugh was there first, his back against it, barring the way. In his upraised hand was the hammer which had clinched Raymond's collar. "Keep back!" he cried. "Don't come any nearer, I warn you!"

The fury in him, brought home by the menace of the weapon, stopped us in our tracks.

"Hugh," the doctor pleaded, "I know what you're thinking, but you can forget that now. The bet's off and I'm opening the door on my own responsibility. You have my word for that."

"Do I? But do you remember the terms of the bet, Doctor? This door must be opened within an hour—*and it doesn't matter what means are used!* Do you understand now? He's fooling both of you. He's faking a death scene so that you'll push open the door and win his bet for him. But it's my bet, not yours, and I have the last word on it!"

I saw from the way he talked, despite the shaking tension in his voice, that he was in perfect command of himself, and it made everything seem that much worse.

"How do you know he's faking?" I demanded. "The man said he had a heart condition. He said there was always a time in a spot like this when he had to fight panic and could feel the strain of it. What right do you have to gamble with his life?"

"Damn it, don't you see he never mentioned any heart condition until he smelled a bet in the wind? Don't you see he set his trap that way, just as he locked the door behind him when he came to dinner! But this time nobody will spring it for him—nobody!"

"Listen to me," the doctor said, and his voice cracked like a whip. "Do you concede that there's one slim possibility of that man being dead in there, or dying?"

"Yes, it is possible—anything is possible."

"I'm not trying to split hairs with you! I'm telling you that if that man is in trouble, every second counts, and you're stealing that time from him! And if that's the case, by God, I'll sit in the witness chair at your trial and swear you murdered him! Is that what you want?"

Hugh's head sank forward on his chest, but his hand still tightly gripped the hammer. I could hear the breath drawing heavily in his throat, and when he raised his head his face was grey and haggard. The torment of indecision was written in every pale sweating line of it.

And then I suddenly understood what Raymond had meant that day when he told Hugh about the revelation he might find in the face of a perfect dilemma. It was the revelation of what a man may learn about himself when he is forced to look into his own depths, and Hugh had found it at last.

In that shadowy cellar, while the relentless seconds thundered louder and louder in our ears, we waited to see what he would do.